ユダヤ系
アメリカ文学研究

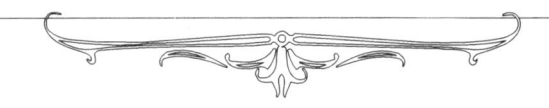

陣﨑克博 著

大学教育出版

ユダヤ系アメリカ文学研究

目　次

第Ⅰ章　序　論 ……………………………………………………………… 5

第Ⅱ章　ユダヤ系アメリカ作家のパイオニア——Abraham Cahan ……………… 10

第Ⅲ章　悪魔的激情の語り手——Isaac Bashevis Singer の3つの短篇 ………… 16

第Ⅳ章　ニューヨークを舞台にした作品の閉塞性・倫理性・
　　　　シュレミール性——Bernard Malamud の5つの短篇を中心にして …… 34

第Ⅴ章　「ユダヤ教への改宗」と「ユダヤ人の改宗」
　　　　——Bernard Malamud, *The Assistant* vs. Philip Roth,
　　　　"The Conversion of the Jews," and "Eli, the Fanatic" ……………… 43

第Ⅵ章　The Ordeal of Jewishness in the Early Works of Bernard Malamud,
　　　　Philip Roth and Saul Bellow ………………………………………… 58
　　　Ⅰ. The Theme of Suffering　58
　　　　　1. Bernard Malamud　58
　　　　　2. Philip Roth　62
　　　　　3. Saul Bellow　69
　　　Ⅱ. A Gallery of Jewish Women　79
　　　　　1. Bernard Malamud　79
　　　　　2. Philip Roth　90
　　　　　3. Saul Bellow　96

第Ⅶ章　崇高なる世界と俗悪の世界——Saul Bellow, *Humboldt's Gift* ………… 105

第Ⅷ章　東西都市文明批判と Corde の内省
　　　　——Saul Bellow, *The Dean's December* ……………………………… 119

第Ⅸ章　結　論 *132*
　　Ⅰ．Cahan, Singer のユダヤ人とユダヤ性　*132*
　　Ⅱ．Malamud, Bellow, Roth のユダヤ人とユダヤ性　*135*

初出一覧 *146*

Selected Bibliography *147*

あとがき *177*

第Ⅰ章
序論

　Philip Rothは，彼のエッセイ集 Reading Myself and Others (1975) のなかの一節 "Writing About Jews" の冒頭で，次のように述べている。「1959年に私の小説が『さようならコロンバス』一巻にまとめられてからというもの，私の作品は，教会の教壇やあちこちの雑誌で，危険，不真面目，無責任なものとたたかれつづけた。」(Ever since some of my first stories were collected in 1959 in a volume called Goodby, Columbus, my work has been attacked from certain pulpits and in certain periodicals as dangerous, dishonest, and irresponsible.) [1] と。彼は，ユダヤ教のラビ (rabbi) や保守的なユダヤ教徒や教育者たちから，彼の小説が「正統ユダヤ主義の基本的価値を著しく歪曲したもの」(a "distorted image of the basic values of Orthodox Judaism," [2] (青山167；149) を創造したと攻撃された。ユダヤ人読者からの手紙のなかにも，Rothを「反ユダヤ主義，"自己憎悪" あるいはいちばんましな場合でも，悪趣味」(being anti-Semitic and "self-hating," or, at least tasteless;) (青山167-68；149) と非難したものが多くあったと，彼自身が述べている。
　「Bellowの作品には全くみられない悪意に満ちた独特の雰囲気が，Roth の作品には覆いかぶさっている . . . .」(An aura of malice hangs over Roth's work which is totally absent from Bellow's . . . .) [3] というような批判は，Roth が常に直面しなければならないものであった。それならなぜ Roth は，ユダヤ人の読

者から非難攻撃されねばならなかったのか？　なぜ怒りと不信に満ちた手紙を受け取らなければならなかったのか？　Robert Alter がその著 After the Tradition のなかで次のような説得力のある説明をしている。

> It is precisely because they were looking in the new novels and short stories for an authentication of their own existence that many members of the great, nonintellectual, Jewish book-buying public were shocked and hurt to find writers representing their institutions as shames, their communities suffused with pettiness, spite, lust, hypocrisy, and pretense—just as human communities always have been. [4]

ユダヤ人読者によるもう一つの批判の理由は，Roth がやったようなユダヤ人批判は「反ユダヤ主義者たちには格好の自己正当化の材料になる，彼らが火の手をあげるさいの"燃料"になる，．．．。立派でもなければ，正常でもないまったく許容しがたい習慣や行為をユダヤ人自身がもっともらしくとりあげているのだから，反ユダヤ主義には渡りに舟だというのである。」(. . . is taken by such anti-Semites as justification of their attitudes, as "fuel" for their fires, particularly as it is a Jew himself who seemingly admits to habits and behavior that are not exemplary, or even normal and acceptable.) [5] というものだった。

　作家と読者の間のこのような関係や相互の反応は，アメリカの他の民族集団には見られない固有のもので，ユダヤ系アメリカ人の社会的・文化的・心理的・宗教的特性を窺わせる。また，ここで強調しておかなければならないのは，「ユダヤ系アメリカ人とは何なのか，またいかに生きるべきか」という考え方が，各人によって非常に大きな差異があるということである。それは，敬虔なユダヤ教徒から好戦的な無神論者，ハシッド (Hasid) [6] から同化政策論者，各ユダヤ系作家とさまざまなタイプの読者の間で共に多種多様である。換言すれば，各人の主張や立場は，ユダヤ的伝統に対する単純な受容やプライドから，ユダヤ性 (Jewishness) に対するアンビヴァレンス (ambivalence) の多彩な段階を経て，アイデンティティ (identity) の危機など全然意識しない徹底した同化主義に至るまで，変化に富んでいるのである。フィールド・ワークなどによる社会科学的調査によるこのテーマの研究も，非常に興味深くまた関心もあるが，

第Ⅰ章　序　論　7

　この調査はもし可能ならば別の機会に譲りたい。そこで本書では，何らかの形でユダヤ性やユダヤ人の生き方に関心を持っている 5 人の作家 Abraham Cahan (1860-1951), Isaac Bashevis Singer (1904-91), Bernard Malamud (1914-86), Saul Bellow (1915-　), Philip Roth (1933-　) のいくつかの作品を取り上げ，各作家（特に Malamud, Bellow, Roth）のユダヤ性に対する態度や取り扱い方の異同を考究することにした。

　生年や活躍した時期に差異はあるが，本質的な違いは Cahan と Singer は東欧で生まれアメリカに移住した一世であり，後の三者はアメリカで生まれた二世と三世[7]だという点である。Lithuania で生育し，1882年22歳のとき渡米，最初に文学作品らしい文学作品をものしたユダヤ系アメリカ文学の先駆者 A. Cahan。東欧で29歳まで過ごし，1935年にアメリカに渡り，イディッシュ (Yiddish) 語で作品を書き続けた I. B. Singer。この 2 人が各々，後の 3 人と全く異なる独特の文学世界を創り上げたことは，その略歴を見ただけでも想像できよう。

　血統の面でユダヤ系出身の作家が，皆すべてユダヤ人を主人公とし，ユダヤ人の諸問題を題材にしている訳ではない。しかしながら，アメリカで生まれた多くのユダヤ系作家群のなかで，登場人物や題材が最もユダヤ的な作家が B. Malamud, S. Bellow（2 人とも二世），そして P. Roth（三世）であろう。彼らは「文学的であれ，宗教的であれ，民族的であれ，ユダヤ的伝統との何らかの関連において重大な問題が提起できる」(a serious question can be raised of a relation to some kind of Jewish tradition whether literary, religious, or national.) [8] 作家たちである。3 人の作家に差異と特質があるにせよ，どの作家の作品も「彼の感受性が，ユダヤ人の生活により真剣に共感するとき」(when his feelings have been more intense about Jewish life,) [9] 最善のものが発揮されている。

　本書で論究する 5 人の作家たちは，それぞれ異なったタイプのユダヤ人を作品のなかで創造した。彼らが考えているユダヤ性なるものの内容は何なのか？彼らの小説や短編小説のなかに表明されているユダヤ性に対する心構えはいかなるものであったのか？「合理的実用主義というアメリカ自家製の道徳体系」(America's home-made moral system of national pragmatism) [10] が，彼らの作品の

なかで伝統的なユダヤ人気質とどのような形で相克したのか？　以下の諸章のなかで，5人の作家のいくつかの選ばれた作品を対象にして，このようなユダヤ性の試練を分析し比較するつもりである。

　繰り返しとなるが，ユダヤ系アメリカ作家のなかで，その作品のユダヤ性が最も濃厚な5人の作家のユダヤ性に対する態度・考え方の共通点と相違点を究明しながら，各作家の作品の特性を比較検討する。特に Malamud, Bellow, Roth の主要作品に重点を置き，同化と疎外の2重性の問題，ユダヤ人としての受難と苦悩，呪縛と解放の循環，独特のユーモア・ペーソス・サタイア，登場人物と文体，読者の受容などの観点から考察する。ユダヤ系アメリカ文学の本質と特有の魅力を浮き彫りにするのが，本書刊行の目的であり意義である。第2次大戦後のユダヤ系アメリカ作家の黄金時代が終焉に近付きつつあるとか，あるいは第Ⅱ幕に入っているとか言われて[11]から久しい現在，この問題にスポットを当てるこの研究は，有意義なものと自覚している。

≪Notes≫

1) フィリップ・ロス，青山南訳『素晴らしいアメリカ作家』（東京：集英社，1980）167. Philip Roth, *Reading Myself and Others* (New York: Farrar Straus and Giroux, 1975)149. 以下この作品からの引用はすべてこの版により，引用英文末尾の括弧内に頁数を記す。和文と英文を併記する場合は（青山167；149）と記す。
2) この引用は，実際には1963年ごろの全米ラビ会議でRabbi Emanuel Rackmanが言った言葉なのだが，Philip Roth はこれを，ユダヤ的伝統を保持しようとする保守的ユダヤ人指導層や一般信徒の共通の考え方のサンプルと考えているようだ。
3) 陣﨑訳；Richard L. Rubenstein, "The Philosophy of Saul Bellow," *The Reconstructionist* XXX (22 January 1965)：7.
4) Robert Alter, *After the Tradition: Essays on Modern Jewish Writing* (New York: E. P. Dutton, 1971) 10.
5) 青山訳168；Roth 149-50.
6) Hasid, Hasidm (plural); Hassid, Hassidm (plural)；Chasid, Chasidim (plural) と種々の表記で書かれる Yiddish。1750年頃ポーランドのユダヤ教徒に起こった信仰復興運動に加わったユダヤ教徒。詳しくは Leo Rosten, *The Joys of Yiddish* (New York: McGraw Hill, 1968) 73-76.を参照。
7) 厳密に言うと Saul Bellow は，1915年カナダの Montreal で生まれ，1924年Chicagoに移

った。
8) 陣﨑訳；Alter 12.
9) 陣﨑訳；Philip Roth's utterance in the Symposium, "The Jewish Intellectual and Jewish Identity," *Congress Bi-Weekly* XXX (16 September 1963): 38.
10) 陣﨑訳；Josephine Zadovsky Knopp, *The Trial of Judaism in Contemporary Jewish Writing* (Chicago: University of Illinois Press, 1975) 108.
11) Ruth R. Wisse, "American Jewish Writing, Act II," *Commentary* LXI (June 1976): 40-46.

第II章
ユダヤ系アメリカ作家のパイオニア
―― Abraham Cahan

　ユダヤ系アメリカ文学の祖とも言うべきパイオニア的作家であり，50年近くにわたって Yiddish 語の新聞 *Jewish Daily Forward* （以下 *Forward* と略記する）の偉大な編集者として活躍し，また社会運動の指導者でもあった Abraham Cahan（1860-1951）は，Lithuania の Vilna に近い寒村で生を受けた。Vilna のユダヤ人学校教師養成所を卒業した彼が，アメリカに亡命する22歳のときまで，ロシアの地で体得したものは，西欧文化であり，ロシア革命の理想であり，またトルストイの文学に対する畏敬の念でもあった。1881年に起こった皇帝アレクサンドル二世暗殺事件とそれに付随する革命運動の余波を受けて，警察に逮捕されそうになったCahanは，1882年ロシアを逃れてニューヨークに辿り着く。
　アメリカに移住してからすぐに彼は社会主義運動に深くかかわるようになり，特に Yiddish 語による演説者として有名になる。入国後6カ月にして早くも Cahan は，ニューヨークの *World* 紙に最初の英語の記事を発表している。2年後にはニューヨークの *Sun* 紙やその他の新聞に定期的に記事を書くようになっていた。1897年に社会主義運動の機関紙とも言うべき Yiddish 語の新聞 *Forward* の創刊にかかわったが，編集上の意見の衝突で数カ月で同紙の編集の仕事を辞めてしまった。その後の5年間は *Century, Scribner's, Cosmopolitan* などの雑誌にニューヨーク East Side のユダヤ人の生活を生き生きと描いた短編

小説を発表し, *Commercial Advertiser*（後に *Globe* となる）紙とも関係を持つようになった。

英語による最初の 2 冊の小説 *Yekl : A Tale of the New York Ghetto*（1896）と *The Imported Bridegroom and Other Stories of the New York Ghetto*（1898）が出版されたのもこのころである。前者の中編小説は, 後に映画 *Hester Street* の種本となったもので, 出版直後 William Dean Howells の好意的書評を得た。独特の素直さとユーモアを混じえた文体でEast Side ghettoのユダヤ系移民の生活をrealisticに叙述したこの小説に, Howellsは大変感銘を受けたのである。2 年後に上梓された後者の短編小説集（1891年から1898年に書かれた 5 作）に対しても, この大作家は *Literature* に賞賛の書評をものし, そのおかげで Cahan は "a new star of realism" として読者の前に華々しく登場することができたのである。ただし, これらの作品は Howells の助力にもかかわらず, 一般読者には当時あまり受け入れられなかったことを付記しておきたい。

1902年 3 月 East Broadway を歩いていた Cahan は, たまたま Forward Press Association の 2 人の役員と出会った。5 年前彼が辞めたときの役員たちである。その頃 Forward 紙の売れ行きは落ち, このままでは廃刊の憂き目をみそうな危機的状態であった。社会主義のお説教じみた記事を満載した面白くもない Yiddish 語の新聞を, 人々はだんだん読まなくなってきていた。古くからのユダヤ系移民のなかには, ニュース源を英語新聞に求める傾向も芽生えていた。2 人の役員は Cahan を手放したことを後悔していて, 彼に再び同紙の編集を手掛けるよう要請した。Cahan は迷った。既にいくらかの名声を確立しさらに輝かしい将来を期待できる作家と新聞記者としてのより広いアメリカ文化の世界を捨てて, 狭い窒息しそうな Yiddish journalism の世界に返ることの意義があるのか。妻 Anna も反対している。懊悩の末, 編集方針に他から口を差し挟まないことなどいくつかの条件を付け, 忙しく編集の仕事に従事することがかえって想像力を増すことを信じて, Cahan は役員の要請を受け入れる決心をする。

1951年に長い生涯を閉じるまで, その後の約50年近くの間 Forward 紙の主任編集者として, 彼はユダヤ系コミュニティの "heart and mind" を形成することに尽力していた。ユダヤ系移民社会の教育者として, ユダヤ人労働運動の指導

者として，また現代文化の紹介者として Forward 紙の果たした役割は大きい。1920年代のピーク時には発行部数が25万部を超え，労働運動，社会主義，人道主義，ならびに優れたYiddish文学やその他の現代文学を擁護してきた。同紙によって紹介されたり支持を受けた作家たちのなかに Sholem Asch, Jonah Rosenfeld, I. J. Singer, Isaac Bashevis Singer の名を挙げることができる。

　Cahan が残したその他の作品として，ロシアを舞台として革命精神の要求と Jewishness の意識を調和させる問題を取り扱った400頁の大冊 The White Terror and the Red: A Novel of Revolutionary Russia (1905)，彼の最高傑作 The Rise of David Levinsky: A Novel (1917)，Yiddish 語で書かれた 5 巻の自伝 Bleter fun Mein Leben (1926-31)（この最初の 2 巻が1969年 The Education of Abraham Cahan として翻訳されている），雑誌や新聞に発表された英語あるいは Yiddish 語で書かれた短編小説や中編小説，批評，記事などがある。

　1910年ごろ Cahan の周辺は，The White Terror and the Red が彼の英語による文学活動の最後を飾るものだと思っていた。ユダヤ系移民の移住が最も多かった1905年から1913年ごろにかけて，Cahan は Forward 紙の有能な編集者として成功し，労働争議を仲裁し，政治的な力を発揮し，文学上の案内者となり，大衆とインテリの仲介者の役割も果たしていた。移民数の増加と社会的地位の向上が，ニューヨーク市内のユダヤ人読者層を増大させていた。このことを考慮に入れた雑誌 McClure's の編集者は1913年にごく軽い気持ちで Cahan に対し「アメリカ・ビジネス界におけるユダヤ系移民の成功」を主題とした記事を書くよう依頼した。Cahan がものしたのは記事ではなく，一人称の形で記述された，衣料産業界の大立者となったユダヤ人の成功物語であった。反ユダヤ主義の復活を誘う危険性を冒して，彼は自分の最もよく知悉した世界を描いた。ユダヤ人の生活をアメリカの社会全般に紹介する仲介者の使命のようなものを，彼は自覚していたのであろう。物語は好評で，McClure's の編集者はさらにもう 2 編書いてくれと要請した。これら一連の 4 作品が修正され拡大されて The Rise of David Levinsky となったのである。[1]

　John Higham が1960年 reprint 版の序文のなかで指摘しているように，この作品には 3 つの文化の素晴らしい融合がみられる。成功のテーマはアメリカ的な

ものであり The Rise of Silas Lapham や Sister Carrie の伝統に属する。Jewishness と Americanism の 2 重性の問題, すなわち acculturation とユダヤ人特有の強烈な identity の危機の主題はユダヤ的である。そのアプローチは Yiddish 文学の伝統に由来するものであり, その芸術的感性はロシア的であると言えよう。この 3 つの要素が統合されて, ユダヤ系移民を素材とした最初の古典的 minor masterpiece[2] が生まれたのである。

 The Rise of David Levinsky は作者 Cahan との identification を思わせる自伝的な作品である。主人公 Levinsky は Cahan と同じくロシアで生まれ, 幼くして父を失い, 母は借金をしながら息子を Talmudic seminary に通わせる。Orthodoxy への piety を叩き込まれる Levinsky の心に, やがてユダヤ教の戒律から離れて, 知的で自由な生活への欲求が, 若い女性との社交生活や性の快楽への憧れが芽生えてくる。そして, 若い女の子と散歩したり, ダンスに興じる異教徒の生活を羨ましく思ったりする。この離反をたしなめる役割を果たすのが, 学友の Reb Sender であり, 彼の助言によって Levinsky は反省し, 以前にも増してタルムード (Talmud)[3] の暗誦に熱中したりする。このような Jewishness に対する固執と離反の揺曳, それに起因する心の悩みは, この小説の中核をなすテーマであるが, 青年に達して渡米するまでのロシア時代のプロットのなかに, すでに暗示的に2重性の基本テーマが示唆されている。さて, Purim の祭りのとき, 異教徒から Levinsky が殴られたことに立腹した母親は抗議に出かけるが, 反対に暴徒に殺されてしまう。孤児となった Levinsky は, ユダヤ人家庭の援助を受けるようになる。この家庭には Matilda という出戻りの娘がおり, 2 人は愛情を持ち始める。しかし, アメリカ行きの夢を捨て切れない Levinsky は, 彼女にこの計画を打ち明ける。一時は反対していた彼女も, アメリカでも Talmud 研究を続けるという約束のもとに, 彼のために渡航費用を準備する。アメリカに渡った Levinsky は, 大変な苦労を重ねながら, 行商人, sweatshop の労働者などと職を転々とし, やがて機を得て独立するようになる。そして, 幾多の辛酸をなめながらも, 持ち前のしたたかさ, 辛抱強さ, 敏捷さ, 時には狡猾さによって, 成功の階段を登りつめ, 遂には衣料産業界の代表的人物の一人となる。この過程が, 524頁 (1960年 reprint 版) に及ぶ長編の大半を

費やして延々と述べられるのだが,その詳細はここでは省略したい。
　この作品の冒頭の一節は,LevinskyのユニークなJewish characterを表明する重要な個所である。主人公のLevinskyは昔を回顧し,1885年には4セントをポケットに入れてアメリカに渡ってきたが,今や200万ドルの財産を持つ成功者となった。しかし,と彼は続ける。「しかし私が心の内なるアイデンティティをしっかりと見つめるとき,それは30年ないし40年前のそれと全く同じであると痛感させられる。私の思いのままになる現在の地位,権力,世俗的な幸福の価値等々も意味がないように思えるのだ。」(And yet when I take a look at my inner identity it impresses me as being precisely the same as it was thirty or forty years ago. My present station, power, the amount of worldly happiness at my command, and the rest of it, seem to be devoid of significance.) [4] 成功と裏あわせの幻滅感,絶えず飢餓感に悩まされながら驀進してきた人生の最後にかち得たworldly successとspiritual decline。小説の最後の部分で,「ユダヤ教会堂でタルムードの経典を体を揺すって読み続ける哀れな少年,デイヴィッドの方が,著名な衣料製造業者の今のデイヴィッド・レヴィンスキーより,はるかに私の内なるアイデンティティと共通点を持っているように思える。」(David, the poor lad swinging over a Talmud volume at the Preacher's Synagogue, seems to have more in common with my inner identity than David Levinsky, the well-known cloak-manufacturer（陣崎；530)) と言う主人公の気持ちは,1902年のForward紙上で「...私は,昔の自分の新鮮未熟さに憧れる。20年の切なる思いをなつかしく思う。」(... I yearn for my greenness of old. I yearn for my yearnings of twenty years ago.) と告白するCahanの心情と一致するものである。後にMalamudやPhilip RothやBellowの作品のなかで,よりsophisticateされた形で提示されたユダヤ人のcrisis of identityの問題が,最も素朴な形で,しかもHoratio Alger的な成功物語という形で提出されたのが,この小説である。
　別の観点からすればこの作品は,ユダヤ教の束縛から解放された移民の孤独の追求とも言えよう。この孤独感はLevinskyの女性遍歴の失敗によって強化される。性の解放はAmericanizationの一つの到達点であり,Jewishnessから最も遠いところにある。彼は,MatildaにもDoraにもAnna Tevkinにも肝心のと

ころで逃げられてしまう。女性との愛の不毛には,シンボリックな社会的な意味が付与されていると考えてもよい。

ユダヤ系アメリカ文学の永遠のテーマである Jewishness と Americanism の2重性の問題を,最初に文学作品らしい文学作品として完成したパイオニア,そこに Cahan の原点的存在価値がある。

≪Notes≫

1) Abaraham Cahan の伝記的事実は, *Dictionary of Literary Biography, Vol.28*：*Twentieth Century American-Jewish Fiction Writers* (Detroit, Mich.: Gale Research Co., 1984) 28-34. 及び Irving Howe, *World of Our Fathers* (New York: Harcourt Brace Jovanovich, 1976) 103-04, 112-12, 138-39, 182-83, 228-29, 523-31, 532-33, 539-42 などを参照した。

2) John Higham, "Introduction" to *The Rise of David Levinsky : A Novel* by Abraham Cahan (New York: Harper and Bros., 1960) x.

3) 本文 Mishnah とその注解 Gemara からなるユダヤ人の生活・宗教・道徳に関する律法の集大成(研究社,新英和大辞典)。

4) 陣﨑訳；Abraham Cahan, *The Rise of David Levinsky* (1917; New York: Harper and Row, 1960) 3. 以下この作品からの引用はすべてこの版により,引用英文末尾の括弧内に頁数を記す。和文と英文を併記する場合は(陣﨑；3)と記す。

第Ⅲ章
悪魔的激情の語り手
── Isaac Bashevis Singerの3つの短篇

I

　1978年のノーベル文学賞受賞者 Isaac Bashevis Singer（1904-91）は，東ポーランドの小さな町で生まれ，ワルシャワの貧しいユダヤ人居住区で成長した。父も祖父も Hasid 派の rabbi，母方の祖父も反 Hasid 派の rabbi で，彼は幼児から宗教教育を受け，聖書や Talmud や cabala を読んだ。一方，Yiddish 語に翻訳された世界の文学にも接し，特にドストエフスキーの『罪と罰』に深い感銘を受けたのであった。[1] 作家だった兄の Israel Joshua から受けた影響も大きかった。

　1935年，兄の後を追ってニューヨークに移住し，Yiddish 語の日刊新聞 *Forward* のフリーランス・ライターとなった。アメリカに渡ってきた Singer は，Yiddish 語の将来性のなさを痛感し，7年間も作品を全然書くことができなかった。1945年から1948年にかけて *Forward* 紙に連載された彼の最初の小説 *The Family Moskat* は，英語に翻訳されて1950年に出版され，3万5000部も売れた。[2] Saul Bellow が *Partisan Review* の1953年5月号に，傑作 "Gimpel the Fool" を翻訳紹介して以来，Singer の名声は徐々に高まり，小説14冊，短編集10冊（選集も含む），戯曲，自伝，児童文学作品などが，次々と英語に翻訳され公刊された。

第Ⅲ章　悪魔的激情の語り手　　17

　ポーランドで過ごした歳月よりも，アメリカに住んだ年月の方がはるかに長いにもかかわらず，Singer の作品は最後まで，まず Yiddish 語で書かれ，英語に翻訳されて読者に提示され，また主たる主人公は Yiddish 語を話す東欧のユダヤ人であった。彼の物語の舞台は，若干の例外を除いて，ポーランドのユダヤ人で構成される小さな村や町，そして時にワルシャワである。時代は19世紀後半か20世紀の初頭。みすぼらしいシナゴーグ (synagogue)，あごひげを生やした敬虔な rabbi，清浄食品 (kosher) を作る儀式屠殺人などが登場する。外界から隔離されたシュテトル (shtetl) [3] の世界である。
　彼は，文学は作家の民族性にその根源を持たなければならないという信念を持っていた。Marshall Breger と Bob Barnhart との会談のなかで Singer は次のように言っている。

> In other words, literature cannot operate in a void above humanity. It is strongly connected with a group, with a clan . . . . I always write about the Jewish people in Poland proper. [4]

　また，1976年に出版された *Passions and Other Stories* の Author's Note のなかでも，こう述べている。

> This is especially important since I deal with unique characters in unique circumstances, a group of people who are still a riddle to the world and often to themselves—the Jews of Eastern Europe, specifically the Yiddish-speaking Jews who perished in Poland and those who emigrated to the U.S.A. The longer I live with them and write about them, the more I am baffled by the richness of their individuality and (since I am one of them) by my own whims and passions. [5]

　さらに，なぜ Yiddish 語で書くのかと問われて，彼はそれが自分の母国語であり，自分が書きたいと思う人たちの言葉であるから，また自分自身の考えを表現する最善の方法であるからという意味の返答をしている。[6]
　世俗化された環境や高まりゆく社会的・文化的変動に接することによって，Singer は彼が育った厳しいユダヤ教の世界からの離脱を図り，また両者の相克の苦悩を味わったのであった。伝統と革新，一方では超世俗的な未来世界や敬

虔な神秘主義に対し,他方では自由思想や懐疑主義やニヒリズムに面しながら,この両者の間を揺曳する苦悩が Singer の作品の主要テーマである。Satan in Goray (1955), The Slave (1962) の長編は,17世紀ユダヤ人社会に発生した正統対異端の葛藤のテーマを取り扱い,The Manor (1967), The Estate (1969) では,ユダヤ教伝統意識と近代的啓蒙思想の相克に苦しむ一家の年代記を展開した。しかし筆者は,彼の長編小説よりも,全部で100を超える彼の短編のなかに,より優れていて面白いものがあると思う。Irving Malin もその著 Isaac Bashevis Singer のなかで次のように適切にこのことを述べているので,以下に引用する。

> Singer is perhaps more effective as a short story writer than as a novelist. By narrowing his focus even more than he does in the closed novels,[7] he can concentrate upon the intense vision of details. He can give us dream, stylization, and parable.[8]

なるほど,Singer の短編には,① "Gimpel the Fool," "The Old Man," "Yanda" のように,極端なシュレミール (schlemiel) やシュリマーゼル (schlimazel)[9],不運な男女,神のように善良過ぎる敗者でありながら,絶望から解放されて生き残ってゆくタイプのもの,② "Jachid and Jechidah," "Cockadoodledoo" のように,人間の肉体を超えた魂とか,人間以外の動物の世界を描いて,人間世界を諷刺する作品,③ "The Lecture," "A Day in Coney Island," "The Son" などのように,彼の自伝的要素が濃い短編群,④そしてさらに,"Blood," "The Witch," "The Gentleman from Cracow" の例にみられるように,悪魔的な激情に魅せられ脅迫され,sexuality や avarice に走る個人や共同体が,黙示録的な恐怖の状況を経験する物語などに大別できる。[10]

筆者にとって最も魅力的なのは,この④のタイプであって,本論では上記3作品について,以下に論述してゆきたい。Yiddish 文学やユダヤの伝統に固執しながらも,その束縛から解放され,人間の本質にかかわる愛欲や貪欲の問題を,悪魔や dybbuk[11] の超自然的な要素と絡み合わせながら描いていく点に,その特色がある。Singer は,文学とは人を楽しませるもの以外の何物でもないと主張している。愛や sex や物欲などの側面に最も顕著に表れる人間の個性,

男女の深層的な，いささか動物的な心の暗黒を明るみに出して，いかに我々の前に提示しているかを考察してみたい。

Ⅱ

Short Friday and Other Stories（1964）のなかの短編 "Blood" の舞台は，Laskev の町からほど遠からぬ所にある広い農園で展開される。この物語は，そのテーマを予言するかのような次の文章で始まる。

> The cabalists know that the passion for blood and the passion for flesh have the same origin, and this is the reason "Thou shalt not kill" is followed by "Thou shalt not commit adultery." 12)

女主人公のRishaは「男ごろし」という噂のある悪玉である。彼女が再婚した農園主 Reb Falik Ehrlichman は，誠実・温和で敬虔・善良な人物であり，既に70歳に近く，Risha より30歳も年上であった。嬶天下の Risha は，でっぷり肥っていて男のように逞しく，今では勝手に農園を取り仕切り，夫に全財産を譲る署名を認めさせていた。

多年に及んで儀式屠殺人を務めた老人 Reb Dan の死に伴い，Risha は新しく，若い Reuben を後任として雇うことを計画する。Reuben は，赤ら首ででっぷり肥満した男で，黒い瞳には冷酷な表情が宿っていた。雄鶏の殺しを頼みにいった Risha の前で，Reuben は即座に鋭利なナイフで雄鶏を殺し，どさっと床の上に倒す。殺戮の血を見た2人は戦慄が体の中をつっ走り，激情に駆られて愛欲の焔を燃え上がらせ，熱烈な愛戯に耽るのであった。

> When Risha finally arose, she said to Reuben: "You certainly murdered me that time."
> "And you me," he answered. (33)

Reuben を Reb Dan の後釜として雇い入れ，すっかり自分のものとするために，Risha は Laskev の町に肉屋を店開きすることを提案する。この計画はRishaの思い通りに進み，Reubenに母屋の一室が与えられ，2人の関係は続い

た。牛の咽喉を切り裂き鮮血がほとばしり出る残酷な情景を眺めたいという渇望が，肉欲と混じり合い，次に行う淫楽の行為を煽り立て駆り立てた。人はひとたび逸脱を冒せば，次々と深みにはまってゆく。ある日，あらゆる恣欲と狡知の父である Satan[13] が，Risha を誘惑し，ついに屠殺行為にまで手を付けさせようとした。Risha は，獣殺しに快楽を覚え，まもなくReuben を助手として働かせ，全部の屠殺を自分で執り行うようになった。獣脂を kosher の脂肪だと偽って販売するなど，町中のユダヤ人を欺くことに満足していた。

She got so much satisfaction from deceiving the community that this soon became as powerful a passion with her as lechery and cruelty. (37)

一方，耳も遠くなり目もほとんど見えなくなった Reb Falik は，自分の建てた学舎で Mishnah[14] を唱えていたが，突然ナイフを手に入ってきた Risha の物凄い形相を見て苦悶に襲われ，立ち上がろうとしたが両足が体を支えきれず，即死した。彼の宗教上の諸研究も悪魔のような妻に対抗できなかったのである。Reuben と Risha の飽くなき罪業は，いつまでも秘密のままでは済まされなかった。騙されて non-kosher の肉を食べさせられた群衆は，怒り心頭に発し，棍棒やナイフで武装し，農園に押し寄せてきた。恐れをなして Reuben は農園から去り逃げていった。農園側も武装し，両者が対峙するなかで，押し寄せた群衆の一人が，もう誰もおまえの肉は買ってやらないぞ、村八分にしてやるからなと叫んだときも，Risha は昂然として，「あんたらの金なんか要らないわよ。あんたらの神も要らないね。宗旨がえするわよ。いまこの場でね！」("I don't need your money. I don't need your God either. I'll convert. Immediately!")（邦高 103；42）と叫ぶ。押し寄せたユダヤ人たちは，転向者の告発によるキリスト教徒たちの怒りと報復を恐れて退却する。

　ある冬のこと，Laskev の町は，夜になるとうろつき回って町の人を襲う人喰い獣の噂が広まっていた。熊だと言う者もあれば，狼と言う者，demon[15] と言う者もあった。ある闇夜のこと，Laskev の肉屋たちは斧やナイフを持って集まり，この怪物を殺そうと決議した。追いかけた男の一人が獲物の姿を発見し，投げつけた斧が命中する。すさまじい叫び声と，ぞっとするような唸り

声がし，皆は she-devil に傷を負わせたものと確信して家路についた。翌朝分かった驚くべきことは，その野獣の正体が Risha であったことである。Risha が狼人間に変じていたのであった。抑えがたい欲望の化身とも言うべきRisha のなかに，血を求める激情と情欲を求める激情が一体化していたのだ。Risha は，Satan によって罰せられ，狼人間に変えられ，村人によって殺され，地獄の火によって焼かれる。

　ここで指摘しておきたいのは，Reuben がそれから数年後，放浪者となって死の間際に，町の rabbi と7人の長老を前にして忌むべき罪業を悔い改めたという，この短編の最後の部分の記述である。Risha の方は，最後まで悔悛するまでに至らなかった。しかし，狼人間になる前，夜になると夢のなかで phantoms が彼女を苦しめた。彼女は十字を切り，子供のころ母に教わったヘブライの呪文を唱えるのであった。また，深夜の空を見上げて，次のように叫ぶこともあった。

"God, come and punish me! Come Satan! Come Asmodeus! [16] Show your might. Carry me to the burning desert behind the dark mountains!" (45)

Risha でさえ，神や悪魔や邪悪な精霊の存在を信じていたのである。

Ⅲ

Passions and Other Stories (1975) のなかの "The Witch" の舞台は，ワルシャワである。主人公の Mark Meitels は40代前半，この地の Gymnasium 女子校の優秀な数学・物理教師で，ユダヤ教に関心はなく，科学のみを信じていた。妻の Lena は，37歳のわがままなナルシストで，子供を産むことを拒否し，sex にも関心がなかった。性交は汚く野獣的なものだと，彼女は考えた。Mark は，運動をすることによってその不満を紛らわした。Lena を見ていると，Mark は彼女が陶磁器製の人形のように思えるのだった。2人の趣味・嗜好は全然合わず，いつも折れさせられるのは Mark の方だった。Mark は Lenaと結婚したことを何回も悔やんだが，離婚することはできなかった。

Markは，女子生徒たちに大変人気があり，彼に夢中になる生徒もいたが，彼は軽率な行動を避け，規律と抑制力に満ちた言動を心掛けた。不倫をすることも可能であったが，彼はそんなことには見向きもせず，あくまで妻に忠実であった。Markの態度は，同僚教師たちの賞賛の的となった。Gymnasiumの娘たちの四肢は，結婚して子供を産みたいという臆することのない欲望を示していた。そういう生徒たちのなかに，極端に成績の悪いBellaがいた。第6学年と第7学年共に，それぞれ1回ずつ留年した。校長はBellaに，職業学校に転校するよう勧めたが，両親が承知しなかった。家は貧しく，彼女の授業料は最低の額まで減額されていた。頭が良くない上に，Bellaは学校中で一番醜い生徒だった。頭は体と不釣り合いに大きく，目は黒くて飛び出しており，鼻は曲がっていて胸は大きく，ヒップは幅広く足は湾曲していた。他の女生徒たちは彼女をFreakと呼んだ。Bellaは，数学の簡単な公式も頭に入らなかったが，生まれながらに持っている優れた領域が一つあった。それは彼女のemotionsであった。彼女はMarkの目をずっと見つめてそらすことなく，その両眼には彼に対する愛と尊敬の念が滲み出ていた。

　Lenaは，脾臓癌にかかっていた。わがままだったLenaが，今や自分の運命を諦め，黙って受容していた。医者は，癌の苦痛を和らげる薬を投与できるだけで，後は死を待つだけだと言った。Gymnasiumの最終試験の直前に，Lenaは亡くなった。Lenaの母は，7日間の喪に服することを提案したが，Markはそのような儀式は信じないと答えた。

> He even declined to say Kaddish over Lena's grave. Why participate in rites in which he didn't believe? What sense did it make to pray to a God who was eternally silent, whose goals could never be established, nor even his existence? [17]

校長は，Bellaが最終試験を受けることを認めなかった。奇妙なことに，Lenaの死の悲しみにもかかわらず，Markの心はどうしようもなくBellaに向いていた。彼女は今何をしているだろうか？ 落第のことをどんなに受け止めているだろうか？ 他の生徒のことは全然頭にないのに，醜いBellaの顔が彼の眼前にちらついて離れなかった。日ごろの自己抑制力も役に立たなかった。

第Ⅲ章　悪魔的激情の語り手　　23

He was consumed by curiosity about that repulsive girl, along with something akin to passion. . . . He listened in astonishment to the chaos raging within his own brain. For reasons that defied explanation, this Bella obsessed him more and more. (119)

時々，Bella が彼を呼んでいるような奇妙な気持ちになることがあった。狂気のようになって，彼女の住む Gnoyna Street に行こうと玄関の戸を締めた途端，電話のベルが鳴った。電話は途中で切れたが，テレパシーによって，それが Bella からだと確信し，"It's she, the beast! . . . "（120）と叫ぶ。彼は今もはや，Mark Meitels ではなく，compulsion に駆られた，あるいはユダヤ伝説の dybbuk に取り憑かれた superstitious dupe に成り下がっていた。

　もう一度掛かってきた電話は，やはり Bella からで，Mark は彼女に自分の家に来るよう勧める。花束を持って訪れた Bella は，先生である Mark に対し，最初に会ったときから愛し求め続けてきたと告白する。そしてまた，自分は魔女であると告白し，死んだ Mark の妻 Lena にずっと呪いをかけてきた罪に対し，神が罰を与えるだろうと言う。そういえば Lena の癌の進行は異常に早く，医者もその早死にを不思議に思っていた，と Mark は回想する。一度は平静に戻った彼は，Bella に 2 度と来るなと宣言する。つれない Mark に対しても，熱い Bella の想いは変わらない。死の間際まで Mark を祝福すると言う彼女に，何か不可解な力に動かされた Mark は，「ぼくの女になれるのかい？」（"Are you ready to become my lover?"）（陣崎；128）と口走る。

　　Something like anger and mockery flashed in Bella's eyes. "You can do what you want with me."
　　"When?"
　　"Now . . . "(128)

　2 人の交合の激しい興奮状態のなかで，Mark は Bella に結婚の約束をしていた。朝早く 3 時ごろ Bella は，Mark が後悔をしているなら自分は Vistula 川で溺死自殺をしてもよい，遊びや冗談で本当に愛していないなら，はっきりそう言ってくれと言う。

"Bella, stay here!" he cried. It was no longer he, Mark Meitels speaking, but some force that had the final say. (130)

彼は新しい激情に圧倒され，2人はじゅうたんの上に倒れ込む。以下は，この短編の最後の部分である。

He said, "If there is such a thing as black magic, maybe there is a God, too."
He couldn't wait to get to the bedroom and pushed her down onto the rug—a witch drenched in blood and semen, a monster that the rising sun transformed into a beauty. (132)

Singer の物語では，女性は，男性を敬虔さや知性から引き離す性衝動の化身として描かれることが多いが，"The Witch" はその好例である。知的で誠実で，自己抑制力も強く，ワルシャワで最も優秀な教師の一人であった Mark Meitels が，魔女の Bella か，あるいは何か不可解な大きな力によって，欲望の虜となるのである。

しかし，上記の引用文にあるように，Mark の心のなかに，まだ God の存在を認める心が残っていることが判明する。また，a monster 以下最後までの部分の記述によって，2人の将来が，魔力から脱して今とは違った明るいものとなる予兆のようなものが窺えるのである。

Ⅳ

Gimpel the Fool and Other Stories（1957）のなかの "The Gentleman from Cracow" は，sexuality に加えて avarice（金銭に対する貪欲さ）への警告である。

Frampol 村のユダヤ人は貧しかった。屋根は瓦葺で，床は汚かった。夏は靴も履かず裸足で，冬はぼろ布で足を包むか，藁のサンダルを履いた。Rabbi Ozer は，立派な教育を受けていたが，受け取る給料は僅かであった。村人のなかの豊かな人々でさえ，安息日以外は肉を食べられなかった。Frampol では金貨を目にすることはめったになかった。ある夏のこと旱魃があった。雨が降

らず，収穫がほとんどないところへ，雹が降って事態をさらに悪くした。Frampol の百姓たちもユダヤ人も，食べる物がなかった。よその大きな町では穀物があったが，誰もそれを買う金がなかった。万策尽きたときに，一つの奇跡が起こった。8頭立ての馬車に乗って，Cracow から一人の紳士が訪れ，村人に金を恵み食物を買う手助けをしてくれたのである。この火のような眼をした紳士は，ユダヤ人の医者で，富裕な妻を産褥で亡くし，a Wonder Rabbi の勧めで悲しみを紛らわすべく，この村を訪れたということであった。彼は，気息奄々として死にかけていた Frampol の村人に活を与えてくれたのである。

　ある日の朝，結婚周旋人たちが，彼の泊まっている宿屋を訪れ，各々手持ちの娘たちの美点を褒め讃えた。それに対して Cracow からやって来た紳士は，満月の暖かい夜，市場で舞踏会を開くことを提案した。娘たちの衣装の費用も何もかも，自分が負担しようと言う。年寄りたちはこの提案に疑念を抱いたが，娘たちは興奮し，若者たちも同意した。母親たちもためらう振りをしたが，結局是認した。年輩の男たちの代表が Rabbi Ozer に同意を求めに行ったとき，Rabbi Ozer は，ユダヤ人にあるまじき行為だと激怒する。あの紳士がこの村に定住してくれれば，村も潤うし，極度の貧困からも救われる。Synagogue も新しい屋根にする必要がありましょうと説得されて，とうとう Rabbi も不承不承折れるのである。今や，その月の半ばに催される舞踏会に向かって，Frampol の村全体が沸いていた。その後も Rabbi Ozer は信徒に向かい，皆は悪魔に誘われて転落の道を辿っているのだと絶えず戒めたが，耳を貸す者はいなかった。

　今は零落して，屑拾いを職としている Lipa という男がいた。その娘の Hodle は，酔っぱらいの父と乞食の母に似て，6歳のころから暴食家で泥棒という風評が立っていた。12歳のとき，Hodle の淫らさが村の女たちの話の種となり，猫や犬の屍肉を食べるという噂も立った。やがて Hodle は村から姿を消し，村人たちは安堵していた。しかし，Frampol の商人たちが，舞踏会の準備として，若い娘たちに無料で布や皮類を配布したとき，Hodle はどこからともなく姿を現した。彼女も今や17歳，十分に成長して女らしくなっていたが，顔はそばかすだらけで，髪の毛はパサパサだった。首にはジプシーの付けるようなビーズの飾りを巻き，手首に狼の歯のブレスレットをはめていた。

ついに舞踏会のその日がやってきた。Rabbi Ozer を除くすべての村人が市場に着飾って集まり、楽隊の音に合わせて踊った。紳士は側近を引き連れ、戦場に赴く騎士のように颯爽と白馬に乗って登場し、娘たちの踊りを眺めていた。Hodle だけが輪に加わらず、皆に無視されて傍らに立っていた。日没が迫ってきた。世界の終焉のように不気味な状況が、火のイメージと共に描写される。

> Never before had Frampol seen such a sunset. Like rivers of burning sulphur, fiery clouds streamed across the heavens, assuming the shapes of elephants, lions, snakes, and monsters. They seemed to be waging a battle in the sky, devouring one another, spitting, breathing fire. It almost seemed to be the River of Fire they watched, where demons tortured the evildoers amidst glowing coals and heaps of ashes. [18]

こういう状態の空を皆が不思議そうに見つめているとき、例の Cracow の紳士が話し始める。自分は世界中で最も金持ちで、金銭は私にとって砂のようなもので、ダイアモンドは小石のごときものだ。イスラエルの失われた十支族の長が、皆の惨状を知って、私を恩恵を施す者として派遣されたのだ。ただ一つだけ条件がある。この村のすべての処女は、この舞踏会に参加し、時計が夜の12時を打つまでに、くじを引くことによって自分の夫を決めなければならない。そうすれば、娘の一人一人に1万ダカットの持参金と膝まで届く一連の真珠を与えようと宣言する。娘は結婚する前に、掟通りの沐浴のため7日間待たなければならない、と大きな声で疑問を呈する老人に対して、紳士はその罪は俺が被ろうと答える。

　組み合わせは奇妙なものだった。比較的豊かな若者と貧しい家の娘、小男と大柄な女、障害者と美人、そして Cracow からやって来た紳士は Hodle が配偶者であった。先ほど大声をあげた老人が、何ということか、Hodle は淫売婦だと叫んだのに対し、紳士は Hodle に、それは真実か、ユダヤ人に対してか異教徒に対してもか、と尋ねる。Hodle は、その通りです、両者に対して行ってきました。パンのためというよりはそれは快楽のためであり、地獄の苦しみなど恐れない、神など存在しない故、後悔もしていないと述べる。

The doctor, leading Hodle by the hand, began to dance. Now, as though the powers of darkness had been summoned, the rain and hail began to fall; . . . But, heedless of the storm, pious men and women embraced without shame, dancing and shouting as though possessed. . . . Suddenly there was a terrific crash. A huge bolt of lightning had simultaneously struck the synagogue, the study house, and the ritual bath. The whole town was on fire. (38)

そこで Cracow からやって来た紳士は，その正体を現す。彼はもはや，村人が歓迎した若者ではなく，悪魔の頭 Ketev Mriti に他ならなかった。体中，うろこに覆われ，胸に一つ目玉が光り，額に猛烈な速度で回転する角を1本生やした怪物であった。

Witches, werewolves, imps, demons, and hobgoblins plummeted from the sky, some on brooms, others on hoops, still others on spiders. . . . Hodle's dress fell from her and she stood naked. (39)

婿の方は「コラー[19]とイシュマエル[20]の冒涜に従い，汝，この指輪をもって，われに悪ならんことを」("With this ring be thou desecrated to me according to the blasphemy of Korah and Ishmael.")（邦高55；39）と宣言した。

Singer は，この物語を Satan の勝利で終わらせていない。夜中に Rabbi Ozer は目覚めた。彼は神聖な人だったので，村を焼き尽くした火も彼の家は襲わなかった。もう夜明けかなと思って外を見たが，空は火のように赤く，野獣の遠吠えに似た叫び声が遠くから聞こえてきた。世界の終わりが訪れたのかなと思いながら，Rabbi は杖を持って信徒を捜し続けた。犬や奇妙な化け物が彼を襲ったが，彼はひるまなかった。市場だった場所は，泥とヘドロと灰だらけの大きな沼となっていた。腰まで沼にはまりこんだ裸の群れが，まだ舞踏の動作に酔いしれていた。Rabbi は，彼らを悪魔の群れだと思い，悪魔払いの文句を唱えようとしたが，そのとき裸の群れが自分の村人なのに気付いた。

Only then did he remember the doctor from Cracow, and the rabbi cried out bitterly, "Jews, for the sake of God, save your souls! You are in the hands of Satan!" (41)

Rabbi Ozer は，悪と戦うよう強く主張した。Torah や呪文や，いくつかの神の名を唱えて祈祷し，一人また一人と迷いから覚醒させた。夜が明けるころまでには，ほとんどの者が常態に復していた。やっと今，村人は悪魔が自分らをたぶらかし，不浄のなかへ引きずりこんだことを悟り，恐怖におののいた。飾り帯で首を締め死のうという男たちや，川に溺れて自殺しようという娘たちを諫め，Rabbi は，遅くならないうちに悔い改めよ，君たちは Satan の誘惑に落ちたのだ，私自身が犠牲の羊となろうと言う。

何もかも泥に変わり，Frampol の村は泥になっていた。幼児たちは死に，村人の住むべき家もなかった。食物もなく，人々は断食して喪に服した。隣町 Yanev のユダヤ人が，Frampol の惨状を知って，食物や衣服を送り，救援の手を差し伸べてきた。材木商人は建材を送り，金持ちは融資をしてくれた。その翌日から，村の再建が始まった。村人が，これほど勤勉に働いたことはこれまでになかった。住民たちは建設の槌を振るい，讃美歌を唱えた。Hodle の住んでいた小屋には人間の住んでいる気配はなく，その丘は雑草と茨に覆われていた。Hodle は，本当は Lilith [21] であり，この女故に，地底の世界の主どもが Frampol に姿を現したのだった。数日後，Rabbi Ozer は亡くなり，村全体が葬儀に参列した。新しい rabbi が赴任し，新しい村ができあがった。時は経ち，老人たちは死んだが，この事件の物語は洋皮紙に書き留められて，いつまでも残された。

> And the events in the story brought their epilogue: the lust for gold had been stifled in Frampol; it was never rekindled. From generation to generation the people remained paupers. A gold coin became an abomination in Frampol, and even silver was looked at askance. (44)

Cracow からやって来た紳士が金を浪費するのは，Satan が昔から使う常套手段である。また，祝日以外に舞踏会に参加し，お祭り騒ぎに耽ることは，ユダヤ性を放棄するに等しい。ユダヤの律法に従わないで，紳士すなわち悪魔の誘惑に負けることは，換言すれば Satan が God に打ち勝ったということである。Hodle の「どだい，神などいないんですから」("There is no God.")（邦高53；

38）という言葉が象徴的である。神に対して犯した冒涜は，大火災によって神に罰せられる。村人の過度の欲望とその処罰が，激しい火のイメージによって強烈に提示される。しかし最後に引用した文章で明らかなように，Frampol のユダヤ人は，その後改悛と反省により再生する。貧困をユダヤ人のバッジとして，勤勉・忍耐・敬神・同情のユダヤ人としての道徳律を回復する。注意しなければならぬのは，これらの徳性は，Cracow から Gentleman-devil がやって来るまでは，Frampol の村にほとんどみられなかったということである。ごく当り前の教訓を得るために，Frampol は何とも大きな犠牲を払ったのであった。

V

　Joel Blocker と Richard Elman との対談のなかで，悪魔的・超自然的なものを作品のなかでなぜ使うのか，その理由を Singer は以下のように説明している。まず，自分の思うことを述べる手助けとなり，無形の物を具体化できる自由がある。それらを通して，他の方法では言えない多くのことが表現できるのだ。例えば，Satan や demon をシンボルとして使うことによって，沢山のことを凝縮した状態に要約できる。また悪魔は，世界すなわち人間と人間の行動の象徴であると私は思っている。私は，象徴的にも実質的にも，彼らの存在を（少なくとも，我々が分からない力や精霊がこの世に存在することを）信じているので，このような文学スタイルが生まれるのは自然である。

> I really love this style and I am always finding new symbols and new stories. . . . I would say that every serious writer is possessed by certain ideas or symbols, and I am possessed by my demons and they add a lot to my vision and my expression.[22]

Singer は，人間は悪魔であると確信しているようにも思われる。
　また，前記 2 人の面接者が，あなたの作品は morality stories ですかと問うたのに対し，Singer は，morality stories と特徴付けることはしたくないが，道徳的な視点から物語を構成していると思っていると答えている。Singer は，自然主義的立場を非難し，善と悪の観点で考えない作家は成功しないと述べ，行動

主義的理論を糾弾している。

> My judgement is that good does not always triumph, that this is very far from being the best of all possible worlds. That's why all my Jews are not good Jews. . . . The Cabbalists say this world is the worst of all possible worlds. They believe there are millions of worlds, but the worst is this one. Here is the very darkness itself. How can you expect that in the blackest darkness, in the deepest abyss of all, everything should turn out nice and proper? From a Cabbalistic point of view, I'm a very realistic writer. . . . [23]

Singer は，文学の最も主要な目的は，読者を楽しませることであると考えている。人が集まると，他人の噂で会話が活気付き，人はそれを楽しむ。噂話を匿名にしたのが物語であり，噂話と違って誰も傷つけない。そしてそれは，人間の特質を取り上げ論じているのである，と言っている。

> The fiction writers who don't discuss character and only discuss social problems take away from literature its very essence. They stop being entertaining. We always love to discuss and reveal character because human character is to us the greatest puzzle. . . . Discussing character constitutes a supreme form of entertainment. [24]

New York Times Book Review の Laurie Colwin とのインタヴューのなかで，Singer文学の最も大切なものは何かと問われ，彼は emotions，特に passions に変化する emotions であると答えている。

> Spinoza says in his *Ethics* that everything can become a passion, and I know that this is true. There is nothing that cannot become a passion. Especially if they are connected either with sex or with the supernatural—and I would say for me sex and the supernatural go very much together. [25]

また，別の個所で，文学とは愛と運命の物語である，つまり「もの狂おしいハリケーンのような人間の激情と，そういった情念との闘争を描くこと」(a description of the mad hurricane of human passions and the struggle with them.) [26] と述べている。また，さらに別のところでは，他の人の人間性と接触する最善の

方法は，愛と性を通してである。愛と性を通して人間性が最も顕著に暴露される故，ここで人生について多くのことを学ぶことができる，という意味のことも言っている。[27]

つまり，彼の最も優れた短編小説の実体をキーワードで示せば，emotions, love, sex, passions, the demonic, the supernatural, とりわけ the demonic passions である。また，passions に取り憑かれるのは，何か目に見えない異常な力，または魔力に動かされた compulsions であり，その結果招来された obsessive, abnormal, unnatural, despairing で grotesque な状況を，結果として振り返ってみれば，それは fate である。ポーランドのユダヤ人の信仰とそれからの逸脱，悪の存在，この宇宙における人間存在の意味などが，悪魔や小悪魔や天使の出没する世界で象徴的に描かれ，謎めいた非現実的な設定のなかに，現実と非現実が境界線もなく交錯し，それでいて時間と空間を超えた普遍性を持って読者に迫ってくる。

人間は本来弱い者であり，天使的な上昇活動よりも，動物的な下向活動に陥りがちである。そこに悪魔が入り込み，人間はさらに罪を重ねて，螺旋状の階段を真っ逆さまに奈落の底に落ち込んでゆく。しかし，世俗的にも宗教的にも絶望の極にありながら，Singer の作品にはどこかに罪悪感と罪の自覚が，仄見える。正統派ユダヤ人の神経を逆撫でする sexuality, criminality, demonology がありながら，Philip Roth の作品とは異なり[28]，どこか遠くで，神がじっと見つめている感がある。悪魔との戦いで，人間は真実を改めて見直し，精神的に一歩向上するという，一抹の希望の曙光が見えるのである。

Singer は，登場人物の行動の具体的な動機を説明することもしないし，フロイド的な心理学的説明もしない。無用な説教や議論を避け，物語ることに徹する storyteller の真骨頂が，悪魔的な激情の発露と，その帰結としての絶望的な惨状，そしてその向こうに仄見えるかすかな希望の光を取り扱うとき，珠玉のような光沢を発して，最も豊かに発揮されるのである。

≪Notes≫

1) Irving Malin, ed., *Critical Views of Isaac Bashevis Singer* (New York University Press, 1969)

14-15.
2) Lawrence S. Friedman, *Understanding Isaac Bashevis Singer* (Columbia, S. C.: University of South Carolina Press, 1988) 6-7.
3) *Yiddish* で Leo Rosten, *The Joys of Yiddish* (New York: McGraw-Hill, 1968) 369. では "Little city, small town, village—in particular, the Jewish communities of eastern Europe, where the culture of the Ashkenazim flourished (before World War II)." と説明している。
4) Malin 36.
5) Isaac Bashevis Singer, *Passions and Other Stories* (London: Jonathan Cape, 1976) v.
6) Malin 14, 17.
7) Irving Malin は Singer の作品を the open novels と the closed novels の2つのタイプに分類している。Malin の著書 *Isaac Bashevis Singer* (New York: Frederick Unger Publishing Co., 1972) 42.の the closed novel の説明を以下に紹介する。I believe that Singer is at his best in the closed novels (and short stories.) These are tight, claustrophobic, and concentrated—they insist upon the detailed, symbolic event, not the comprehensive sweep of history, and they consequently force us to read closely. They tend to deal with faith in an "obsessive" way because they limit themselves to an exploration of one "center of consciousness." Although they are far removed from the "all-encompassing" generational novels previously discussed, they do represent the recurring themes of freedom and slavery, the nature of Jewishness.
8) Irving Malin, *Isaac Bashevis Singer* (New York: Frederick Unger Publishing Co., 1972) 70.
9) シュレミールもシュリマーザルも共に Yiddish 語で，不運につきまとわれ，へまばかりやらかす人の意であるが，厳密に言うと，シュレミールはスープを膝の上にこぼす人で，シュリマーザルはこぼされる人である。前者は不運の種をまき散らす人で，後者はそれを受ける犠牲者である。なお，さらに詳しい説明は，第Ⅴ章のNote 5.を参照。
10) Edward Alexander はその著，*Isaac Bashevis Singer, A Study of the Short Fiction* (Boston: Twayne Publishers, 1990) PartⅠで，Singer の短編小説を9のタイプに分類している。
11) ユダヤ伝説で人の心につく悪霊，または安住所を得ず人の心に乗り移って働く死人の霊。
12) Isaac Bashevis Singer, *Short Friday and Other Stories* (New York: Farrar, Satraus and Giroux, 1964) 26. 以下この作品からの引用はすべてこの版により，引用英文末尾の括弧内に頁数を記す。和文と英文を併記する場合は（邦高103;42）と記す。和文はアイザック・B・シンガー，邦高忠二訳『短い金曜日』（東京：晶文社，1971）による。
13) 通俗的なデーモン学では，Satan は大いなる悪魔であって，demon の軍勢の指揮官である。Devil, Lucifer と同一視されることもある。
14) 2世紀末にユダヤ教の口伝を収集し，生活・宗教に関する規則を編集したもので，後に Talmud の基となった。

15) ユダヤ教・キリスト教では悪霊。鬼, 鬼神, 悪魔も意味し, 今では devil と大体同じ意味に使われている。かつて両者の間には厳然とした区別があり, demon は神々と人間との間に介在する一種の霊を指した。
16) デーモン学のいくつかの流れのなかで重要な devil。
17) Isaac Bashevis Singer, *Passions and Other Stories* (London: Jonathan Cape, 1976) 117. New York: Farrar, Straus and Giroux, 1975年版は入手できなかったので, 以下この作品からの引用はすべて Jonathan Cape 版により, 引用文末尾の括弧内に頁数を記す。和文と英文を併記する場合は（陣﨑；117）と記す。
18) Isaac Bashevis Singer, *Gimpel the Fool and Other Stories* (New York: Farrar, Straus and Giroux, 1957) 34-35. 以下この作品からの引用はすべてこの版により, 引用英文末尾の括弧内に頁数を記す。和文と英文を併記する場合は（邦高49；34-35）と記す。和文はアイザック・B・シンガー, 邦高忠二訳『短い金曜日』(東京：晶文社, 1971) による。
19) Moses と Aaron に対する反乱を指揮したレビ人。 Cf.《聖書》*Num.* 16.
20) Abraham がその侍女 Hagar に生ませた子。妻Sarahによって母と共に追放された。 Cf.《聖書》*Gen.* 16:11.
21) ユダヤ伝説で, Eve が作られる前の Adam の妻で, devil の母と言われている。
22) Malin, *Critical Views of Isaac Bashevis Singer*, 23.
23) Malin 25.
24) Isaac Bashevis Singer and Richard Burgin, *Conversations with Isaac Bashevis Singer* (New York: Doubleday & Company, Inc., 1985) 47.
25) *New York Times Book Review* (23 July 1978): 24.
26) 陣﨑訳；Isaac Bashevis Singer, *The Image and Other Stories* (New York: Farrar, Straus and Giroux, 1985) vii.
27) Singer and Burgin 33.
28) Phillip Roth も, その小説がユダヤ人社会を中傷するものとして非難攻撃を受けたが, Singer も同じような批判を浴びた。Joel Blocker と Richard Elman との対談（Irving Malin, ed., *Critical Views of Isaac Bashevis Singer*, 12）のなかで, Singer は宗教について次のように述べている。自分は, God と the Higher Powers の存在は信じるけれども, 人間が神性なものとして創り出した教義や制度や慣例には, 疑念をいだいている。それが, 父親に勧められても, Hasid 派の rabbi にならなかった理由である, と。

第IV章
ニューヨークを舞台にした作品の閉塞性・倫理性・シュレミール性
―― Bernard Malamudの5つの短編を中心にして

　Bernard Malamud の作品，特にその短編には，ニューヨークの貧しい下町のどこかを舞台にしたものが多い。しかし比較的具体的に場所が明示されているのは，グリニッチ・ヴィレッジは Prince 通りの小菓子屋の主人公 Tommy Castelliとその店で万引きをする少女との微妙な関係を描いた短編 "The Prison"（1950）や，イースト・サイドにある古ぼけたアパートに住んでいる年金暮らしの Kessler の苦悩を記した "The Mourners"（1955）ぐらいのものであろうか。"The Bill"（1951），"The Loan"（1952），"Take Pity"（1958），"Angel Levine"（1955），"The First Seven Years"（1950），"The Magic Barrel"（1954）などの短編の舞台も，*The Assistant*（1957）などの長編のそれも，ニューヨークのどこかということは分かるのだが，特定のどこでもない，大抵ごみごみした古ぼけた町の一隅である。Malamud が創り上げたシュールレアリスティックな靄に包まれてはいるが，それだけにかえって，いかにもニューヨークらしい，いやニューヨークでなくてはならないリアリティーを，これらの作品は持っている。
　大都市の持つ特性の一つは，貧富の差の激しさであろうが，Malamud は好んで極貧のユダヤ系アメリカ人を主人公として選ぶ。彼らは，ニューヨークの貧相な貸しアパートに住んでいるか，倒産寸前の小店でお客の来るのを待っているかである。大抵，しみったれていて，重々しく，陰うつな，同化していない一世か二世のユダヤ人である。馬鹿に近いお人好しで，しばしば人に騙され，

第Ⅳ章　ニューヨークを舞台にした作品の閉塞性・倫理性・シュレミール性　　35

一生働いても文無しで終わる。教育と将来性に，娘のより良き結婚に夢を託し，営々として働くが，その努力は報われず，何か不運が振りかかってきて，ささやかな成功の夢も無残に打ち砕かれる。生まれながら不運を背負って生きているような犠牲者の一生であるが，その苦悩と貧困にじっと耐え，より貧しくより悲惨な近隣の人々に憐憫を持ち，ささやかな援助の手を差し伸べる。貧乏を美しい女のように愛する男たちとその人間関係が，現実と幻想の交錯したニューヨークを背景にして繰り広げられるのである。

　極度の貧困と闘い，狭いアパートの一室か店のなかに閉じ込められ，孤独感や絶望感に打ちひしがれ，不運をかこちながら，それでいて清く正しく生きていこうとする人たち——こういう人たちをユーモアとペーソスを交えて描くことにかけて，おそらくMalamudの右に出る者はあるまい。この貧困性，閉塞性， schlemiel あるいは schlimazel 性，そして，そういう状態のなかでの倫理性は，ニューヨークのような大都会において，最も極限状況を露呈するのであるが，以下具体的にこれらの諸点をMalamudの作品のなかで探求してみたい。

　"The Mourners"のKesslerは65歳，以前鶏卵鑑別を職としていたが，今は老人年金だけで一人で細々と暮らしているユダヤ人である。ある時期には家庭を持ったこともあったが，妻や子供はいつも彼の気にいらぬ存在でしかなく，幾年かすると彼は家族を捨てて出ていってしまった。10年間も住み慣れたイースト・サイドのこの古アパートの5階に訪れる友もなく孤独な毎日である。管理人と家主は，Kesslerの不潔を理由に，彼をアパートから追い出そうとする。立ち退き命令に異議を申し立てなかったため，執行官はKesslerを無理やり連れ出し，貧しい家具類も舗道に運び出して並べる。雨やみぞれの降りしきるなか，持ち出された椅子の一つに，上着も着ず帽子もかぶらず，Kesslerは座っている。見兼ねた隣人たちが，部屋の錠を引き切ってKesslerを部屋に運び込み，家具を元に戻す。高血圧が持病の家主Gruberは，怒ってKesslerを追い出そうと詰問する。しかし老人は聞いていなかった。体を前後に揺すり，30年前に捨てた家族のことを想い，その罪深さに我と我が身をかきむしっている。Kesslerの苦悩の激しさに恐怖を感じたGruberは発作を起こす。体をゆっくり揺らしているKesslerは誰かの喪に服しているのだが，それは他ならぬ自分の

ためだ，とGruberは気付く。家主は，Kesslerのベッドにある敷布をはぎ取り，それを大きな体に巻きつけ，床にどんと倒れて哀悼者となる。

　"The Loan"は，同じ移民船の3等船客としてニューヨークにやって来た旧友のKobotskyが，貧しいパン屋のLiebに，200ドルほど貸して欲しいと頼みにくる話である。Liebは，この30年間一文なしのパン屋であった。ある日，あまりの惨めさに，練り粉の上に涙をこぼした。それから後は，涙で味を付けたパンが，よく売れるようになり，今では小金を貯めている。しかし脱腸やそこひに苦しむLiebは，健康には恵まれていない。15年前借りた100ドルをいまだに返さず，今また無心にきたKobotskyに対して，Liebは昔の怒りを忘れ，旧友の不幸を助けたいと思う。しかし，Liebの後妻のBessieは，ロシアやドイツでユダヤ人として受けた辛酸，アメリカでのこれまでの苦労と将来の不安を吐露して，要求に応じようとしない。自分はアメリカに来て，この貧しいパン屋に会った。貧乏の味しか知らなくて，人生にお金も楽しみも持たない哀れな人，そんな人とどうした訳か結婚してしまった。それからは，昼も夜も働いて，どうやら曲がりなりにも店が持てるまでになり，12年目の今，やっと息がつけるようになった。しかし，Liebは健康ではない。目は両方とも手術しなければならない。それに万が一，Liebが今死んだら，自分はどこへ行けばいいの？　一文無しだったら，面倒は誰がみてくれるの？　Bessieの説得力ある悲しい物語を聞いているうちに，焼いていたパンが黒焦げとなる。Kobotskyとパン屋は，互いの消え果てた青春を溜息と共に嘆き合い，抱き合って，永久に別れる。

　"The Bill"のPanessa夫妻は，工場勤めを定年退職したPanessa氏の3000ドルの預金を基にして，デリカテッセンを開いている。地下へ石段を5つ降りたところにあるこの店は，実際は壁のなかの穴とでもいった体のものであった。その通りは河に近かったけれどもその気配はなく，ただ時代がかった煉瓦造りのアパートの続く狭い曲がりくねった横町である。ボールを真っすぐ投げ上げる子供だけが薄青い空の断片を見ることができる暗い環境である。近所のセルフサーヴィスの店に押されて，Panessaの店の売り上げは少ない。その数少ないお客の一人Willy Schlegelに掛売りを始めたことが原因で，その額が合計83ドル

となり、店の経営も行き詰まって食べる物にも不自由する状態のなかで、Panessa氏は老衰のため死亡する。Panessa夫妻は、店の繁盛のために積極的に行動するでもなく、ただ受身にお客の来るのを待ち、しかも異教徒の客Schlegelに善意と信頼を提供し、それが原因で破滅するのである。

"Take Pity"は、生活調査員の質問に答える、以前コーヒーのセールスマンだったRosenの語りという形で進められる。38歳の未亡人Evaの亡夫は、ポーランドから来た避難移民で、アメリカに着くと盲の馬みたいに働いて、3000ドルぐらいを貯めた。その金で彼は、壁に囲まれた穴蔵みたいな食料品店を買ったのだが、その店はてんで商売になるような所ではなかった。結局、店はつぶれて彼は死亡し、Evaは、残された1000ドルの保険金で2人の子供を養っていかねばならない。夫の死後も食料品店を続けるEvaであったが、近くのスーパーマーケットに圧迫され、利益は上がらず、保険金の1000ドルもやがてなくなってしまう。Evaを愛しているRosenは、結婚を申し込んで断られ、それでも可能な限りの援助を提供しようとして拒絶される。ついにRosenは自分の弁護士のところへ行って遺書を作成する。Rosenの持っているものを全部——株券も、2つの家も、当座預金も、保険金も——彼女に与えるように署名をして家に帰り、台所でガスの栓を開けて自殺を図るが未遂に終わるのである。

"The Cost of Living"（1950）の主人公Sam Tomashevskyは東欧から移住して27年間、不運な食料品店を妻となんとか守ってきた。生まれてこのかた、生きることの楽しみなんてなかったような人生である。この貧しい夫婦の最近の悩みは、隣の空き家にどんな店が引っ越してくるかということである。隣は、イタリア系の靴修理屋が倒産して、冬の間中空っぽであった。Samには、そのことが寝ても覚めても心のなかのしこりとなって、重苦しくのし掛かっている。悪夢は現実となり、5月になって最新式の設備を調えたチェーン・ストアの食料品店が乗り込んでくる。Samの店の顧客は、1人減り2人減り、秋になるとますます店は不景気となって、ほとんど客は来なくなる。とうとうSamは店を競売に付し、どこへともなく去って行く。

貧困性、閉塞性、schlemiel・schlimazel性、ユダヤ的な倫理性といった特色が、その各々の重点の置き方や組み合わせの度合いは異なるにしても、これま

で考慮してきた短編群のなかに顕著に見られることは，個々に具体的に指摘するまでもなかろう。

長編 The Assistant は，これら初期の短編を基盤にして集大成したものと言えるが，この作品については都合によりここでは言及せず，第V章において詳述する。ともあれ，これまで，先に列挙した4つの特色が，ニューヨークを舞台とした初期の短編に，どのように顕現されているかを考察してきた。以下，Malamud 自身のニューヨークとの関係と，その後の作品のこの大都市との関係を追いながら論を進めてゆきたい。

Malamud は，1914年，ロシアのウクライナ地方からのユダヤ系移民の子として，ニューヨークのブルックリンで生まれた。ブルックリンの Erasmus Hall 高校を経てニューヨーク市立大学で英文学を専攻し，コロンビア大学の大学院で学んで修士号を得た。母校の Erasmus Hall 夜間高校などに勤務し，昼間は創作に従事していたが，1949年，生活の安定のため35年間住み慣れたニューヨークを後にして，オレゴン州 Corvallis にあるオレゴン州立大学 Corvallis 校に英作文の講師として赴任する。1943年に2つの習作短編を発表しているが，これは世の認めるところとならなかった。Harper's Bazaar に "The Cost of Living" を，Partisan Review に "The First Seven Years"，"The Magic Barrel" などを，Commentary に "The Prison"，"The Bill"，"The Loan" などを次々に公表して，作家としての地位を確立し始めたのは，1950年以降すなわち，彼がオレゴン州に移り住んでからのことである。そのほんの一部分がニューヨーク時代に書かれた可能性はなきにしもあらずであるが，大部分の初期の短編や The Assistant は，西部の果ての Corvallis 時代に書かれたと推定される。これらの作品に描かれているニューヨークが，シャガールの絵のような幻想性を秘めているのは，ここにその要因の一つがあるのかもしれない。

異常な野球の才能を持った田舎少年の人生の浮沈を描いた幻想的・寓意的な処女長編 The Natural (1952)，The Assistant，これまで雑誌に発表した12の短編に "Take Pity" を加えて本の形にした The Magic Barrel (1958)，それにオレゴン州立大学での教員生活を題材にした A New Life (1961) などが次々と出版され，Malamud は確固たる地位を文壇に確立するが，これらの作品は，Corvallis 時代

第Ⅳ章　ニューヨークを舞台にした作品の閉塞性・倫理性・シュレミール性　39

の12年間に執筆されたものである。

　1961年に Malamud は，オレゴン州立大学準教授の職を辞し，ヴァーモント州の Bennington 大学の教授として迎えられる。その後は，Bennington とニューヨークのアパートの間を行ったり来たりしていたようである。その後，短編集 *Idiots First*（1963），1910年代初め，革命前のロシアを舞台にした残忍で不条理な迫害の物語 *The Fixer*（1966），イタリア物のオムニバス小説 *Pictures of Fidelman*（1969），再びニューヨークを舞台としてユダヤ系作家と作家志望の黒人との確執や人種間の微妙な対立感情を描いた *The Tenants*（1971），第3の短編集 *Rembrandt's Hat*（1973），ニューヨーク州の田舎町 Center Campobello に住む熟年の伝記作家を主人公とした自伝的小説 *Dubin's Lives*（1977）が続刊された。それに最終作 *God's Grace*（1982）は，水爆戦争後の大洪水のため，地球上にただ一人生き残ったユダヤ系古代学者が潜水艇に乗って，話のできるチンパンジーと太平洋と覚しき所を漂流し，無人島に着き，ヒヒやチンパンジーや猿やゴリラと生活するプロセスを描いた想像的・予言的物語である。

　話を元に戻して1961年に出版された *A New Life* に返ることにしよう。地方大学英文科の保守性と堕落した状況を諷刺したこの小説の主人公 Seymour Levin は，この小説の作者と同じく，ニューヨークから新しい生活を求めて北西部の田舎大学に赴任する。所は，Cascadia という架空の州にある Easchester, 人口１万足らずの小さな町にある Cascadia 州立大学 Easchester 校であり，時は，これまでの作品の特色であった「時代のない」世界から，はっきりと1950年の晩夏から翌年の初夏までと明記してある。

　これまでのニューヨーク物やイタリア物と比べて，全く新しい世界，牧歌的な自然の背景がふんだんに提示される。プロットの場面転換の要所要所には，壮大で詳細な自然描写と季節の移り変わりが描かれ，随所にニューヨークとの比較がなされる。最初に Easchester に着いたとき，Levin は次のように感じる。「ほんとに西部だな，とレヴィンは思った。開拓者たちが，この谷間にはじめて幌馬車を乗り入れた場面を想像しただけで胸が熱くなる。まだおれは，自然の懐で暮らしたことはほとんどないが，昔から自然は好きだった。だから，ニューヨークを離れたのは間違いではなかったと改めてそう思った。彼は幸福感

に身をふるわせた。」(My God, the West, Levin thought. He imagined the pioneers in covered wagons entering this valley for the first time, and found it a moving thought. Although he had lived little in nature Levin had always loved it, and the sense of having done the right thing in leaving New York was renewed in him. He shuddered at his good fortune.)[1] Levinは，下宿の家の芝生を刈り，落葉の大掃除をし，ウォールデンの森に小宇宙を認めた晩年のThoreauになったような気分に浸ったりする。室内と戸外とが交流し合い，外出するときも錠を掛けないでもよい生活が気に入っている。自然と親しむうちに，心にはゆとりが生まれ，裕福さに浸ることができる。そして，大自然の風景の変化の魔術的な素晴らしさに感嘆する。

都会的な慌ただしさを逃れることが，Easchesterに来た喜びの大きな部分を占めているのだが，しかし一方では，都会にある期待と神秘を恋しく思い，死んでいるように静まりかえっているこの町にいると，自分が老け込んでくるように感じる。自分は雑多な移民が交流している大都会の出身なのに，この大学の学生はどれもこれも似たような顔付きが集まっている町や小都市の出身だ，と考えたりもする。

恋に破れ泥酔者となって，ニューヨークの夜をうろつき回った過去の苦悩と恥辱を清算し逃れるべく，Levinは西部にやって来た。最初は，大学の英作文担当講師として一応満足し，同じ過ちを繰り返さないよう努力をしようと思っている。節操を持った人間として，学部長・学科長・作文主任などによって支えられている体制に，おとなしく順応し，自分を抑えなければと考える。しかし段々と慣れるにつれて，ここの社交生活も学問的な生活も，退屈で活気のないものだということが分かってくる。学科主任は文法教科書とその改訂だけに熱意を示し，自分の編集したその教科書を学科指定として30年間も，皆に使わせるよう仕向けている。学問的研究への情熱も努力も，ここでは認められない。過去の苦悩の追憶と，現在の倦怠と孤独のなかで，徐々にLevinの悪の虫が首をもたげてくる。柄にもなく，前任者Leo Duffyの歩んだ道を辿って，英文科教室の改革に乗り出すまではまだ良かった。酒場の女，独身の女性同僚教師，教えている女子学生との性遍歴までは，ことが露顕せずに済んだ。しかし，

作文主任教授の妻 Pauline Gilley との森のなかや Levin の下宿での度重なる逢瀬は，ついに周囲の知るところとなり，学科長選挙出馬にも失敗して，大学を追放される羽目となる。小説全体を通じて，Leo Duffy のイメージが，Pauline にも Levin にも付きまとって離れない。Pauline にとっては Leo Duffy の代役に過ぎなかったかもしれない Levin は，Leo と同じような運命を辿ってゆく。いや，Leo よりも，もっともっとルフトメンシュ（luftmensh）[2] 的要素，schlemiel 的要素が強い。あまり気の進まないまま，Pauline と 2 人の養子，それに Pauline のお腹のなかの子供の運命をも背負って，彼らの救済者，犠牲者となり，牧歌的田園の地を去ってゆく結末は滑稽味さえある。

　だめな男はどこにいてもだめだと，Malamud は言っているのかもしれない。しかし，西部からニューヨークにやって来たという違いはあるにしても，*The Assistant* の Frank Alpine は，同じような汚辱の過去から立ち上がって，新しい生活を求めている。Levin よりも，もっと悲惨な環境のなかで，聖人のような努力と忍耐でもって苦難を切り抜けてゆく徳性がある。罪を告白しようとする欲求も，Levin よりはるかに強烈である。道化の要素の強い Levin にはない感動がある。小説に一貫して流れている強烈に読者に訴えるものを，より強く *The Assistant* のなかに感じるのは，ここら辺りに原因があるのであろう。

　なるほど Malamud の作品における農村対都市の関係図式は，*The Assistant* と *A New Life* とのそれぐらいしか，存在しないかもしれない。また，Malamud は，都市の問題を真正面から取り扱っている作家ではないのかもしれない。都市に対する憧憬も，都市の持つ破壊的要素に対する批判・攻撃・幻滅も真っ向からは記述されていないかもしれない。しかし，現実と幻想の混合した Malamud の創り上げたニューヨークと，そこにうごめく貧しい人間像は，至高の芸術的芳香を持つものである。多民族で構成されているニューヨークの民族的伝統を留める生活の一端を描き，この大都会の栄光と発展のかげにかくれ大資本に抑圧されている個人の貧困と苦悩をものして，Malamud より優れた作家はあるまい。Malamud のニューヨークは，アメリカ文学と都市の系譜のなかで永遠に生き続けることであろう。

≪Notes≫

1) バーナード・マラマッド，宮本陽吉訳『もうひとつの生活』(東京：新潮社，1970) 4.
   Bernard Malamud, *A New Life* (New York: Farrar, Straus and Giroux, 1961) 4-5.
2) Yiddish語で，空の男の意。転じて，夢想家で感受性が強く詩人タイプの人，楽天的だが非実際的な人をいう。なお，*A New Life* については，第Ⅵ章においても若干言及する。

第V章
「ユダヤ教への改宗」と「ユダヤ人の改宗」
—— Bernard Malamud, *The Assistant* vs. Philip Roth, "The Conversion of the Jews," and "Eli, the Fanatic"

　Bernard Malamud の初期の小説の世界は，貧乏たらしく陰欝で，ヘブライ臭を芬々と漂わせている。登場人物は，大抵ニューヨーク市に居住する，東欧から移住してきた一世のユダヤ人か，その二世である。廃業寸前のしみったれた小売店主か，貧乏な大学生や作家修業中の男であったりする。

　Malamud の主人公の一生は，不運な事柄の連続である。彼らは生まれながらの負け犬であり，敗北者（born loser）である。しばしば人に騙されるのだが，決して人を騙すことはせず，あくまでも誠実な人生を貫く。惨めな貧困に苦しみながら，より貧しくより悲惨な隣人に憐憫をかけ，援助する。彼らは，善良な行為に対して報われることもない。物質的な貧しさは甘受しているが，精神的な貧困に陥ることはない。Malamud は，人は自分の運命に忠実でなければならない，「苦難はユダヤ人であることのあかしであり，まさに宿命だと言っている」（. . . to speak of suffering as the mark of the Jew and as his very fate.）[1] ようである。

　Malamud は Martin Buber の哲学を彼の作品の中に採り入れていると言われている。Buber も信じているように，苦難は人間生活に欠くことのできないものであり，苦難によって神は人間を罪から救いたまう[2] のである。Malamud の主人公の人生航路は苦難に満ち，彼はそれらを乗り越え，人間として成長してゆかねばならないのである。

Malamud の第2作であり，代表作とも言うべき *The Assistant* の主人公の1人 Morris Bober は，その典型的な登場人物である。貧しい60歳の病身な食料品店主で，若いころユダヤ人としてロシアに育ち，徴兵を逃れて希望の国アメリカに渡ってきた。この小説のストーリーが展開するよりずっと以前，Morris は，斜視で抜け目のない共同事業者 Charlie Sobeloff に騙され，ごまかされて，店を乗っ取られてしまう。そこで Morris 一家はユダヤ人居住地から，周りは皆異教徒（gentiles）ばかりが住んでいるこの地区に移ってきた。その後どうした訳か，酒屋の Karp 一家とキャンディ・ストアの Pearl 一家が隣り合って住みつき，この3軒が小さなユダヤ人集団を造っている。Bober 家はこれまで不景気のときを何とか切り抜け，生き延びてきた。

しかし最近になって，ピカピカの最新式装備を誇るデリカテッセン兼食料品店が近くに開店し，Morris の店は閉鎖寸前に追い込まれている。正直に，長時間働いたが，得たものはほとんど何もなかった。苦しい期待，果てしれぬ失望，煙と消えた幾年，自分では数えることもできない数々の不運，今や60歳になって，30歳の時よりも貧しくなっている。彼の23歳の娘 Helen は，自分の給料小切手を父に渡し，家計を助けていた。

> The grocer, on the other hand, had never altered his fortune, unless degrees of poverty meant alteration, for luck and he were, if not natural enemies, not good friends. He labored long hours, was the soul of honesty . . . , yet he trusted cheaters — coveted nobody's nothing and always got poorer . . . . At the end you were sixty and had less than at thirty. It was, she〔Helen〕thought, surely a talent.[3]

酔っ払いが Julius Karp の酒屋に石を投げると，それは Bober の店に当たって，窓ガラスを壊す。Karp が恐れていた2人の強盗は，繁盛している酒屋に押し入ろうとして，結局は不景気な Morris の店を選ぶ。強盗の1人は拳銃を振り上げ，Morris の顔をめがけて打ち下ろした。

> He fell without a cry. The end fitted the day. It was his luck, others had better. (27)

他のユダヤ人は，もっと運が良かった。Julius Karp は運が向いてきて，今は

繁盛する酒屋を経営している。彼の息子 Louis は「のんびりと暮らすタイプで，父親の苦労の果実が膝に落ちてくるのを待っているといった様子だった。」（. . . made a relaxed living letting the fruit of his father's investment fall into his lap.)[4] 手に触れるものすべてを純金に変える才能を持つ Julius は，太り過ぎの妻を店の上の貧相なげた履き住宅から公園通りの大きな家に移したのだった。Sam Pearl のキャンディ・ストアは Karp の酒屋ほど成功していなかったが，息子の Nat はハンサムで野心的なコロンビア大学法学部の学生で，将来を嘱望される有望株である。

　Morris Bober は，彼らの，特に Julius Karp の幸運に対し，愛憎併存の揺曳する微妙な心境であった。何年もの間，彼はこの男の幸運に腹を立てまいとしてきたが，最近では相手が少しは不運に見舞われればよいという気にもなった。しかしそのすぐ後で彼は反省するのであった。

> God bless Julius Karp, the grocer thought. Without him I would have my life too easy. God made Karp so a poor grocery man will not forget his life is hard. (23)

それからまた再び，schlimazel [5] の Morris は，何年も報いなく働いてきたという思いに周期的に悩まされるのであった。この小説の終わりに近くなって，Ward Minogue の失火で Karp の酒屋が灰塵に帰してしまう。空ろな，水を滴らす抜け殻になってしまった Karp の財産を眼前にして，Morris は罪の苛責にさいなまれる。

> Afterward Morris couldn't sleep. He stood at his bedroom window in his long underwear, looking down at the pile of burned and broken fixtures on the sidewalk. With a frozen hand the grocer clawed at a live pain in his breast. He felt an overwhelming hatred of himself. He had wished it on Karp—just this. His anguish was terrible. (218-19)

　より貧しい人たちに対する寛大さにおいて，Morris Bober はアンビヴァレンスの兆候も示さない。毎朝6時にたった3セントの種なしパンを買いに来るユダヤ人嫌いのポーランド女にも，貧しい母親が掛けで買いによこす小さな女の

子にも，妻が弟と駆け落ちした電球行商人にも，彼の店に押し入った強盗の片割れであり結局は彼の店と苦悩の哲学を引き継ぐ Frank Alpine に対しても，等しく差別することなく Morris は慈善と親切と寛容さを注ぎかけるのである。

　The Assistant のメイン・プロットは，Frank Alpine に対する Morris の関係と，Frank と Helen との関係という，2つの流れが交錯しながら展開していく。後者は，Frank が Helen に対する肉体的な欲情から精神的な愛情を持つに至る過程であり，犯した罪に対する悔恨と Helen に対する真の愛情から，Morris の死後も無欲の献身的奉仕をなす人間に変身するプロセスである。前者は，イタリア系カトリック教徒の Frank が，Morris のユダヤ教徒らしい人間観に感動し，欲望と情熱と悔恨と罪悪感の混ざり合った苦悩の長い試練の後に，ユダヤ教に改宗して店を継ぎ，Morris の後継者となる展開である。P. L. Hays がいみじくも指摘しているように，「フランクはユダヤ教（精神）とヘレンに強く惹かれ，この両者と一体になることを切望した」(Frank was strongly attracted to Judaism and Helen, and wished to 'belong' to both.)[6] のである。換言すれば，この小説は，最後に Frank が割礼を施しユダヤ教に改宗する結末となるまで，Frank が両者と一体となる試みの過程であると言えよう。

　Frank Alpine は25歳のイタリア系アメリカ人である。孤児院でカトリック教徒として育てられ，後に放浪者となり，最近より良いチャンスを求めてブルックリンに来た。ある11月初旬の朝，Frank は Ward Minogue と2人で Morris の店に強盗に入り，Morris がユダヤ人であるというただそれだけの理由で，彼を犠牲者として選ぶ。Morris の寛容さに訴え，自分が強盗に入った事実を隠して，Frank はやがて Morris のアシスタントとして働くようになる。ある朝馬鈴薯の皮をむきながら，ユダヤ人とはどんなものか，ユダヤ人は何を信じているのか，と Frank が Morris に質問する。Morris は次のような返答をする。

> "My father used to say to be a Jew all you need is a good heart. . . . The important thing is the Torah. This is the Law—a Jew must believe in the Law. . . . But I don't worry about kosher, which is to me old-fashioned. What I worry is to follow the Jewish Law. . . . This means to do what is right, to be honest, to be good. This means to other people. Our life is hard enough. Why should we hurt somebody else? . . . . We ain't

animals. This is why we need the Law. This is what a Jew believes. . . . If a Jew forgets the Law, . . . , he is not a good Jew, and not a good man." (124-25)

　Morris の言う律法は，必ずしも Talmud やトーラー (Torah) にその起源のすべてをさかのぼるものではない。Morris は清浄食品を食べないし，ユダヤ教の休日にも，贖罪の日 (Yom Kipper) を除いて，店を開く。Frank は彼が synagogue に出かける姿を見たことがない。しかし，Morris の葬儀の際, rabbi によって述べられたように，Morris は，ユダヤ人の形式的な慣習には従わなかったかもしれないが，ユダヤ人の体験のなかに生き，ユダヤ人の精神に忠実であり，苦しみながらも希望を持って耐えてきたが故に，本当のユダヤ人であった。Malamud にとって，善良なユダヤ人であることは善良な人間であるのと同義であった。Ihab Hassan は，「マラマッドの小説の第一の，そして最も明白な特徴は，その善良さである」(The first and most obvious quality of his 〔Malamud's〕 fiction is its goodness.)[7]と言っているが，この善良さを最も典型的に体現しているのが，馬鹿に近い誠実なユダヤ人，Morris Bober なのである。

　この小説の初めから終わりまで，Morris Bober の人生は，精神的には平安であったにしても，救いようもなく徹底した苦難の連続であった。一方，Frank Alpine は，苦難の試練を乗り越えてゆかねばならなかった。Malamud の小説の他の多くの登場人物がそうであるように，Frank は最初，自己中心的で挫折した駄目人間として出発し，やがて新しい生活を求めて東部に来る。鼻もちならぬ悪臭を放ってきた過去から抜け出してやり直したい，その悪臭が彼を窒息させぬ前に自分の人生を変えたいと，もう一人の schlimazel たる Frank は願っている。彼は食料品店主に自分の過去を次のように説明する。

". . . . With me one wrong thing leads to another and it ends in a trap. I want the moon so all I get is cheese." (36)

Frank の話は，Morris の琴線に触れ，この男は61歳の俺とまるで同じようなことをしゃべるな，と思ったりする。
　Alpine は，彼自身の悲劇的過去から逃れ，古い自分の揺曳する残像を払拭し

ようと努力する。しかし時々は，またぞろ悪の道の誘惑に屈服する。Morris の店のレジから金を盗み始め，Helen のヌードを覗き見し，ついには彼女をレイプする。Morris に対する強盗傷害の罪を告白したいという欲求に，繰り返しさいなまれる。揺れ動いて相克する欲望と意志のはざまで，その苛責と苦悶の過程のなかで，Frank が徐々に関心を持つに至ったのは，Morris の常軌を逸脱した辛抱強さであり善良さであった。Frank は心のなかで Morris のことを考える。

What kind of a man did you have to be born to shut yourself up in an overgrown coffin and never once during the day . . . poke your beak out of the door for a snootful of air? The answer wasn't hard to say—you had to be a Jew. They were born prisoners. That was what Morris was, with his deadly patience, or endurance, or whatever the hell it was; . . . . (86)

欲求と情欲と悔恨と自責の混ざり合った苦悶の長いドストエフスキー的な試練の後に，Frank はだんだんと自己抑制を身に付けていく。Morris の人生の重荷と苦悩を受け継ぎ，Helen の愛をかち取るために，昼も夜も超人的な働きぶりで貧困と戦い，Morris 亡き後の母娘を養い，Helen を夜学に通わせる。そんなある日，Frank は自分にも分からぬ理由から，空気坑をよじ登って Helen を覗くことをやめ，そして店にいるときも正直な人間となる。Frank は，都市小説のパターンによく見られるように，都市の悪に染まって堕落するのではなく，貧困にもめげず，自己の精神的再生，自己救済を実現する。Morris と同じように，物質的にどんなに貧しくても心のなかは豊かになるのである。この小説の最後の個所で，Frank はユダヤ教徒に改宗する。この改宗によって，Frank は Morris が背負っていた重荷の一切を継承することになる。Frank の割礼は，Helen に対する献身，そして正統派ユダヤ教というよりはむしろ Morris の律法に対する傾倒の印である。前にも記したように，善良なユダヤ人であることは善良な人間であることである。Frank は割礼によって，彼の新しい道徳規範が，子供時代の理想であったアッシジの聖フランシスの信条と異ならないことを，再確認するのである。

Frank 自身の貪欲とわがままは，ついに克服される。過去の自分を清算し，

ささやかな平安と生活の秩序を得ようとした長年の願いが達成される。彼の再生，苦悩による自己救済が実現される。Frank の改宗によって，苦悩の結果得られる自己贖罪のプロセスが終わりを告げる。しかし，彼の人間であるが故の苦悩は，彼の師 Morris Bober が言うように，生きている限り続くのである。

The Assistant 全般に，重苦しく陰気な雰囲気が支配しているが，その要因の一つに，牢獄，墓，棺のメタファーの頻用がある。Morris の店は，牢獄や墓や棺に比せられる。大きな棺みたいな店に閉じこもって，Yiddish 語の新聞を買いに行くときだけ鼻先に外の空気を嗅ぐだけの暮らしなんて，ユダヤ人でなければできない。彼らは生まれつき囚人なのだ，と Frank は考える。Helen でさえも，Frank が臭い店に入れられ，囚人に仕立てられたのだと言う。ガス自殺未遂後入院した Morris も，病院から帰ってきて，2 階の寝室で階下の店の重苦しい沈黙に耐えきれず，下には物言えぬ墓石がしっかり植え込まれていて，死のにおいが床の隙間から滲み上がってくると感じる。

この小説の登場人物たちは，皆，辛抱強く何かを待っている。Bober 家の人たちは，しみったれた店のなかで，同じようにしみったれたお客が店のなかに入ってくるのを，昼も夜も忍耐強く待っている。娘の Helen は，勤め先から帰宅するとき，ドアを開けながら「私よ」と大きな声で両親に言う。小さいときからの習慣で，お客が来たと思って両親をぬか喜びさせないためである。Frank は，最初Helenと話し一緒に過ごせるチャンスを待ち，彼女の愛を待ち続ける。悪漢に強姦されそうになった Helen を助けた直後，Frank は，渇望と情熱に満ちた愛を口にし，果てしなく待つ辛さを訴えながら，彼女を犯すのである。Helen の愛を喪失した Frank は，いつか彼女の精神的な愛が芽ばえてくるのを，自分は生まれつき待つようにできている人間だなと思いながら，待ち続ける。Helen は，ボーイフレンドからの誘いの電話を待ち，より良き教育と将来性という彼女の理想の実現を待ち焦がれ，Helen の母親は，Frank が家を去るのを待っている。皆が実現の可能性をあまり期待しないで何かを待っている状況も，この小説のトーンを暗いものにする役割を演じている。

Malamud の小説や短編が，「未熟から円熟に至る，苦痛に満ちたプロセスの寓話，あるいは譬え話」(fables or parables of the painful process from immaturity to maturity)⁸⁾であるならば，Philip Roth は紛れもなく，半ば同化したユダヤ系アメリカ人のアイデンティティの危機について書いている。Malamud の小説の世界が, 苦悩するユダヤ人の窒息しそうな窮乏に色付けられているとすれば，Yiddish 文学の類似性から解放された Roth の世界には，かなり同化したユダヤ系アメリカ人の物質的豊かさに起因する明るさがある。

Philip Roth の主人公の苦悩は，物質的なものではなく精神的なものである。彼らの苦悩は，現代のぜいたくな社会，その浅薄な皮相性，その無意味な居心地良さに対する拒絶反応にその源がある。彼らはそのなかで精神的平安を得ることができないのである。Roth は，*Reading Myself and Others* の一節 "Writing American Fiction" のなかで「しかし, フィクションの書き手としてのマラマッドは，現代アメリカのユダヤ人，いかにもわれわれの時代らしいユダヤ人につきまとう不安やジレンマや堕落にはさしたる関心をしめさない。」(But Malamud, as a writer of fiction, has not shown specific interest in the anxieties and dilemmas and corruptions of the contemporary American Jew, the Jew we think of as characteristic of our times.)⁹⁾ と Malamud を批判している。

Philip Roth の作品においては，伝統的なユダヤ的価値，ユダヤ的遺産，そしてこれらを保持していこうとするユダヤ人社会に疑問を抱き，挑戦し，批判する若者が登場する。その典型的な人物の一人が *Goodbye, Columbus and Five Short Stories* (1959) のなかの "The Conversion of the Jews" の主人公 Ozzie Freedman である。

Ozzie は，ユダヤ教で成人期の象徴的な年齢，13歳に近付いている。ヘブライ語学校で Ozzie は，rabbi の Binder 先生に対し，宗教についての当惑させるような質問を呈する。独立宣言には人間は平等であるとはっきり書いてあるのに，Binder 先生はどうしてユダヤ人を「選ばれた人」("the Chosen People")¹⁰⁾ と呼ぶことができるのか。飛行機事故の死亡者リストにユダヤ人の名前を発見したときのみ，彼の家族が飛行機事故のことを悲劇だと言うのはなぜなのか。Ozzie が難しい質問をする度ごとに，Ozzie の母親は Binder 先生に呼び出される。母親が3度目に呼び出しを受けたのは，Ozzie が，神様は6日間で世界を創ることができるのに，性交しなくても女性に赤ん坊を生ませることができな

第Ⅴ章 「ユダヤ教への改宗」と「ユダヤ人の改宗」   51

いのか,と質問したときであった。自由討論の時間になって,先生は Ozzie に意見を述べるように強制する。Binder 先生に対する Ozzie の鬱積した不信が爆発する。「先生は知らないんだ！ 神様のことなんか何も知らないんだ！」("You don't know！ You don't know anything about God！")（佐伯・宮本137；158）と叫ぶ。Binder 先生の手が Ozzie の頬に飛び,手の平がまともに鼻を叩いた。Ozzie は「馬鹿野郎！ 馬鹿野郎！」("You bastard, you bastard！")（佐伯・宮本138；159）と叫びながら,追いかける先生の腕をかいくぐり,synagogue の屋根の上に逃げ,屋根に付いている上げ蓋をしっかりとロックする。

「小型の破壊活動分子」("a pint-sized subversive") [11] Ozzie は,陳腐なユダヤ教信仰と彼が見なすものに疑問を投げかける。最後の手段として彼は synagogue の屋根に登ることによって,Binder 先生,彼の母,71歳の小使の Yakov Blotnik に代表される「偏狭で不毛な宗教性」(the narrow and sterile religiosity) [12] から逃れようとする。

> Yakov Blotnik's old mind hobbled slowly, as if on crutches, and though he couldn't decide precisely what the boy was doing on the roof, he knew it wasn't good—that is, it wasn't-good-for-the-Jews. For Yakov Blotnik life had fractionated itself simply: things were either good-for-the-Jews or no-good-for-the-Jews. (162)

Ozzie は,こういった精神的に空虚なユダヤ人——祈りの言葉は覚えているが,神については忘れてしまったユダヤ人に満足していない。屋根の上から Ozzie は,下にいる群衆の皆に——ラビ,母親,消防士,級友の皆に異教徒の祈りの姿勢で跪くことを要求する。そしてまた Ozzie は,下の群衆の皆に,神を信じます,神様は何でもできると信じます,神様は性交をしなくても子供が作れると信じます,イエス・キリストを信じます,と大きな声で言わせる。しばらくの間,この少年は synagogue の屋根の上で,キリストと聖者と殉教者と Martin Buber が一体となった存在となる。下にいる皆の「ユダヤ人の改宗」を強制し,一時的にせよ,いささか喜劇的な信仰復興を皆に成し遂げさせた少年は,やっと降りることを承諾する。「小型の破壊活動分子」は,「夕闇に縁どられて,聖像を包む大きな光輪のように輝く黄色いネットのちょうど真ん中へ」

(. . . right into the center of the yellow net that glowed in the evening's edge like an overgrown halo.)（佐伯・宮本155；171）飛び降り，帰っていく。

　Philip Roth の主人公は，程度の差はあれいくぶん狂気じみている。少なくとも正常の世界からみると，そう思える。*Goodbye, Columbus and Five Short Stories* のなかの "Eli, the Fanatic" の主人公も例外ではない。Ozzie と同じように，Eli Peck の狂気の行動は，精神的アイデンティティを求め，殉教の責任を取ることに由来する。Eli は神経質な弁護士で，ニューヨーク州 Woodenton という反ユダヤ主義もみられない裕福で無事泰平な郊外に，美しい妻と住んでいるユダヤ人である。Eli 弁護士は，最近丘の上にできた Hasid のユダヤ教神学校をこの町から追い出すよう，町の人から依頼を受ける。ユダヤ教神学校には校長の Leo Tzuref と18人の子供たち，黒い帽子と黒い衣服を身にまとった一人の「グリーニー」（"greenie"）がいて，彼らはナチの迫害を受けた難民であった。

　Woodenton は，ユダヤ系と非ユダヤ系が共に仲よく住んでいる進歩的な町である。町民は，彼らの家族が安楽と美と落ち着きのうちに暮らすことを望んでいた。ユダヤ教神学校の出現は，進歩的ユダヤ人社会が不安を感じる脅威であった。それは，ほとんど同化したユダヤ人に過去の苦難を思い起こさせ，彼らの出自を痛ましく暴いてみせるからである。そのなかでも最も率直に歯に衣を着せず Eli に意見を言うのが，友人の Ted Heller であった。Heller を始め Woodenton のユダヤ人を最も動転させたのは，異様な黒い帽子と衣服の「グリーニー」が，町なかを訪れることであった。Eli は，頑固なユダヤ教神学校長に手紙を書いて，次の2つの条件が入れられれば，神学校に対して退去の法的手続きを取らないことを約束する。条件とは「1. ウッデントン・ユダヤ教神学校の宗教的・教育的・社会的活動は，神学校敷地内に限ること。2. ユダヤ教神学校職員は，二十世紀アメリカの生活にふさわしい服装をする限りにおいて，通りにおいても店においても歓迎される。」(1. The religious, educational, and social activities of the Yeshivah of Woodenton will be confined to the Yeshivah grounds. 2. The Yeshivah personnel are welcomed in the streets and stores of Woodenton provided they are attired in clothing usually associated with American life

第V章 「ユダヤ教への改宗」と「ユダヤ人の改宗」　53

in the 20th century.)（佐伯・宮本68；276）というものである。Eli の提示した妥協案は，平凡な常識の支配する世界では納得のいくものであったろうが，ユダヤ教神学校の世界には受け入れられなかった。2日後に Eli は，Tzuref 校長から拒絶の返事を受け取る。「あの紳士が着ている背広は，持っている衣類のすべてであります。」(The suit the gentleman wears is all he's got.)（佐伯・宮本69；277）と。

　法についての Eli と校長の両者の見解は，著しい対照をなすものである。

　　"We make the law, Mr. Tzuref. It is our community. These are my neighbors. I am their attorney. They pay me. Without law there is chaos."
　　"What you call law, I call shame. The heart, Mr. Peck, the heart is law! God!" he announced. (280)

心の真実の探求，これこそ，時代の風潮に合わせて彼らの信仰を変容してきた Woodenton のユダヤ人が失ってしまったものであった。世俗化したユダヤ人の代表者であり代弁者である Eli は，宗教心のスポークスマンたる Tzuref 校長や「グリーニー」を説得することができるどころか，彼らの Talmud 的な英知によって煙に巻かれてしまう。俗物的な Ted Heller と異なり，Eli がこの短編の終わりの所で，本当の生き方を掴もうとして狂気に近い状態に走ることの伏線は，彼が以前にも何度かノイローゼになったことで暗示されている。

　妻の Miriam が出産のために入院したその晩，Eli は自分の洋服2着を箱に詰め，ユダヤ教神学校の正面玄関の上り口の所に置く。そこで2度目に「グリーニー」の姿を見かけた Eli は，心のなかに痛みを感じ始める。翌朝「グリーニー」は，Eli が与えた緑のツイードを着て町の通りを練り歩き，町の人々を驚かす。さらに Eli がびっくりしたことは，「グリーニー」が自分の異様な黒い衣裳を，Eli の家の玄関に置いていたことであった。

　「わたしはみんなの代りですし，みんなはわたしと同じですよ，ツュレフさん。」("I am them, they are me, Mr. Tzuref.")（佐伯・宮本73；279）と言って，Woodenton の現代的なユダヤ人と自分を同一視していた Eli Peck は，今やアイデンティティ・クライシスを感じ始める。彼は改宗，換言すれば，人間の苦悩

の運命を受け入れることによって信仰の殉教者的擁護者となる過程をスタートさせるのである。異様な衝動に駆られて，Eliは「グリーニー」の黒い衣裳と黒い帽子を身に着け，彼と対面するために出かけていく。Eli が啓示を受けるのは，まさにそのときである。「グリーニー」との対面で彼から異常な，夢を見るような暗示を受け，Eli はそのままの服装で Woodenton のメインストリート，Coach House Road を練り歩く。Eli 自身を除く町の人は誰もが，この美しい妻を持つ若い弁護士Eli の神経がおかしくなったことに気付いていた。

> He knew what he did was not insane, though he felt every inch of its strangeness. He felt those black clothes as if they were the skin of his skin—the give and pull as they got used to where he bulged and buckled. (307-08)

家の前まで辿り着いた Eli は，家のなかに入らず，そのまま向きを変えて病院に行き，生まれたばかりの長男と会おうとする。当惑する看護婦，妻のMiriam，Ted Heller，インターンの前で，Eli は赤ん坊と対面し，最後は上着を脱がされ，注射針を打ち込まれる。「薬で心が和らいだが，あの黒さが滲みとおったところまで薬はとどかなかった。」(The drug calmed his soul, but did not touch it down where the blackness had reached.) (佐伯・宮本125；313) という文章で，この短編は終わっている。

Bernard Malamud と Philip Roth の数ある作品のなかで，同じように改宗をテーマとし，1957，1958，1959年とほぼ同じころに書かれた3つの作品を取り上げてみた。*The Assistant* の Frank Alipne は，カトリックでありながら，自分の人生に空虚さを感じて，苦しみながらも希望を持って耐えてきた Morris Bober のユダヤ人としての生き方に興味を持ち始め，やがて苦悶と懊悩の過去を清算すべくユダヤ教に改宗する。しかし，Malamud の言う善良なユダヤ人とは善良な人間ということである。Frank の改宗したユダヤ教も決して戒律や慣習に固執する頑迷で保守的なユダヤ教信仰ではない。もっと普遍的な道徳，宗教的価値観のようなものである。Frank は，小説が終わった後の余生も，馬鹿に近い善人として，Morris の生き方を継承していくことであろう。

Philip Roth の "Eli, the Fanatic" の主人公は，鈍感な彼の友人 Ted Heller と異なり，ノーマルシーとノイローゼの間を揺曳する，感受性が強く，傷つきやすいユダヤ人である。Eli の改宗は，Hasid によって脱ぎ捨てられた宗教的な黒い衣裳を身にまとうことによってなされる。形式や慣習のみを重んじ，心を忘れた現代ユダヤ人社会への痛烈な批判であり，諷刺であるが，この Eli の改宗はほんの一時的でしかない。それは "The Conversion of the Jews" の Ozzie が，synagogue の屋根の上で，下にいる偏狭なユダヤ教徒たちを，その不毛な宗教性から解放させるのが，ほんの僅かな時間でしかないのと似ている。Eli は狂気と判断されて鎮静剤を注射され，Ozzie は消防夫の広げている大きなネットに飛び込んでいく。2人とも，本当の生き方を掴み取ろうとする極限状況から，すぐに惰性的な現実の世界に帰っていくのである。Eli にしても Ozzie にしても，周囲の者が彼らを狂気あるいは異常として取り扱うこともそうであるが，一時的な極限状況から現実世界への回帰もまた，Roth のユダヤ人社会への痛烈な批判である。

貧しく暗く苦しい世界を乗り越えた Frank の将来は，貧しく苦しくともなぜか曙光が感じられ，安定した人生がいつまでも継続していくような重量感がある。内面的な強靭ささえ窺われる。それに反し，Eli や Ozzie や周囲のユダヤ人の世界は，豊かで明るそうに見えながら，内面的には何と儚く浅薄に映ることであろうか。現実のユダヤ人社会の偏狭な閉鎖性・俗物性に対する移民三世 Roth の批判とペシミズム，それに反し二世の Malamud が抱くユダヤ教精神への揺るぎなき信頼感，この両者の落差がこのように感じさせるのであろうか。ユダヤ的伝統や慣習を保持しようとする rabbi を核としたユダヤ人社会が Roth の作品に向けている非難（と Roth の反論）と，Malamud の小説に向けている肯定的態度の差もまた対照的である。

古くさいユダヤ人を数多く登場させ，重苦しいユダヤ臭が作品の至るところに漂っている Malamud の *The Assistant* が，ユダヤ人の問題だけでなく，より普遍的な人間の根本問題を取り扱い，特殊から普遍を指向しているのに反し，現代的で明るい雰囲気ながら，しかしいくぶんの皮肉と狂気を秘めたタッチで描かれている Roth の2つの短編が，現代アメリカでユダヤ人であることの意

味，ユダヤ人のアイデンティティの危機という特殊な問題に（我々の時代の特色を最も体現しているという意図で書かれたとすれば，普遍を内包した特殊ということになるが）迫っていることも，まことに興味深い対照と言えよう。

≪Notes≫
1) 陣﨑訳；Philip Rahv, "Introduction," *A Malamud Reader*, ed. Philip Rahv (New York: Farrar, Straus and Giroux, 1967) x.
2) Peter L. Hays, "The Complex Pattern of Redemption in *The Assistant*," *The Centennial Review* 13 (Spring 1969) : 200-14
3) Bernard Malamud, *The Assistant* (New York: Farrar, Straus and Giroux, 1957) 16-17. 以下この作品からの引用はすべてこの版により，引用英文末尾の括弧内に頁数を記す。
4) マラマッド，加島祥三訳『アシスタント』（東京：新潮文庫，1972) 63. Malamud 41.
5) Yiddish 語の schlimazel は，Ruth R. Wisse, *The Schlemiel as Modern Hero* (Chicago: University of Chicago Press, 1971) 14. において，次のように定義されている。「シュレミールとシュリマーゼルのアメリカにおける区別は，前者がスープを膝の上にこぼす人，後者がこぼされる人とする大雑把な指針に要約されていて，定義に対する有用な根拠を提供してくれる。シュレミールは積極的に悪運をまき散らす人であり，シュリマーゼルは受動的な犠牲者である。もっと厳密に定義すれば，シュリマーゼルは災難に出くわし，不運に立ち向かう強い傾向を持っているが，不幸な状況は彼の外にあるのであり，常に意外性のどたばた喜劇的要素を暗示している。シュレミールの不運は性格的なものである。偶然的なものではなく本質的なものである。シュリマーゼルを含むコメディが状況的であるのに対し，シュレミールのコメディは実存的であり，現実との対決において彼の本性そのものに起源を求める。」
6) 陣﨑訳；Peter L. Hays 205.
7) 陣﨑訳；Ihab Hassan, *Radical Innocence: Studies in the Contemporary American Novel* (Princeton, N. J.: Princeton University Press, 1961) 161.
8) 陣﨑訳；Tonny Tanner, *City of Words: American Fiction 1950-1970* (London: Jonathan Cape, 1971) 323.
9) フィリップ・ロス，青山南訳『素晴らしいアメリカ作家』（東京：集英社，1980) 145. Philip Roth, *Reading Myself and Others* (New York: Farrar, Straus and Giroux, 1975) 127.
10) フィリップ・ロス，佐伯彰一・宮本陽吉訳『狂信者イーライ』（東京：集英社，1973) 131. Philip Roth, *Goodbye, Columbus and Five Short Stories* (Boston: Houghton Mifflin, 1959) 153. 以下この作品からの引用はすべてこの版により，引用英文末尾の括弧内に頁数を記す。和文と英文を併記する場合は（佐伯・宮本131 ; 153）と記す。

11）陣﨑訳；Sanford Pinsker, *The Comedy That "Hoits"; An Essay on the Fiction of Philip Roth* (Columbia, University of Missouri, 1975) 13.
12）陣﨑訳；John N. McDaniel, *The Fiction of Philip Roth* (Haddonfield, N. J.: Haddonfield House, 1974) 57.

第Ⅵ章

The Ordeal of Jewishness in the Early Works of Bernard Malamud, Philip Roth and Saul Bellow

Ⅰ. THE THEME OF SUFFERING [1]

1. BERNARD MALAMUD

Characters in Malamud's fiction seem as if they had appeared in the American scene from the East European *shtetl* through a timetunnel. They are usually unassimilated first- and second-generation American Jews of New York City. They live in small, meager tenant apartments or keep tiny, wretched stores which are nearly failing. They anchor their hopes in their children's future by seeking a foothold in education and marriage as a ladder for social success and status. Their dream, however, is mercilessly shattered, running against the severe realities of life. The lives of Malamud's protagonists are a series of unfortunate events. They are born losers. Being often taken in but never deceiving others, they persistently lead an honest life. Suffering from abject poverty, they still extend active sympathy and help toward the suffering of poorer and more miserable neighbors. For their good conduct they are not rewarded. They are caught in a material poverty, but they do not confuse it with a spiritual poverty. Malamud's characters are filled to the brim with suffering and have to transcend it. Those in *The Assistant* and *A New Life*, including minor characters, are no exception. However, as the details were discussed in Chapter Ⅳ and Ⅴ, the description here is limited to what is not yet discussed. Especially as to *The Assistant*, suffice it to say here in Part I its style has a Hemingway clarity, "a kind of humility and courage, but also a softness Hemingway never strove to communicate," [2] and that this novel is the most apocalyptic and most Jewish and probably the best one written by Bernard Malamud.

From 1949 through 1961 Bernard Malamud taught English composition at the Department of English, Oregon State University, Corvallis. During this period of his life in the West he published his first two novels (*The Natural* and *The Assistant*) and the collection of short stories, *The Magic Barrel*. His next novel, *A New Life*, an academic satire, a love story and a quest for escape from the past, was based on his experience at Oregon State University. A little before the publication of *A New Life*, Philip Roth criticized Malamud in speech delivered at Stanford University in 1960 that "he does not—or has not yet—found the *contemporary* scene a proper or sufficient backdrop for his tales of heartlessness and heartache, of suffering and regeneration." [3] Though it is not clear whether Malamud knew about Roth's speech or not, *A New Life* might have been his experiment to "find a more persuasive frame by which to demonstrate his theme of suffering and regeneration." [4]

Thirty-year-old Seymour Levin, formerly a drunkard comes to teach at the new world of Cascadia in 1950 with his Master's degree from New York University. At the opening of the novel, just like Frank Alpine, S. Levin is filled with an anguished discontent about his past and throughout the novel tries to escape from its shame. In his youth, his father, a thief, died in prison; and his mother, being shocked, went crazy and killed herself. Then Levin failed in a love affair with an unhappy, embittered woman. He mourned the loss of them and became a drunk. Later in the novel Seymour confesses his past to the colleague's wife who has become his mistress, Pauline Gilley:

> "For two years I lived in self-hatred, willing to part with life. I won't tell you what I had come to. But one morning in somebody's filthy cellar, I awoke under burlap bags and saw my rotting shoes on a broken chair. They were lit in dim sunlight from a shaft or

window. I stared at the chair, it looked like a painting, a thing with a value of its own. I squeezed what was left of my brain to understand why this should move me so deeply, why I was crying. Then I thought, Levin, if you were dead there would be no light on your shoes in this cellar. I came to believe what I had often wanted to, that life is holy. I then became a man of principle."[5]

Thus it is as a man of principle, with a beard grown in a deliberate attempt to stave off his past, that he gets off the train at Marathon, Cascadia after a long and tiring transcontinental journey. He is a fledgling English lecturer enamored of the nature of the wild West, and he makes a fresh determination to live an honest and meaningful life without making the same mistakes. However, like Morris and Frank and many other protagonists in the short stories in *The Magic Barrel*, Levin finds himself a slapstick *schlimazel*.

Met at the station by Gerald Gilley, Director of Freshman Composition, and his wife Pauline, he spends one evening at their house. Mrs. Gilley "missed Levin's plate and dropped a hot gob of tuna fish and potato into his lap"(10). While Levin is telling a story for their adopted son, Erik, the boy wets Levin's pants. One month later, during his first class, he forgets to zip up his fly and gains the unusual attention of students. On his second day in the Northwest, Seymour learns that Cascadia College is not really a liberal arts college. Its social and academic life is dull, inert and easy-going. An aged and temperamental chairman, Orville Fairchild, dexterously urges the English faculty to use his *The Elements of Grammar*, revised, thirteenth edition which has been the department's textbook for thirty years. At this cow college in a backwoods town, there is no "publish or perish" hanging over each faculty member's head. Gradually Levin becomes entangled in the election of chairman and he tries in vain to reform the English Department. In his commitment to love, lacking self-control, he goes on making the same mistakes. In a mixed agony of dark past and present loneliness he succumbs to the lure of the other sex. Two sexual adventures, one in the barn with a waitress and one in his office with a lady colleague, end unsatisfied by interruption. Levin's assignation with a willing coed and his cuckoldry with Pauline Gilley evict him from his "career as college professor, sweet dream of his life" (278).

S. Levin is clearly Jewish though there is no overt mention of this in the novel. Throughout *A New Life*, the word "Jewish" is used only once, in Pauline's answer to Levin's question why she picked his application out of the cards her husband had discarded and then persuaded him to employ Levin as a lecturer:

> "I needed one. Your picture reminded me of a Jewish boy I knew in college who was very kind to me during a trying time in my life." (361)

Levin's suffering, unlike that of Morris and Frank, is not directly related to the suffering of a Jew. He goes through his series of struggles with his drenched old self, with the corrupt academic world and with over-sexed women. In the course of his ordeal, he suffers for self-salvation. One sleepless night during the winter vacation, Levin thinks in his lonely bed:

> Levin felt himself grow depressed. He thought of Nadalee endlessly, had got her without deserving to—fruit for teacher—a mean way to win a lay. His escape to the West had thus far come to nothing, space corrupted by time, the past-contaminated self. Mold memories, bad habits, worse luck. He recalled in dirty detail each disgusting defeat from boyhood, his weaknesses, impoverishment, undiscipline—the limp self entangled in the fabric of a will-less life. (163-64)

Levin suffers; but his suffering, his remorse, his feelings of guilt are far less intense and persuasive than those of Frank Alpine. For example, Levin's idea on sex is not as moral as Frank's. [6]

> Levin had only casually tied morality to sex, the act, that is. Sex was where it grew, where with luck he found it, manna when least expected. What was for free was for free so long as nobody got hurt. (222)

Frank's way of thinking is more honest, more convincing and more appealing. After many loveless carnal acts with four women, S. Levin leaves the campus of the land-grant college with a pregnant Pauline whom he loves now only as a matter of principle, together with her two children and a defamed and jobless future. At the end of the novel, it is not certain whether he has completed a rebirth or not, whether his pure and frequent resolutions to change himself have been realized or not. He may be a slapstick *schlemiel*; he may be a born loser. But he is neither the fool of goodness nor a secular *tzaddik*. The element of farce in him overshadows that of the saint-elect. Levin does not have as much patience and endurance as Frank Alpine, and his desire to confess his crime is not as strong. Something holy about the grocer's assistant does not surround the lecturer of Freshman Composition. Compare Morris's "Law" with Levin's self-pitying version: "Levin's Law Ⅰ: Weak leaders favor weak leaders, the mirror principle in politics"(302). "Levin's Law Ⅱ: One becomes his victim's victim. Ⅲ. Stand for something and somebody around will feel persecuted"(308).

Malamud was ambitious in trying to extend the range of his concerns and to create a portrait of society in a realistic technique. His new attempt, however, resulted in a limited success. In comparison with *The Assistant* and such short stories as "The Magic Barrel," "The First Seven Years," and "The Loan," *A New Life* is deficient in the power and vitality to fascinate the reader. Malamud creates his best Malamudian heroes when he limits his fictional world to the suffering and irony of timeless and placeless imprisoned poor Jews.

2. PHILIP ROTH

In the novels and short stories of Philip Roth, young men appear who challenge traditional Jewish values, Jewish heritage and the American Jewish community. Two of the most typical figures, as were already discussed in Chapter V, are Ozzie Freedman of "The Conversion of the Jews" and Eli Peck of "Eli, the Fanatic" in *Goodbye, Columbus and Five Short Stories*.

In May of 1945, after the fighting ended in Europe, Sergeant Nathan Marx in "Defender of the Faith" of the *Goodbye, Columbus* collection was rotated back to a training camp at Camp Crowder, Missouri. Marx, who has no special sense of Jewish identity, has in his company three Jewish trainees named Sheldon Grossbart, Larry Fishbein and Mickey Halpern. Grossbart is a complete strategic stinker, and begins to manipulate Marx's sympathies on the basis of their common Jewish background. Grossbart is "more a defender of his own advantage than of faith; Fishbein and Halpern merely provide a convenient rationale." [7] Marx's ambivalent Jewishness is tested by Private Grossbart's cunning tactics. Grossbart's egoistic and chauvinistic goal with regard to Sergeant Marx is, first of all, to get formal permission from him to attend Friday night religious services without having to do barracks cleaning. The second and third claims of Grossbart's are, respectively, to request *kosher* food on the pretext of following dietary laws instead of eating *trafe*[8] in the chow of the army, and to obtain a weekend pass in order to attend belated *Seder* at his aunt's. These special favors solicited by the shrewd young private displeases the veteran sergeant. When disgusted Marx refuses one of these requests, Grossbart whines:

> "Ashamed, that's what you are," he said. "So you take it out on the rest of us. They say Hitler himself was half a Jew. Hearing you, I wouldn't doubt it.". . . . Tears came to his [Grossbart's] eyes. "It's hard thing to be a Jew. But now I understand what Mickey says—it's a harder thing to stay one. He raised a hand sadly toward me. "Look at *you*."
> "Stop crying!"
> "Stop this, stop that, stop the other thing! *You* stop, Sergeant. Stop closing your heart to your own!" [9]

Marx's dormant sense of Jewish identity is now wakened.

Nathan Marx is no less repelled by "a crude streak of casual prejudice" [10] which is manifested by his commanding officer, Captain Paul Barrett: "Marx, I'd fight side by side with a nigger if the fella proved to me he was a man"(179), and "Sir—Marx, here, tells me Jews have a tendency to be pushy"(190). Trapped between two different attitudes toward Jewishness, Marx is forced to define his identity. He struggles and is torn between his desire to be a good American soldier and his feeling of loyalty to fellow Jews.

Marx, following Grossbart's tracks to Chapel No. 3, soon learns that Grossbart goes to services chiefly because he appreciates the wine. He also discovers that the obnoxious and selfish private, when the request of *kosher* food backfires, "tries to put the Sergeant in his debt by sending his Congressman a letter praising the Sergeant."[11] The weekend outing on the pretext of attending his aunt's *Seder* in Kansas City proves to consist of pleasure-seeking in St. Louis. He brings back Chinese egg rolls instead of the *gefilte* fish [12] he promised to!

> Rage came charging at me. I didn't sidestep. "Grossbart, you're a liar!" I said. "You're a schemer and a crook. You've got no respect for anything. Nothing at all. Not for me, for the truth—not even for poor Halpern! You use us all—" (210)

Finally, when Marx discovers that Grossbart pulls his string on a Jewish noncom in charge of Classification and Assignment and succeeds in avoiding dangerous duty in the Pacific, he calls up a friendly sergeant and takes an action that appears to be anti-Semitic:

> "This may sound crazy, Bob, but I got a kid here on orders to Monmouth who wants them changed. He had a brother killed in Europe, and he's hot to go to the Pacific. Says he'd feel like a coward if he wound up Stateside. I don't know, Bob—can anything be done? Put somebody else in the Monmouth slot?" (212)

The following day he receives the corrected orders. To the infuriated Grossbart, Marx explains that he did have the orders reversed "not to satisfy his vindictiveness, but to stop the use of Jewish tradition and belief for selfish, irresponsible purposes." [13]

> I stood outside the orderly room, and I heard Grossbart weeping behind me. Over in the barracks, in the lighted windows, I could see the boys in their T shirts sitting on their bunks talking about their orders, as they'd been doing for the past two days. With a kind of quiet nervousness, they polished shoes, shined belt buckles, squared away underwear, trying as best they could to accept their fate. Behind me, Grossbart swallowed hard, accepting his. And then, resisting with all my will and impulse to turn and seek pardon

for my vindictiveness, I accepted my own. (214)

"Defender of the Faith" has the same insistence as Roth's other stories. We have to accept the suffering which life requires of man, and "faith and martyrdom, affirmation of life and acceptance of suffering are in the Jewish tradition." [14]

The subject of "Goodbye, Columbus" is "the social and cultural conflict that arises in the experience of Jews as they make their way from the lower-middle class communities of the cities to the prosperous country-club civilization of the suburbs." [15] Neil Klugman, a graduate of Newark College of Rutgers University, now works in a library and lives with his Aunt Gladys and Uncle Max in a small apartment in a lower-middle class neighborhood. His feelings toward life are tentative and ambivalent. He knows that the library is not going to be his lifework. And, when asked by Mrs. Patimkin whether he is Orthodox or Conservative, he answers, "I'm just Jewish"(99). His attachment to Newark, however, is very deep—he "felt a deep knowledge of Newark, an attachment so rooted that it could not help but branch out into affection"(41).

A poor Jewish boy from Newark, Neil Klugman, one summer falls in love with a rich Jewish girl from Short Hills, Brenda Patimkin. Brenda is a student of Radcliffe College. While Neil is a guest of Brenda's family at Short Hills during the summer vacation, they enjoy both the psychological and sensual satisfactions that their relations provide. His affair with her [16] finally proves unsuccessful.

Through the eyes of Neil Klugman, Philip Roth satirizes the absurdities and incongruities of the Patimkins' daily life. Their vulgar materialism is manifested by an emphasis on gigantic athleticism and expensive quantities of sports equipment and fresh fruits in their refrigerator. Brenda's father is a manufacturer of kitchen and bathroom sinks.

> Mr. Patimkin reminded me of my father, except that when he spoke he did not surround each syllable with a wheeze. He was tall, strong, ungrammatical, and a ferocious eater.

> When he attacked his salad—after drenching it in bottled French dressing—the veins swelled under the heavy skin of his forearm. He ate three helpings of salad, Ron had four, Brenda and Julie had two, and only Mrs. Patimkin and I had one each. (31)

While Mr. Patimkin is proud of his bumpy nose as a vestige of visible Jewishness, he is also proud of being able to spend a lot of money to have his daughter's nose bobbed. He professes his business ethic that one needs a little of the *gonif*.[17]

Brenda's mother, a second generation American, "busies herself with the Ladies' Benevolent Society, Hadassah, and the Orthodox synagogue,"[18] and has never heard of Martin Buber. Brenda's brother, Ron, is an immense Jewish athlete, a former football hero at Ohio State. In the pool when he pushes his palm flat into the water, a small hurricane beats up against Brenda and Neil. Ron faithfully intends to follow his father's occupation.

The Patimkins lived in Newark when Brenda was a baby, and after Pearl Harbor they moved up to Short Hills; "Patimkin Kitchen and Bathroom Sinks had gone to war: no new barracks was complete until it had a squad of Patimkin sinks lined up in its latrine"(53). Brenda's careless words, "She [Mrs. Patimkin] still thinks we live in Newark"(36), repels Neil.

> I did not intend to allow myself such unfaithful thoughts, to line up with Mrs. Patimkin while I sat beside Brenda, but I could not shake from my elephant's brain that she-still-thinks-we-live-in-Newark remark. (36-37)

Neil's first generation American Aunt Gladys warns him that Jewish people living in Short Hills could not be real Jews. Coming to the Patimkins' house and coming into close contact with the family's materialism and their phoney standards of success and happiness, Neil harbors a sense of unbelongingness:

> For a while I remained in the hall, bitten with the urge to slide quietly out of the house, into my car, and back to Newark, where I might even sit in the alley and break candy with my own. I felt like Carlota; no, not even as comfortable as that. (50)

What oppresses Neil Klugman is not only the empty and insignificant lives of the Patimkins living in Short Hills. He is also displeased by his regulation-ridden and mean-spirited fellow librarians such as John McKee, Mr. Scapello and Miss Winney. He finds solace only with an illiterate Negro boy who shares his enthusiasm for Gauguin and the island of Tahiti. At the end of the story, he breaks off with Brenda Patimkin and Short Hills, returns to Newark and his job in the Public Library, on the first day of the Jewish New Year. Apparently he has shown evidence of growth as a man and probably as a Jew as well.

As Dan Isaac has said, this title story "marks the successful working of a significant theme: the rejection of Jewish life, not because it is too Jewish, but because it is not Jewish enough, because it is so dominated by and infused with the American ethos that it partakes of the same corruption, offering no significant alternative." [19]

Portnoy's Complaint was published in 1969. This story is told in the form of a long monologue given by one Alexander Portnoy to a New York psychiatrist, Dr. Spielvogel. Alexander Portnoy is an unmarried able lawyer: he graduated at the head of his class at the Columbia School of Law and has an I.Q. of 158. He is now thirty-three years old and has recently been appointed by the Mayor to be Assistant Commissioner for the City of New York Commission on Human Opportunity. Certainly a central concern of the novel is, as John N. McDaniel maintains, "the absurd state of helplessness, crippledness and victimization in which Portnoy finds himself." [20] Alexander is repelled by the traditional Jewish values of his parents and the exclusiveness of the Jew, and as a reaction he derives some consolation in masturbatory acts and then female conquests. Alex, like a sex maniac, seeks for unrestrained sexual adventures with various types of *shikses*. [21]

Alexander Portnoy's father, Jake, worked for Boston & Northeasten Life and appeared forever "crushed by the colossus known as the insurance company." [22] He peddled promises of security among the skeptical Negroes of Newark. Jake is now living on a pension, and he is an incompetent, "kindly, anxious, uncomprehending," [23] permanently constipated *schlimazel* whose greatest hope is to have a grandson before he dies. Alexander complains about his father:

> And his [Jake Portnoy's] grasp. No money, no schooling, no language, no learning, curiosity without culture, drive without opportunity, experience without wisdom. . . . How easily his inadequacies can move me to tears. As easily as they move me to anger! (26)

Jake Portnoy is a poor object of his son's disenchantment. Alex's mother, Sophie,[24] has the qualities of the stereotypical Jewish mother in every respect. She is very deeply imbedded in Alex's consciousness.

According to Alex, a "Jewish man with his parents alive is half the time a helpless *infant!*"(111). The final passage of "Whacking Off" opens with these words:

> Doctor Spielvogel, this is my life, my only life, and I'm living it in the middle of a Jewish joke! I am the son in the Jewish joke—*only it ain't no joke!* Please, who crippled us like this? Who made us so morbid and hysterical and weak? Why, why are they screaming still, "Watch out! Don't do it! Alex—*no!*" and why, alone on my bed in New York, why am I still hopelessly beating my meat? Doctor, what do you call this sickness I have? Is this the Jewish suffering I used to hear so much about? Is this what has come down to me from the pogroms and the persecution? from the mockery and abuse bestowed by the *goyim* over these two thousand lovely years? Oh my secrets, my shame, my palpitations, my flushes, my sweats! The way I respond to the simple vicissitudes of human life! Doctor, I can't stand any more being frightened like this over nothing! Bless me with manhood! Make me brave! Make me strong! Make me *whole!* Enough being a nice Jewish boy, publicly pleasing my parents while privately pulling my putz! Enough! (36-37)

In this way Alexander Portnoy satirically describes the pleasures and pains of his childhood, his daily struggles with his parents and his religion, his masturbatory fantasies, and his heterosexual experiences. He feels repugnance to severe *kosher* laws and "*goyische* this and *goyische* that!"(75). He is disgusted with the saga of the suffering Jews. He feels sick of Jews who are, by being ultra-assimilated into the

American life, intimidated, self-critical, self-defensive, emasculated and degraded. He is tired of the idea that we are Jews and we are superior and that we cannot commit our hearts to victory in such a thuggish game as football. He doesn't believe in God and he doesn't believe in the Jewish religion or in any religion. But he believes in the principle of equality, and if someone ever uses the word "nigger" in his presence, he will drive a real dagger into his heart.

Alex has had a lot of loveless sex with gentile girls, a phenomenon he refers to as "Hating Your Goy and Eating One Too"(233). This is his effort to be emancipated from his Jewish parents, and the Jewish community, but for all his struggles he cannot escape from being a Jew. The more relations he has with gentile girls, the more he suffers. In Israel with Naomi, a female Israeli soldier, Alex finds himself twice impotent. He is still too Jewish to be an American. In spite of his protestations, he is more essentially Jewish than he appears. Guilt and fear are terms that Alex constantly but ineffectively defies. He is also a *schlemiel.*

Philip Roth grapples with the serious problem of Jewish identity through extreme behaviors in ordinary situations: how to reconcile the contradictory demands of being a Jew on the one hand and of being a member of the insane, modern American community on the other. Roth's heroes are in various ways victims; and through these victims he intends to dramatize "how insane American public life is and how adversely it affects its members."[25] Though Philip Roth says, "I am not a Jewish writer; I am a writer who is a Jew,"[26] he is most brilliant when he devoted himself to the details of American Jewish life.

3. SAUL BELLOW

At first glance, Bellow's second novel, *The Victim*, seems to be an analysis of anti-Semitism. However, it penetrates to a far deeper theme of the burden of guilt and responsibility, mainly through the complex relationship between a Jew and a gentile. The main plot of this novel deals with the reciprocal victim-and-victimizer relationship between the Jewish Asa Leventhal and non-Jewish Kirby Allbee.

Leventhal, an editor of a small trade magazine in lower Manhattan, is plagued with a persecution complex because of his early hard times, his character, and his Jewishness. He comes originally from Hartford. His father, an owner of a small dry-goods store, was "a turbulent man, harsh and selfish toward his sons."[27] His mother died in an insane asylum when Asa was eight and his brother Max was six. After graduating from high school, Asa Leventhal came to New York, where "for a time he worked for an auctioneer named Harkavy, a friend of his Uncle Schacter"(13). Under his protection Leventhal went to college at night and took a prelegal course. When Harkavy died of pneumonia and the shop was shut down, he began to drift and for a few months lived "in a dirty hall bedroom on the East Side, starved and thin"(14).

> He began in a spirit of utter hopelessness. The smaller trade papers simply turned him away. The larger gave him applications to fill out; occasionally he spent a few minutes with a personnel manager and had the opportunity to shake someone's hand. Gradually he became peculiarly aggressive and, avoiding the receptionists, he would make his way into an inner office, stop anyone who appeared to have authority, and introduce himself. He was met with astonishment, with coldness, and with anger. He often grew angry himself. (18-19)

Even now many years later while he is working for Burke-Beard and Company as an editor, he still cannot forget the days in the hotel on lower Broadway. So, on account of his own past experience, he is intently aware of the precariousness, fragility and instability of his position. He persistently fears a blacklist which might be distributed among big shots in the business world. He is sensitive, nervous, suspicious, defensive, vulnerable, quick to take offense and to feel he is not being given his due respect. He is lonely (his wife being away for the summer), isolated and alienated. As is often the case with this type of man, he is liable to sympathize disproportionately with a person in his predicament, and cannot take a determined step even against unjustified accusations. He is ambivalent and vacillating. It is these characteristics of Asa Leventhal that result in his becoming a victim and lead him to be vulnerable to the accusations of Kirby Allbee.

During Leventhal's jobhunting period (and a few years before the action of the story begins), the anti-Semitic Allbee, a gentile from an old New England family, arranged a job interview for Leventhal with his own employer, Mr. Rudiger. The interview, however, ended in the most abject failure. Leventhal knew that Rudiger did not want him even before he uttered his first word. Rudiger was too rude for Leventhal to restrain himself. There was "an atmosphere of infliction and injury from which neither could withdraw"(44). In the ensuing discussion Leventhal enraged Rudiger by insulting him. A few days later Rudiger dismissed Allbee himself, convincing that the two had planned the course of the interview and making this event a convenient excuse for the discharge of drunkard Allbee.

At the beginning of the story, Asa Leventhal has to take care of his absent brother's family. Asa's wife, Mary, is temporarily visiting her mother in Charleston. The setting of the novel is placed in an extremely hot New York summer. The arrangements for Leventhal's being off balance are nearly complete.

Kirby Allbee, who has lost his job and then his wife and what little money she has left, one day appears before Asa Leventhal, and then haunts him persistently, demanding that he make amends. Allbee insists that Leventhal is the real cause of his wife's death and his own degradation because Leventhal intentionally and maliciously contrived the interview with Rudiger for the purpose of revenging Allbee's anti-Semitic remark to Leventhal made earlier at a party.

> When they reached the lower hall, Allbee stopped and said, "You try to put all the blame on me, but you know it's true that you're to blame. You and you only. For everything. You ruined me. Ruined! Because that's what I am, ruined! You're the one that's responsible. You did it to me deliberately, out of hate. Out of pure hate!" (77-78)

Leventhal knows that Allbee's neurotic and persistent accusations are groundless and thinks with anger and disgust that Allbee must have been fired for drunkenness and that Allbee is turning wrongs or faults of his own into wrongs against himself.

When his anger subsides, however, he begins to be puzzled.

> The senselessness of it perturbed him most of all. "Why me?" he thought, frowning. "Of course, he has to have someone to blame; that's how it starts. But when he goes over everybody he knows, in that brain of his, how does he wind up with me? "(79)

In spite of the seeming unreasonableness of Allbee's complaints, Leventhal is "not convinced of his own innocence."[28] He gradually comes to suppose that it is "necessary for him to accept some of the blame for Allbee's comedown"(119-20), and he suffers from this understanding.

Leventhal is nervous about his friends' estimation. When he hears that Williston who once helped him hinted that his troublemaking at the interview with Rudiger was intentional, he comes to Williston and tells him in excitement:

> "You may think you have a different slant on it than Allbee has, but it comes out the same. If you believe I did it on purpose, to get even, then it's not only because I'm terrible personally but because I'm a Jew."(116)

As the story develops Leventhal is exposed to many explicit anti-Semitic remarks by Kirbee Allbee and Mr. Beard, his employer, and is pestered with implicit anti-Semitic gestures and hostility by the Catholic mother of Max's wife. Leventhal's fear and suffering are "intensified by the vulnerability he feels as a Jew in what seems to him an environment charged with anti-Semitism."[29]

Leventhal in scene after scene allows Allbee to practice upon his weakness. He meets Allbee with complex and ambivalent feelings of guilt, fear, anger, disgust, and a touch of compassion. Leventhal sees in Allbee an image of his own possible failure and a projection of his own self-hatred. Allbee cunningly insinuates himself into the life of Leventhal. Allbee slovenly dressed turns up before Leventhal first in the park, the next day at Leventhal's apartment, and then in a restaurant where Leventhal is with Max's eldest son. Finally after being thrown out of his room by his landlord, the ruined bum forcibly stays at Leventhal's apartment. The half-alcoholic Allbee becomes increasingly audacious. He is impudent enough to read intimate letters from

Leventhal's wife, and sleeps with a prostitute in Leventhal's bed while he is away. Severe and at times violent confrontations between the victim and the oppressor culminate when Leventhal finds Allbee in the kitchen about to commit suicide by gassing himself—apparently "a murder attempt thinly veiled as suicide."[30] Even Leventhal now can no longer put up with him. The accused kicks out the accuser and "wrenches them both free from the tangle of the accusation and guilt."[31] Now both Leventhal and Allbee unknowingly assume the dual role of the victim and the victimizer, namely the *schlimazel* and *schlemiel*.

In a Broadway theatre a few years later, Asa Leventhal and his wife Mary happen to meet Kirby Allbee escorting a once famous actress. Leventhal has changed in his appearance and character. He is now one of the editors of young Harkavy's paper, *Antique Horizons*. He is satisfied with his present job. His health is better and he looks years younger. Something recalcitrant in him has left him, and his obstinately unrevealing expression has softened. Mary is now pregnant and he is going to be a father in the near future. They now live in the uptown end of Central Park West. Now he seems to be released from the burden of guilt and responsibility and the persecution complex caused by anti-Semitism, real and imagined. On the other hand, Kirby Allbee, now a gigolo of a seemingly wealthy former actress, Yvonne Crane, has changed superficially but not substantially, and he comments on Mary's pregnancy: "Congratulations. I see you're following orders. 'Increase and multiply' "(292). To Leventhal Allbee looks "more than moderately prosperous in the dinner jacket and the silk-seamed formal trousers"(290). On nearer sight, however, Allbee doesn't look good; Leventhal can recognize the decay of something in his unhealthy color. During the intermission Allbee expresses his gratitude to Leventhal, and after telling the latter that he is now engaged in radio advertising, goes on:

". . . . I'm not the type that runs things. I never could be. I realized that long ago. I'm the type that comes to terms with whoever runs things. What do I care? The world wasn't made exactly for me. What am I going to do about it?"(294)

Leventhal cries as Allbee is leaving, "Wait a minute, what's your idea of who runs things?"(294) But Allbee runs in and springs up the stairs, and the question remains unanswered.

As is indicated by the prefaced epigraphs from the *Thousand and One Nights* and from De Quincey's *The Pains of Opium*, Saul Bellow expects the reader to learn through the work that we live in the world where events are unpredictable and responsibility is inescapable and that each man is one way or another the victim of the other and must come to terms with deliberate and accidental victimization. Bellow desires also to clarify in the novel that not only Jews but all men are in a precarious plight in the modern world and have to suffer to live under the burdens and pressures of society and must be "run" by systems and organizations. What most impresses the reader of *The Victim* is Leventhal's insistence that to be "human" consists in the ability ultimately to make his accounting, in other words to be responsible for what he has done.

Tommy Wilhelm in *Seize the Day* is, like Asa Leventhal in *The Victim* and Joseph in *Dangling Man*, a victim hero, a slob, a *schlimazel*, or another pathetic dangling man. He is a middle-aged Jew, thrown out of a well-established sales position with a large Eastern manufacturing company. He is a failure as actor, as salesman, as husband and father and son, and probably as a man; and he suffers for it.

The story of the novella begins when Tommy has lost wife, children, mistress, and most of his money. He now lives at the Hotel Gloriana, an aging residence hotel in Central Park West, where his retired father resides. Tommy's father, Dr. Adler, was a distinguished medical professor, and is even now respected among the residents of the hotel. To Dr. Adler, Tommy Wilhelm who has changed his name from Wilky Adler as a sign of rebellion against his father, is a perpetual source of disappointment. Tommy, an impulsive and childlike man, laments to his father his past fate and present suffering. He hopes for paternal love of any kind: monetary assistance, mercy, tenderness, acknowledgement of his existence, even just the feeling. Dr. Alder, a self-made man, however, doesn't like to be bothered by this slovenly son and shrinks from assuming the responsibility. His response is nothing but an angry and analytical denunciation of Tommy's past failures and present ignominy. Though he has a considerable fortune and can easily help his son, he rejects Tommy's pleas and shatters Tommy's illusions. Tommy's complaint is that Dr. Adler's one and only son cannot speak his mind or ease his heart to his father.

> As his father did not answer this avowal and turned away his glance, Wilhelm suddenly burst out, "No, but you hate me. And if I had money you wouldn't. By God, you have to admit it. The money makes the difference. Then we would be a fine father and son, if I was a credit to you—so you could boast and brag about me all over the hotel. But I'm not the right type of son. I'm too old, I'm too old and too unlucky."
>
> His father said, "I can't give you any money. There would be no end to it if I started. . . . I'm still alive, not dead. I am still here. Life isn't over yet. I am as much alive as you or anyone. And I want nobody on my back. Get off! And I give you the same advice, Wilky. Carry nobody on your back." [32]

The above citation significantly represents a dramatic confrontation of son and father, which is one of the important themes of *Seize the Day*.

Dr. Tamkin, a fraud, psychiatrist, idealist, is the only person Tommy can talk to. He assumes the role of Tommy's spiritual father instead of Dr. Adler. Dr. Tamkin, an enigmatic person who represent both a father and a betrayer, promises Tommy riches and salvation. He teaches Tommy: "The past is no good to us. The future is full of anxiety. Only the present is real—the here-and-now. Seize the day"(66). Harboring a suspicion against his sanity and true identity, Tommy has to admit that there is a great deal of truth in Tamkin's words. Over Tamkin's psychiatric advice on life Tommy contemplates:

> Yes, thought Wilhelm, suffering is the only kind of life they are sure they can have, and if they quit suffering they're afraid they'll have nothing. He [Dr. Tamkin] knows it. This time the faker knows what he's talking about. (98)

Believing that Tamkin will get through this crisis and bring him to safety, Tommy entrusts his last seven hundred dollars to Tamkin and speculates in the commodities market. Tamkin disappears with his money. Dr. Adler refuses his final solicitation for help. His wife Margaret hangs up on him when he phoned her. He has now lost everything. Desperately he pursues Tamkin into a church, where he misses him in a large funeral crowd. Tommy Wilhelm weeps at a stranger's funeral he has just stumbled into by accident.

> Soon he was past words, past reason, coherence. He could not stop. The source of all tears had suddenly sprung open within him, black, deep, and hot, and they were pouring out and convulsed his body, bending his stubborn head, bowing his shoulders, twisting his face, crippling the very hands with which he held the handkerchief. His efforts to collet himself were useless. The great knot of ill and grief in his throat swelled upward and he gave in utterly and held his face and wept. He cried with all his heart.(117-18)

The last paragraph of this novella ends with the following sentence: "He heard it [the heavy sea-like music] and sank deeper than sorrow, through torn sobs and cries toward the consummation of his heart's ultimate need"(118). Whether this signifies the defeated acceptance of his status as victim, or his death, or a kind of his rebirth or resurrection after washing away all his sufferings by tears, is ambivalent.

Moses Elkanah Herzog is a Canadian-born Jewish professor whose second marriage has just broken up. He is a good, steady, hopeful, rational, diligent, dignified, yet childish person. He is impulsive, overbearing, gloomy, and always brooding. This middle-aged highly intellectual Jew, hedged in by brutal circumstances and burdened by his many failures, is a real sufferer and on the verge of insanity. The novel Herzog centers around his desperate efforts to shake off his neuroses and to revenge himself.

Herzog in the novel restlessly and impulsively moves from place to place: from New York to Martha's Vineyard, back to New York, from there to Chicago and then to Ludeyville, Massachusettes, all within a few days. The novel consists of Herzog's actions during the days of these trips and the nightmarish recollections of his past failures that run through his mind during that time.

Until middle age, he lived a normal and rather successful life. He made "a brilliant start in his Ph. D. thesis—*The State of Nature in 17th and 18th Century English and French Political Philosophy*. He had to his credit also several articles and a book, *Romanticism and Christianity*." [33] Fortune, however, began to cease to smile on him after his divorce from his first wife Daisy. His suffering is intensified and his mental health is aggravated by his second ex-wife Madeleine's adultery with Valentine Gersbach, his best friend.

Valentine and Madeleine spread the rumor that Herzog's sanity has collapsed. Herzog is obsessed with "the need to explain, to have it out, to justify, to put in perspective, to clarify, to make amends"(2), and so he writes endlessly and frantically dozens of unmailed letters to the great and to the obscure, to his friends, and to his ex-wives and mistresses. The anger and despair and crisis of identity of this child-man is vented in writing letters. In these letters the readers are given not only the confession of his suffering but also full-flown discussions of Bellow-through-Herzog's essential beliefs in defense of man.

Herzog suffers deeply just as do Asa Leventhal in *The Victim* and Tommy Wilhelm in *Seize the Day*, but unlike them Herzog is not totally immersed in his suffering and tries to see it from a philosophical view-point. Herzog incessantly mediates. He is absorbed in the true, the good and the beautiful, avoiding a cruel and nasty world. The Jewish passion for ideological moralism can be seen very characteristically in him. He knows that he is an innocent, unpractical man, and he is thrown into masochistic self hatred. He levels unremitting self-criticism and self-examination against himself.

> Resuming his self-examination, he admitted that he had been a bad husband—twice. Daisy, his first wife, he had treated miserably. Madeleine, his second, had tried to do *him* in. To his son and his daughter he was a loving but bad father. To his own parents he had been an ungrateful child. To his country, an indifferent citizen. To his brothers and his sister, affectionate but remote. With his friends, an egoist. With love, lazy. With

> brightness, dull. With power, passive. With his own soul, evasive.(4-5)

He lacks confidence in the value of self, and suffers from self-doubts concerning his own social relevance.

Peter M. Axthelm is right in contending that "Bellow approaches the problem of suffering with the sensitive insight of Jewish tradition,"[34] and that "the Jewish legacy of suffering is an important theme of *Herzog*."[35] He is nostalgically haunted by the memories of his Jewish parents, his brothers and his sister, his friends and the experiences of his childhood and youth in a ghetto street in Montreal and Chicago. He remembers his father, Jonah Herzog, who emigrated from Russia to Canada. There he tried many jobs only to fail in any of them until he became a bootlegger; and again as a bootlegger he blundered. Herzog inherited from his father a bluntness and a short-temper, and from his mother his dreamy and romantic nature.

> Napoleon Street, rotten, toylike, crazy and filthy, riddled, flogged with harsh weather —the bootlegger's boys reciting ancient prayers. To this Moses' heart was attached with great power. Here was a wider range of human feelings than he had ever again been able to find. The children of the race, by a never-failing miracle, opened their eyes on one strange world after another, age after age, and uttered the same prayer in each, eagerly loving what they found. What was wrong with Napoleon Street? thought Herzog. All he ever wanted was there.(140)

The richness of his Jewish past is firmly kept in the innermost part of his heart.

Herzog indiscriminately seeks advice and help from his successful brothers and sister, his Jewish friends, his psychiatrist, his lawyer, and his doctor. They all pity him, and want to teach him about reality. Sandor Himmelstein, Herzog's Chicago lawyer who handled his affairs during the divorce, is one of these reality-instructors. Sandor tells Herzog:

> "Well, when you suffer, you really suffer. You're a real, genuine old Jewish type that digs the emotions. I'll give you that. I understand it. I grew up on Sangamon Street,

remember, when a Jew was still a Jew. I know about suffering—we're on the same identical network."(84)

After many other instructions in reality by his New York lawyer Simkin, his friend, and his wife's adulterer Valentine Gersbach, and several women attending to him, Herzog overcomes his emotional trouble and finally returns to normalcy.

In the final passage of the novel Herzog decides to stop writing letters:

> He went around and entered from the front, wondering what further evidence of his sanity, besides refusing to go to the hospital, he could show. Perhaps he'd stop writing letters. Yes, that was what was coming, in fact. The knowledge that he was done with these letters. Whatever had come over him during these last months, the spell, really seemed to be passing, really going.(341)

The end of writing letters means the end of his alienation and his acceptance of reality. He has ultimately terminated a melodramatic struggle against his own being and has mastered the courage to live.

The typical Bellow protagonist is part bum, part neurotic, and part philosopher. He often indulges in discursive speculation. He is compulsively indecisive. He is a troubled sufferer, and his kinship is with the fool. He continues in a desperate struggle for life, and tries to find meaning in life. The question he ask is: "How is it possible today for a good man to live?" or "How can one resist the controls of this vast society *without* turning into a nihilist, avoiding the absurdity of empty rebellion?"[36] He also tries with some intellectual detachment to understand the whole mysterious ordeal of Jewishness, and finally he converts his suffering into an acceptance of life.

II. A GALLERY OF JEWISH WOMEN

1. BERNARD MALAMUD

Frank Alpine's interest and hunger for Helen Bober is motivated at first by her flower-like panties and restless brassières moving idly in the wind on the clothesline above the store. He begins to think of her as an object for his sexual satisfaction. His transformation from seducer to lover and provider, his "process of maturation from *eros* to *caritas*" [1] is another important theme of *The Assistant*.

The first time Frank laid eyes on her, "he was at once aware of something starved about her, a hunger in her eyes he couldn't forget because it made him remember his own." [2] In the fly-specked, worm-eaten shop, his desire to get to know her begins to grow.

> She had a pretty face and a good figure, small-breasted, neat, as if she had meant herself to look that way. He liked to watch her brisk, awkward walk till she turned the corner. It was a sexy walk, with a wobble in it, a strange movement, . . . Her legs were just a bit bowed, and maybe that was the sexy part of it. She stayed in his mind after she had turned the corner; her legs and small breasts and the pink brassières that covered them.(62)

He tries to "think of schemes of getting her inside the store"(63). Two weeks after Morris's accident, Frank tricks Helen into answering the empty phone just in order to see her figure. The intervention of Ida, Helen's mother, who expects her daughter to marry Nat Pearl or Louis Karp and who regards every gentile as dangerous, intensifies his desire and frustration.

One evening, driven by an irresistible passion, Frank climbs an elevator shaft to spy on her in the bathroom. Seeing her naked body through the uncurtained cross sash window, he felt a throb of pain, "an overwhelming desire to love her, at the same time an awareness of loss, of never having had what he had wanted most, and other such memories he didn't care to recall"(75). One time he is tormented with the conscience-stricken desire to confess his past crime to Helen and Morris. At the same time, however, he frequently feels a pleasure in doing something he knows he ought not to do. Suffering, he waits for her company for a long time.

> He wanted her but the facts made a terrible construction. They were Jews and he was not. If he started going out with Helen her mother would throw a double fit and Morris

another. And Helen made him feel, from the way she carried herself, even when she seemed most lonely, that she had plans for something big in her life—nobody like F. Alpine. He had nothing, a backbreaking past, had committed a crime against her old man, and in spite of his touchy conscience, was stealing from him too. How complicated could impossible get?(89)

Helen Bober, Morris' daughter, is a pretty but lonely New Yorker. She wanted a larger and better life, a college education as well as an educated, prospective husband. But now with little promise of a future, she works as a secretary with a ladies undergarment manufacturer. She is poor and unhappy, but she is proud. She never compromises with her ideals; "Life *has* to have some meaning"(43) to her. After working hours, she takes night courses at New York University, mostly literature courses; and she dreams of the day when something will happen. At first she shows no interest at all in a poor grocery clerk; her interest is more manifested in the well-groomed Nat Pearl and Mercury-driving Louis Karp. In the summer she offered her virginity to handsome and ambitious Nat Pearl, and now she regrets her lost virginity with torments of conscience. She is not satisfied with the carnal love that Nat offered. Her ideal in sex is "first mutual love, then loving"(14). She cannot tolerate Nat Pearl who thinks of her merely as a means of sexual gratification. She also declines Louis's marriage proposal for the reason that she does not want a storekeeper for a husband.

A few days after Christmas Helen and Frank meet at the library and take a walk in the park together. Helen's icy attitude toward Frank gradually begins to thaw. She bears a touch of tender feelings to him. In spite of his devouring eyes she feels she owes him gratitude. She also feels ashamed she has never thanked him for the help he has given her father. She thinks that his clothes show taste. She suggests that he should not make a career of a grocery, since there is no future in it. Frank tells her a sad story of his old carnival girl friend and about his ambitions and plans for college. In the same evening when she was in bed, Helen thinks of their walk that they took together:

> Thinking about Frank, she tried to see him straight but came up with a confusing image: the grocery clerk with the greedy eyes, on top of the ex-carnival hand and future serious college student, a man of possibilities.(101)

The first step of Frank's wooing process results in success.

Helen's good will toward Frank by slow degrees seems to be transformed into something akin to love. She comes to think that he is obviously more than an ordinary person. One night, after he told Helen his resolution to start college in the fall, she cannot stop thinking about it and imagines herself invited by him to a campus concert or play. Besides, Helen is willing to talk at length about books he is reading. The third time they meet, Frank hands her a package containing his presents. As she holds it against her breast, she feels a throb of desire for Frank. His presents are expensive things—disproportionate for his means—and much lovelier than anyone else has ever given her. This touches her; but she thinks she cannot take them, because they place her under obligation to him. The next evening she returns them to Frank. When she sees him bitterly hurt, she becomes aware of her responsibility for having encouraged him, out of her loneliness.

> The strange thing was there were times she felt she liked him very much. He was, in many ways, a worthwhile person, and where a man gave off honest feeling, was she a machine to shut off her own? Yet she knew she mustn't become seriously attracted to him because there would be trouble in buckets. Trouble, thank you, she had had enough of. She wanted now a peaceful life without worry—any more worries. Friends they could be, in a minor key; she might on a moonlit night even hold hands with him, but beyond that nothing.(113-14)

After all, complying with Frank's offer for a deal, she decides to keep one of his presents, a red leather copy of Shakespeare's plays.

Helen thinks Frank is not the kind of man she wants to be in love with, and tells him not to forget that she is Jewish. However, she feels herself, "despite the strongest doubts, falling in love with Frank"(130). She also feels that she has changed him and this affects her. Then one night in the park they exchanges the first impassioned kisses. Yet at the moment of sweetest joy she feels she still cannot fully accept him.

> He wasn't, for instance, Jewish. Not too long ago this was the great barrier, her protection against ever talking him seriously; now it no longer seemed such an urgently important thing—how could it in times like these? How could anything be important but love and fulfillment? It had lately come to her that her worry he was a gentile was less for her own sake than for her mother and father. Although she had only loosely been brought up as Jewish she felt loyal to the Jews, more for what they had gone through than what she knew of their history or theology—loved them as a people, thought with pride of herself as one of them; she had never imagined she would marry anybody but a Jew. But she had recently come to think that in such unhappy times . . . . to find love was miraculous, and to fulfill it as best two people could was what really mattered.(132)

She dreams of the day when they will marry and she will "help him realize his wish to be somebody"(133). But she postpones making any important decisions.

When she returns Frank's presents, he wonders what the payoff will be of his marrying Helen and of having to do with Jews the rest of his life. But it is a fickle idea. Her naked image in the bathroom seen through the window sorely afflicts him. He is "the victim of the sharp edge of his hunger"(135). Out of his physical loneliness, he wants to take her completely: he wants "satisfaction, relief, a stake in the future"(135). Through his solicitation, one Friday evening Helen sneaks up to his room. Contrary to his hungry expectation, he cannot satisfy his natural urge resisted by her idea of sex—"Loving should come with love"(139). She thinks she loves him but sometimes she is not sure; she instinctively senses something hidden and evasive about him.

Helen's remark at his room that Frank must discipline himself strangely haunts his mind, and bangs around in his head "like a stick against a drum"(157). He makes up "his mind to return, bit by bit until all paid up, the hundred and forty-odd bucks"(157) he pilfered from Morris. However, Frank is not fortunate enough to enjoy good luck. Julius Karp, pitying Morris's hard luck life, suggests that his assistant is filching the meager take of the grocery. The next day Morris witnesses a theft by his assistant. With a violent sense of outrage he orders Frank to leave the store. Desperate but with a slightly bright expectation that Helen is at last ready to surrender herself freely to him, Frank hurries to their regular dating place in front of the lilac trees around midnight of the same day.

A stereotyped nagging Jewish mother and wife, Ida Bober, repeatedly warns her husband to expel the *goy* from the store. To Ida, the idea of Helen and Frank together represents some potential evil; the husband of a Jewish girl must be a Jew. She suspects that Helen is interested in him instead of her ideal future son-in-law, Nat Pearl. One dark and windy night Ida follows her daughter to see if she is dating the gentile, and watches them kissing on the bench in the deserted park. Complying with Ida's weeping appeal to give Nat another chance, Helen goes out with him. While they are driving into Long Island or stop off for a drink at a roadside tavern, Helen's thoughts are still on Frank whom she is to meet at the regular place around midnight after this unwanted drive; and she feels she is truly in love with Frank.

While waiting for Frank in the park at one in the morning, Helen is attacked by a drunkard bum, Ward Minogue. The moment she is going to be violated, Frank Alpine appears at the place and after a struggle drives away Minogue. Helen is crying in his arms, saying at last that she loves him. Feeling hopelessly that it is the end and he will never see her again, and thinking he must love her before she is lost to him, Frank Alpine succumbs to an act of near-rape.

> Even as he spoke the thought of her as beyond his reach, forever in the bathroom as he spied, so he stopped her pleas with kisses. . . .
> Afterward, she cried, "Dog—uncircumcised dog!" (168)

When he finally satisfies his carnal desire, he has lost everything he has sought for and almost had, Helen's love. Both Frank and Helen suffer and moan in a gnawing remorse. When their eyes meet several days after the incident, her eyes show disgust. Observing her, Frank feels "a pang of loss, shame, regret"(179).

The next day Morris Bober attempts suicide by inhaling gas. He is saved from the gas by Frank Alpine and Nick Fuso, but he develops pneumonia and is sent to the hospital by ambulance. By getting Frank to promise not to bother Helen any more, Ida permits him to stay in the store. Strangely enough, neither Helen nor Morris has told Ida what Frank has done. Frank thinks he will promise anything to stay in the grocery.

> He would do anything she [Helen] wanted, and if she wanted nothing he would do something, what he should do; and he would do it all on his own will, nobody pushing him but himself. He would do it with discipline and with love.(184)

Helen now lives "in hatred of herself for having loved the clerk against her better judgement"(192). What has happened has put her in another world. Though his presence makes Helen sick, and even though business is terrible, Frank tries all sorts of schemes to hang on. He sells specials; he extends the opening hours; he repaints the wall and the ceiling of the store; he cuts down on expenses; and he even works at a coffee shop as a counterman from ten p.m. to six a.m. after he closes the grocery. In spite of these superhuman efforts, business is terrible. To make the matters worst, Morris finally suspects that Frank was one of the robbers who held him up; he demands that Frank leave the store.

At the beginning of April Morris dies of "double pneumonia from shoveling snow in front of his place of business so people could pass by on the sidewalk"(228). At his funeral Frank Alpine appears and stands behind the dead man's relatives, old friends and *landsleit*[3] who were "drawn by funeral notices in the Jewish morning papers"(226). In the cemetery Frank loses his balance, slips and lands feet first onto Morris's coffin. Frank reflects the burden and suffering of his Jewish master, Morris Bober, a typical *schlimazel*. Frank sneaks back into store; and works without sparing himself, until he grows "thin, his neck scrawny, face bones prominent, his broken nose sharp"(241). He works for love and for his predecessor's penniless bereaved family. He lives and works so that, in the future, he would be forgiven. All he asks for himself is "the privilege of giving her something"(237) she cannot give back. For himself he spends only for the barest necessities.

> When he could no longer sew up the holes in his undershirts he threw them away and wore none. He soaked his laundry in the sink and hung it to dry in the kitchen.(240-41)

Sacrificing his personal opportunities and even his existence including meals and sleep, he helps Helen get her night college education. One August night he even suggests that she go to college during the day. He confesses his crime to Helen. She reacts with contempt and disgust for him.

Frank has an additional concern. Recently Nat Pearl has been hanging around Helen. They often go out for rides at night. Sometimes Frank listens at the side door to their whispering and necking. This makes him jealous and he cannot sleep, desiring her so much. Again he climbs up the air shaft to spy on Helen in the bathroom.

> He swore to himself that he would never spy on her again, but he did. And in the store he took to cheating customers. When they weren't watching the scale he short-weighted them. A couple of times he shortchanged an old dame who never knew how much she had in her purse.
> Then one day, for no reason he could give, though the reason felt familiar, he stopped climbing up the air shaft to peek at Helen, and he was honest in the store.(242)

One night in January Helen happens to see Frank at the counter of the Coffee Pot resting his head on his arms and going drunkenly back to sleep. "Groggy from overwork, thin, unhappy"(243), he is working for her. Because of him she has enough to go to college at night. She is charmed with his superhuman will and effort, patience and potentiality. In bed she says to herself that he has changed into somebody else, and that since he has changed in his heart he owes her nothing. On her way to work one morning a week later, Helen enters the grocery and thanks him for the help he is giving them. Again he mentions his idea of her going to day college. Helen answers that she will think about it, and before leaving she takes a leather-bound book out of the brief case and tells him she is still using *his* Shakespeare. The next night, listening at the side door, Frank hears Nat say something harsh, after which Helen slaps him.

"You bitch," Nat called after her. (244)

One day in April, about one year after Morris's death, Frank goes to the hospital and has himself circumcised. He becomes a Jew, a sign of unselfish devotion to Helen and of his commitment of the Law of Judaism as it was told to him by Morris Bober. Frank's ultimate reformation has taken place and he is now a "circumcised" semi-St. Francis.

As Edwin M. Eigner points out, a "Mistress Poverty, Helen is haughty and bitter,"[4] and when she plays this part "Malamud phrases her speech in the rhythms of her mother, a discontented, bigoted, and unforgiving woman."[5] She is affectionate to her parents especially to her father;[6] but she behaves somewhat coldly toward her suitors: Frank Alpine, Nat Pearl and Louis Karp. With Frank she is especially harsh even one year after his act of rape-seduction. Although during that night she wished to give herself to Frank, as she later realizes, she still appears to be severe with Frank who is an unselfish giver of himself. Writing in *The Midwest Quarterly*, Walter Shear gives a convincing explanation:

> For her, love with Frank becomes a resignation to fate, an accepting of the present with all its disappointments as a permanent condition, and therefore love turns to hatred—as she realizes, to divert hatred from herself.[7]

She hates poverty and she seeks a new life and a higher status; she dreams an American dream of success. However, when Nat Pearl criticizes her on the phone, she reverts to some old-fashioned values of "a hot and heavy conscience in these times"(109). She was brought up as Jewish. She must make her life meaningful. She has an ideal in sex. It is true that she is more practical and more independent than her parents. After the oratory of the rabbi at Morris's funeral, she says of her father:

> He was no saint; he was in a way weak, his only true strength in his sweet nature and his

understanding. He knew, at least, what was good. . . . People liked him, but who can admire a man passing his life in such a store? . . . He made himself a victim. He could, with a little more courage, have been more than he was.(230)

However, she has never imagined that she will marry a gentile. She is a good Jew; and like the women in several of Malamud's other stories—Miriam Feld in "The First Seven Years," and Isabella del Dongo in "The Lady of the Lake"—she is proud to be a Jew. The result of Frank's courtship is mystified in surrealistic haziness; Helen Bober probably chooses as her spouse Frank Alpine who is a convert to Judaism and who as a successor to her father's Law and suffering lives a life of material but not spiritual poverty, rather than either of the two materialistic young Jewish suitors.

The initial short story in the collection titled *The Magic Barrel*, "The First Seven Years," is similar to *The Assistant* in the development of narrative and in the arrangement of characters, though of course the scale, length and intensity are quite different. Feld, the shoemaker, is an immigrant from the Polish *shtetl* and wants his single daughter, Miriam, to marry an educated man and live a better life. Feld and Morris Bober have something in common with their personal ill-health and with having a daughter instead of a son. Max is the son of a Jewish peddlar, now "taking a business course leading to a degree in accountancy."[8] Feld regards him with respect and good will because of the sacrifices he has made "throughout the years—in winter or direst heat—to further his education"(3). His rival, Sobel, bald and thirty-year-old refugee from Poland, "had by the skin of his teeth escaped Hitler's incinerators"(15). Just like Frank Alpine, Sobel appears off the street one night at the shoemaker's and begs for work. Sobel learns the trade from Feld. Again like Frank, it is only because of his love of Miriam that Sobel works five years for meager wages. He is more interested in books than in money.

Miriam's father regards Max as the future provider of a better life and ask him to date her. Miriam, however, who has already been won by Sobel through his books and commentary, displays no interest in Max whom she perceives after two dates to be an inveterate materialist having no soul. Feld's approach to Max infuriates the assistant. Sobel breaks the shoemaker's last and rushes out into the snow vowing that he will never return to work. When his new helper proves a thief, Feld reluctantly drags himself to the old helper's rooming house, and asks him to come back to work. Feld's anger turns into pity for the old helper. Sobel's shouldres shakes sobbingly when he asks Feld if he can marry Miriam.

"She is only nineteen," Feld said brokenly. "This is too young yet to get married. Don't ask her for two years more, till she is twenty-one, then you can talk to her."(15)

Feld feels that all his dreams for his daughter are dead, but "with a stronger stride"(15), he walks back home. The next morning shoemaker finds his assistant already seated at the last, "pounding leather for his love"(16).

The setting of "The Lady of the Lake" in the same collection is laid in Italy. Henry Levin, an employee at Macy's book department, who has "recently come into a small inheritance"(105), quits and goes to Europe "seeking romance"(105). In order to hide his Jewish identity, he takes to calling himself Henry R. Freeman. In pursuit of a new life, just as Frank Alpine went to New York from San Francisco, Seymour Levin from New York to Cascadia, Freeman comes to the Stresa shore on beautiful Lake Maggiore. Every time he gazes with a sense of awe at the gorgeous gardens and the luxuriant vegetation of the island Del Dongo, he experiences "a painful, contracting remembrance. . . of personal poverty"(111), and at the same time he recalls "a sad memory of unlived life, his own, of all that had slipped through his fingers"(109). When for the first time Freeman meets Isabella del Dongo whose dark, sharp Italian face has "that quality of beauty which hold the mark of history, the beauty of a people and civilization"(113), he discovers "in her eyes a hidden hunger, or memory thereof"(113). The girl with high-arched breasts[9] studies him for a full minute, and then hesitantly asks him: "Are you, perhaps, Jewish?"(113). Though shocked by the question, Freeman lies on fear of losing her favor. Having told a lie to the beloved afflicts him. At the top of Mt. Mottarone when Isabella compares the Alpine peaks to a *Menorah* ,[10] he pretends not to know Hebrew.

Freeman fails in Isabella's second test. At the lake front on their way back from Mt. Mottarone, Isabella confesses to him that she is not the daughter of the famous family who owns the island, but the daughter of the poor caretaker of the palace. In the same evening at the garden of the lake's edge, Isabella again asks Freeman, who has come to marry her, "Are you a Jew?"(132). In response to the denial of his identification, she unbuttons her bodice, baring her breast branded at Buchenwald by the Nazis, and then says:

> "I can't marry you. We are Jews. My past is meaningful to me. I treasure what I suffered for."(132)

Again, what he hoped to win has slipped through the fingers of Henry R. Freeman, both the *schlemiel* and *schlimazel.*

Among Malamud's women characters, there are some seductive lothsome ladies who drive heroes finally into a miserable or despairing condition. They are, for example, Memo Paris and Harriet Bird in *The Natural,* Pauline Gilley in *A New Life,* Stella Salzman in "The Magic Barrel." However, it is on another type of woman character that Malamud lavishes his love and praise. They are Helen Bober, Miriam Feld, Isabella della Setta, characters who value and remain loyal to traditional Jewish way of life.

2. PHILIP ROTH

Ida Bober in *The Assistant* is the stereotyped Jewish mother always nagging because her family is poor and unfortunate. She is characterized by her muted suffering, her extreme courage in her struggle against poverty, and her fine sense of balance and stability. Sophie Portnoy and Neil Klugman's Aunt Gladys also have the qualities of the stereotyped Jewish mother. They share with Ida Bober in their devotion to the family and in their loyalty to the Jewish tradition, but none of them is poor nor illfated. They are very different from Ida Bober in that they live in an affluent society and have an self-possessed urban sophistication. One more important difference to be noted here is that Roth's Jewish mothers are portrayed as exaggerated comic figures.

Sophie Portnoy, a freckled and redheaded descendant of Polish Jews and the dispenser of Judaic and family law, attaches herself to her son like a cancer. She dedicates her unlimited leisure to two allowable passions: love of the male child and hatred of the *goyim*. Just like every Jewish mother, she smothers her son, Alexander.

> You should have watched her at work during polio season! She should have gotten medals from the March of Dimes! Open your mouth. Why is your throat red? Do you have a headache you're not telling me about? You're not going to any baseball game, Alex, until I see you move your neck. Is your neck stiff? Then why are you moving it that way? You ate like you were nauseous, are you nauseous? Well, you ate like you were nauseous. I don't want you drinking from the drinking fountain in that playground. If you're thirsty wait until you're home . . . . I don't want you running around, and that's final. Or eating hamburgers out. Or mayonnaise. Or chopped liver. Or tuna. Not everybody is careful the way your mother is about spoilage. You're used to a spotless house, you don't begin to know what goes on in restaurants.[11]

The love of this Jewish mother is generous, forceful but destructive, and thus spoils her son. She has the dual role of nurturer and devourer. Sometimes she is a sardonic, castrating, omnipotent matriarch. She points a bread knife at Alex's heart because he will not eat some string beans and a baked potato. Alex comes to feel disgust at his mother and thinks she is too much to bear.

> If it's bad it's the *goyim*, if it's good it's the Jews! Can't you see, my dear parents, from whose loins I somehow leaped, that such thinking is a trifle barbaric? . . . . The very first distinction I learned from you, I'm sure, was not night and day, or hot and cold, but *goyische* and Jewish! . . . . Jew Jew Jew Jew Jew Jew! It is coming out of my ears already, the saga of the suffering Jews! Do me a favor, my people, and stick your suffering heritage up your suffering ass—*I happen also to be a human being!* (75-76)

Melvin J. Friedman has remarked that following the publication of *Portnoy's Complaint* every Jewish son including himself received from his mother a note with the following rhetorical question, "am I a Mrs. Portnoy?"[12] Though somewhat satirically distorted and a little different from Alfred Kazin's mother in his *A Walker in the City* and Norman Podhoretz's in his *Making It* both of whom are depicted with a kind of respect and sympathy, Sophie in *Portnoy's Complaint* "has given a conclusive form and texture to the image of the Jewish mother,"[13] parhaps of all mothers. Sophie is one of the most striking women characters of the decade.

Always obsessed with the guilt and fear implanted by his mother, Alexander Portnoy goes through revengeful sex adventures with gentile and Israeli girls in order to make sexual liberation as the key to total freedom from his mother, his past, and his religion. Portnoy's complaint is that all this sex is unsatisfying. Philip Roth defines his hero's complaint as a "disorder in which strongly-felt ethical and altruistic impulses are perpetually warring with extreme sexual longings, often of a perverse nature"(iv).

The first gentile girl with whom Alexander Portnoy, a lustridden, mother-addicted young Jewish bachelor, has relations is Kay Campbell. Kay, alias "the Pumpkin," a prototype of the Midwestern *shikse*, is big-bottomed, lipstickless, barefooted, artless, sweet-tempered, round and ample and sun-colored, and without a trace of morbidity or egoism. She has never raised her voice in an argument. Alex continues to portray her character:

> Slight as a butterfly through the rib cage and neck, but planted like a bear beneath! *Rooted*, that's what I'm getting at! Joined by those lineman's legs to this American ground!(218)

When Kay thinks she is pregnant, Alex says to her:

> "And you'll convert, right?"
> I intended the question to be received as ironic, or thought I had. But Kay took it seriously. Not solemnly, mind you, just seriously.
> Kay Campbell, Davenport, Iowa: "Why would I want to do a thing like that?"(230)

Her words put Portnoy into a rage. As a result he decides not to see her any more. Sarah Abbott Maulsby, the "Pilgrim," a product of New Canaan; Foxcroft and Vassar, is another gentile heart broken by Alex. "A tall, gentle, decorous twenty-two-year-old, fresh from college, and working as a receptionist in the office of the Senator from Connecticut"(232), Sarah is an aristocratic Yankee beauty whose ancestors arrived in America in the seventeenth century. Alex spends three months forcing her to suck his cock. When at last she succumbs to his coercion, Alex says to Sarah:

> "I love you too, my baby," but of course it couldn't have been clearer to me that despite all her many qualities and charms—her devotion, her beauty, her deerlike grace, her place in American history—there could never be any "love" in me for The Pilgrim. Intolerant of her frailities. Jealous of her accomplishments. Resentful of her family. No, not much room there for love.(240)

To love her only for pleasure is Alex's little vengeance on Mr. Lindabury, Boston & Northeastern Life's president, for all those nights and Sundays his father spent collecting insurance premiums down in the colored district.

Alex's third and sexually most attracted *shikse* is Mary Jane Reed, "the Monky," a hyper-erotic fashion model. She is from an impoverished family of West Virginia. She is outrageously vulgar and uneducated. Alex indulges in loose erotic and sometimes grotesque pleasures with her.

> Ten months. Incredible. For in that time not a day—very likely, not an hour—passed that I did not ask myself, "Why continue with this person? This brutalized woman! This coarse, tormented, self-loathing, bewildered, lost, identityless—" and so on. The list was inexhaustible, I reviewed it interminably. And to remember the ease with which I had plucked her off the street (the sexual triumph of my life!), well, that made me groan with disgust. How can I go on and on with someone whose reason and judgment and behavior I can't possibly respect?(214)

After many undescribably profligate adventures with the Monkey, he suffers with remorse and guilt. Finally, Alex abandons her in Greece.

Alexander Portnoy goes to Israel aboard an El Al flight in order to convert himself from a "bewildered runaway into a man once again."(252) In a world where every one is a Jew, he befriends Naomi, "the Heroine," a famale lieutenant in the Jewish army. Her parents are Zionists from Philadelphia who came to Palestine just before the outbreak of World War II. She is determined, humorless and self-possessed, but he is excited by her "*small, voluptuous figure nipped at the middle by the wide webbing of her khaki belt*"(256).

> But how naturally she [Naomi] wore her idealism, I [Alex] thought. Yes, this was my kind of girl, all right—innocent, good-hearted, *zaftig*,[14] unsophisticated and unfucked-up. Of course! I don't want movie stars and mannequins and whores, or any combination thereof. I don't want a sexual extravaganza for a life, or a continuation of this masochistic extravaganza I've been living, either. No, I want simplicity, I want health, I want her!(259)

Alex finds himself saying, "I want to marry you"(263), to Naomi whom he hardly knows and doesn't even like. He tries to find his salvation in her. Then, after listening to her idealistic lectures on the superiority of Israeli socialism, he attempts to rape her; but he finds himself sexually helpless. She resembles his mother and accordingly renders him impotent. Naomi blames and criticizes him for being self-deprecating and self-mocking. He is made to understand that he is the epitome of what is most shameful in the culture of the Diaspora. She kicks him; then he think to himself:

> My head went spinning, the vilest juices rose in my throat. Ow, my heart! And in Israel! Where other Jews find refuge, sanctuary and peace, Portnoy now perishes! Where other Jews flourish, I now expire! And all I wanted was to give a little pleasure—and make a little for myself. Why, why can I not have some pleasure without the retribution following behind like a caboose!(271)

Alex who is incurably but simulatively sick, is a victim of the Diaspora, a *schlemiel* discarded by an Israeli tomboy.

Usually the traditional *schlemiel* is a cuckold, but Alex is at least sexually an activist hero, though at the end of the novel he is impotent before Naomi. This is quite different from most of Malamud's and Bellow's protagonists who are all the time vexed and tormented by women.

Roth's Jewish female characters can be categorically divided into two groups. The first consists of traditional Jewish mothers like Sophie Portnoy, Neil Klugman's Aunt Gladys and Ozzie Freedman's mother. The second group consists of second or third generation native Americans and almost entirely assimilated Jewish women. They represent the vulgar materialism of middle class Jewish life. Examples of this type are Brenda Patimkin, her mother, and Miriam Peck who believes that if only he goes to a psychiatrist, Eli's mental trouble will be remedied.

Brenda Patimkin is an angel to Neil Klugman. He is attracted to her and to the Patimkins's wealth. She is, however, looking for a transient, romantic free-love relationship rather than "the permanent, responsible relationship that Neil is trying to establish."[15] Neil's romantic infatuation is manipulated by Brenda's bourgeois calculatingness. He is her errand boy, emergency baby-sitter, and an outlet for her sexual deire. He obeys her. When the Patimkins find that their daughter has been sleeping with Neil all summer, they are indignant. Brenda tells Neil in a hotel room in Boston.

> "Neil, you don't understand. They're still my parents. They did send me to the best schools, didn't they? They have given me everything I've wanted, haven't they?"[16]

The "Cinderella story turned upside down"[17] ends here. Standing in front of Harvard's Lamont Library and seeing his reflection in the glass front of the building, Neil entertains some doubts as to his own identity. He perceives for the first time how his success dream for a better life has distorted his spiritual quest.

Jewish women characters of Philip Roth are akin to actresses in a satirical comedy; they are more fantasy than actuality. With the exception of Sophie Portnoy and Brenda Patimkin, his Jewish women are neither as colorful nor as real and vivid as Helen Bober, Miriam Feld and Stella Salzman are in Malamud's stories. It is ironic that the heroines of Philip Roth, who is committed to social realism, are less real than those of Bernard Malamud whose protagonists, Roth criticizes, as living "in a timeless depression and a placeless Lower East Side." [18]

3. SAUL BELLOW

Victoria Sullivan is correct in maintaining that the women characters of Saul Bellow's novels necessarily "fall into two basic categories: the victims and the victimizers." [19]

Most of the latter type can be lethal on the phone. The story of *The Victim* opens with Elena's phone call to Leventhal in his office. Elena, his brother's wife, implores him with terrible cries over the phone to come to her home on Staten Island. Her younger son Mickey is seriously sick and she needs his help. While her husband Max is working away from home in a shipyard at Galveston, Texas, Elena is burdened with the care of the children. Several times leaving work during a rush period, Leventhal makes his way to Staten Island and finds that Elena, despite her unquestionable love for Mickey, is not able to handle Mickey's illness. She is slovenly, and she herself needs taking care of; and like most of Bellow's women she is a little crazy and a little perverse. In the following statement, however, there is a slightly overstated distortion of Leventhal.

> For the present he preferred to be cautious about Elena and assume that her nerves were overworked. She gave way without control to what any parent with a sick child was liable to feel. But when he allowed himself to go further, to think of more than overworked nerves and Italian emotions, he saw the parallel between her and his mother .
> . . . At least you could say of them that they were both extraordinary when they were disturbed (he had not forgotten his mother's screaming)—whatever the right word for it was. [20]

Leventhal persuades Elena that Mickey should be taken to a hospital; but Elena resists, saying that she can look after him better than a nurse can. Leventhal is forced to take on an additional conflicting burden. He thinks that this burden, after all, belongs to

Max and he has no right to be away. In spite of her pleading, Leventhal makes a crucial decision in getting his nephew away from his mother and into the hospital. This well-meant action, however, leads to Mickey's subsequent death in the hospital.

At Mickey's funeral, Leventhal suffers pangs of guilt and dreads his being blamed by Elena. He feels she will hold him responsible for the death of her young child. He knows that the accusation is utterly wrong and probably groundless. But it is precisely because of the unreasonableness of the blame that he fears her. Her unpredictable behavior "frightens him because he sees that it is part of his nature."[21] He sees a reflection of his own madness in Elena just as he does in Kirby Allbee. Max and Elena are simply benign versions of Allbee, which leads Leventhal into the plights that "compel him to ponder the nature and extent of the individual's responsibility towards others."[22] The subtheme dealing with Elena's family intensifies the primary theme.

Max is married to an Italian woman, Elena. Her mother is a rigidly strict Catholic, who is unfriendly and feels antagonism to Max and Leventhal, because of Elena's intermarriage. She feels that a Jew, a man of wrong blood, has given her daughter two children. Her understanding is that Mickey's death is an inevitable punishment on her daughter's impure marriage.

Leventhal does not observe Jewish holidays. He does not carry with him a constant awareness of his role and background as a Jew. But all of his thinking is channeled along the lines of defensive Jewishness. Subconsciously he disapproves of his brother's mixed marriage. After Mickey's funeral he is lost in the thought that his deceased father would be amazed if he knew that his grandson was buried in a Catholic cemetery. And he is afraid that Elena and her mother will "use his Jewishness as an excuse for blaming him for the death of Mickey."[23]

Tommy Wilhelm in *Seize the Day* stays at a hotel, leaving his wife and two children at home. His wife Margaret is cold, measured, insufferable, remorsely unbending, and goes out with other men; and so he feels unable to continue to live with her. Margaret, who has more survival capacity than her indecisive husband, will not give him a divorce, and he has to support her and their two children. She warns him not to send post-dated checks nor to skip any payments. Tommy complains to his father: "Whenever she can hit me, she hits, and she seems to live for that alone. And she demands more and more, and still more."[24] Tommy feels that she hates, chokes, and is strangling him, and that he, her husband, is a slave with an iron collar around his neck. The following remark of Dr. Tamkin about women is a pertinent criticism of Tommy's plight:

> ". . . . Innately, the female knows how to cripple by sickening a man with guilt. It is a very special destruct, and she sends her curse to make a fellow impotent. As if she says, 'Unless I allow it, you will never more be a man.' But men like my old dad or Mr. Rappaport answer, 'Woman, what art thou to me?' You can't do that yet. You're a halfway case. You want to follow your instinct, but you're too worried still. . . ."(97)

And he advises Tommy not to marry suffering.

After Tommy has lost his last money, he calls up Margaret and asks her to get a job. She absolutely rejects his request for the reason that she is not going to have two young children, fourteen and ten, running loose. She hangs up saying that she will listen when he can speak normally and has something sensibly to say. Tommy tries to tear the telephone apparatus from the wall. Margaret is one of the representative type of victimized women who apply "one more pressure on his already over-burdened psyche."[25]

Madeleine Pontritter, Herzog's second wife, has recently divorced him. She is the most virulent and the most insidious of Bellow's women characters in his three fictional works, *The Victim, Seize the Day*, and *Herzog*, all of whom cause additional suffering for the male protagonists. She is beautiful, sensuous, hysterical, cunning, extravagant, irresponsible, and fiercely unsympathetic.

Several years previously Madeleine had made a fresh start in life with Herzog by converting to Judaism from Catholicism. Herzog, to please his wife, quit a professorship with a brilliant future in New York and bought a big old house in Ludeyville, Massachusetts, with the twenty thousand dollars he inherited from his father. Madeleine didn't want him to be an ordinary professor, but she changed her mind after they lived in Ludeyville for a year. She "considered herself too young, too intelligent, too vital, too sociable to be buried in the remote Berkshires."[26] He wrote to Chicago to find jobs both for Valentine Gersbach and for himself.

Madeleine had never loved him, and "after about a year of this new Chicago life, Madeleine decided that she and Moses couldn't make it after all—she wanted a divorce"(6). The hitherto unsuspecting Herzog, after he returned from Europe, discovered that Madeleine and Gersbach were lovers before they moved to Chicago. She repeatedly committed cuckoldry with his best friend Gersbach, but he believed in his wife's innocence. As soon as Herzog left her, she sent his picture to the police. If he ever set foot on the porch again to see his daughter June, she was going to call the squad car.

Herzog, convinced that his daughter June is being mistreated, conceives a murderous design against the adulterous pair. He goes to his father's home in Chicago. From his father's desk, Herzog takes a pistol and some Czarist money that his father brought over from the old country. He then sets out to kill Valentine Gersbach. Finding him gently bathing June, he withdraws. The next day Lucas Asphalter, Herzog's zoologist friend, arranges for him to spend an afternoon with June. The father and child have a heartwarming time until his rental car is involved in a minor collision. Herzog, accompanying June, is required to report to the precinct station on a charge of carrying an unregistered loaded pistol with him.

Madeleine appears at the police station to accuse him and tries to incriminate him. She recognizes two bullets on the sergeant's desk and insinuates that his original intention was to kill her. The sergeant asks her:

"He make any threats?"

Herzog waited, tense, for her reply. She would consider the support money—the rent. She was canny, a superbly cunning, very canny woman. But there was also the violence of her hatred, and that hatred had a fringe of insanity.(299)

Her eyes expresses "a total will that he should die."(301) She takes everything from him—child, money, fame, profession, learning, and even life. He writhes under her sharp elegant heel. Madeleine is the archetype of domineering women who "eat green salad and drink human blood"(42).

Herzog cannot get along very well with women, yet there is always a woman tending him. There is his first wife Daisy, a conventional Jewish woman whom he divorced because he was bored, and who now takes care of their son, Marco. Daisy is a strict, moody woman but dependable; and Marco has come through all right. "Stability, symmetry, order, containment"(126) are Daisy's strength. Herzog knows that he deserves what he suffers considering what he did to Daisy.

His mistresses extend from plump and pink Wanda in Poland to Sono Oguki, a tender-hearted Japanese who speaks broken French. But the most important figure to Herzog is Ramona Donsell, a Jewess of mixed heritage from Argentina, who seeks to heal his wounds inflicted by Madeleine. Ramona is lovely, fragrant and seductive, and besides she is a practical, capable and successful New York businesswoman. To Ramona Herzog's willingness to suffer is beyond comprehension. In her French-Russian-Argentine-Jewish and overwhelmingly attractive ways, she gives him "asylum, shrimp, wine, music, flowers, sympathy, . . . room, so to speak, in her soul, and finally the embrace of her body"(199). She is the counterbalance of Madeleine. She tries to reassure him of his intelligence and masculinity. She offers him peace and happiness, and finally saves him from insanity.

In Saul Bellow's novels loathsome ladies are more colorfully depicted than are submissive and attractive women. And he seems to view women causing pain and suffering to men. On this Jewish Orthodox suspicion of womankind, Malamud and Roth as well as Bellow have a commonly shared opinion. They hint and warn that a Jewish man cannot have sex for fun without being prepared for future trouble and suffering.

≪Notes≫

Ⅰ.

1) The attitude toward suffering is one of the major distinguishing factors between Judaism and Christianity. In Judaism, according to the *Encyclopaedia Judaica* ("Suffering," Vol.15), "man is challenged to remedy suffering wherever it can be remedied, and to endure it without complaining wherever it is irremediable." The existence of suffering is explained that "it is a process of purification." Such suffering is termed in the Talmud "afflictions of love" (*vissurin shel ahavah*). Another explanation is "to formulate a doctrine of reward and punishment in the afterlife."

2) Ihab Hassan, *Radical Innocence:Studies in the Contemporary American Novel* (Princeton, N. J.: Princeton University Press, 1961) 168.

3) Philip Roth, *Reading Myself and Others* (New York: Farrar, Straus and Giroux, 1975) 128.

4) Sidney Richman, *Bernard Malamud* (New Haven, Conn.:College & University Press, 1966) 79.

5) Bernard Malamud, *A New Life* (New York: Farrar, Straus and Cudahy,1961) 201. All the subsequent quotations from *A New Life* are from this edition, followed by page numbers in parentheses.

6) The love and sex lives of Malamud's characters will be discussed in Part Ⅱ of this Chapter.

7) Sanford Pinsker, *The Comedy That "Hoits"; An Essay on the Fiction of Philip Roth* (Colombia: University of Missouri Press, 1975) 19.

8) A Yiddish term meaning "any food which is not *kosher*."

9) Philip Roth, *Goodbye, Columbus and Five Short Stories* (Boston: Houghton, Mifflin, 1959) 202-03. All the subsequent quotations from *Goodbye, Columbus and Five Short Stories* are from this edition, followed by page numbers in parentheses.

10) Dan Isaac, "In Defense of Philip Roth," *Chicago Review* XVII (Nos. 2 & 3, 1964) : 91.

11) Irving and Harriet Deer, "Philip Roth and the Crisis in American Fiction," *The Minnesota Review* VI (No. 4, 1966) : 355.

12) "*Gefilte* fish" means "fish cakes or fish loaf, made of various fishes which are chopped or ground and miced with eggs, and lots of onions and pepper; the traditional Friday night fish, served at the Sabbath dinner."

13) Deer 356.

14) Joseph C. Landis, "The Sadness of Philip Roth: An Interim Report," *The Massachusetts Review* III (Winter 1962): 267.

15) Baruch Hochman, "Child and Man in Philip Roth," *Midstream* XIII (December 1967): 68.

16) The more detailed reference appears in Part Ⅱ of this Chapter.

17) A Yiddish term meaning "thief."

18) Bernard Sherman, *The Invention of the Jew: Jewish-American Education Novels* (1916-1964) (New York: Thomas Yoseloff, 1969) 171.
19) Isaac 90.
20) John N. McDaniel, *The Fiction of Philip Roth* (Haddonfield, N. J.: Haddonfield House, 1974) 143.
21) "Shikse" is a Yiddish term meaning "a non-Jewish woman, especially a young one."
22) Maurice Wohlgelernter, "Mama and Papa and All the Complaints," *Tradition* X (Fall 1969) : 74.
23) Philip Roth, *Portnoy's Complaint* (New York: Random House, 1969) 39. All the subsequent quotations from *Portnoy's Complaint* are from this edition, followed by page numbers in parentheses.
24) The more detailed reference about Sophie Portnoy appears in Part II of this Chapter.
25) McDaniel 143.
26) "The Jewish Intellectual and Jewish Identity," *Congress Bi-Weekly* XXX (16 September 1963): 35.
27) Saul Bellow, *The Victim* (New York: Vanguard Press, 1947) 13. All the subsequent quotations from *The Victim* are from this edition, followed by page numbers in parentheses.
28) Robert R. Dutton, *Saul Bellow* (New York: Twayne Publishers, 1971) 39.
29) Gilbert M. Porter, *Whence the Power?: The Artistry and Humanity of Saul Bellow* (Columbia: University of Missouri Press, 1974) 34.
30) Porter 29.
31) Robert Detweiler, *Saul Bellow: A Critical Essay* (Grand Rapids, Mich.: W. B. Eerdmans, 1967) 14.
32) Saul Bellow, *Seize the Day* (New York: Viking Press, 1956) 55. All the subsequent quotations from *Seize the Day* are from this edition, followed by page numbers in parentheses.
33) Saul Bellow, *Herzog* (New York: Viking Press, 1964) 4. All the subsequent quotations from *Herzog* are from this edition, followed by page numbers in parentheses.
34) Peter M. Axthelm, *The Modern Confessional Novel* (New Haven, Conn.: Yale University Press, 1967) 131.
35) Axthelm 135.
36) Saul Bellow's answer for the interviewer's question in *Writers at Work: The "Paris Review" Interviews*, Third Series (New York: Viking Press, 1967) 196.

II.

1) Sandy Cohen, *Bernard Malamud and the Trial by Love* (Amsterdam: Rodopi N. V., 1974) 10.

2) Bernard Malamud, *The Assistant* (New York: Farrar, Straus and Giroux, 1957) 61. All the subsequent quotations from *The Assistant* are from this edition, followed by page numbers in parentheses.
3) The plural form of "landsman," a Yiddish term meaning "someone who comes from the same home town."
4) Edwin M. Eigner, "Malamud's Use of the Quest Romance," *Genre* I (January 1968): 64.
5) Loc. cit.
6) Louis A. Berman writers in his *Jews and Intermarriage: A Study in Personality and Culture* (New York: Thomas Yoseloff, 1968) 341:

Perhaps the delicate balance between the strong mother and the gentle father may require the traditional value system of the *shtetl*; perhaps this norm does not transplant well into the soil of the Western world.

7) Walter Shear, "Culture Conflict in *The Assistant*," *The Midwest Quarterly* VII (Summer 1966): 377.
8) Bernard Malamud, *The Magic Barrel* (New York: Farrar, Straus and Giroux, 1958) 11. All the subsequent quotations from *The Magic Barrel* are from this edition, followed by page numbers in parentheses.
9) Edwin M. Eigner writes in his "Malamud's Use of the Quest Romance," *Genre* I (January 1968) 57, as follows:

The interest which Levin takes in Isaballa's breasts is typical of Malamud's heroes, who always characterize their women by the size, shape, quality, even by the health of their breasts. From *The Natural* through *The Fixer*, Malamud's power of invention in this particular is remarkable: besides breasts that are described as sick, well stacked, hard, neat, little, and full, there are also breasts that pierce and breasts that beat like hearts; some are like flowers or like small birds; there are even green breasts. Moreover when at the conclusion of *A New Life* the heroin changes her role in relation to the hero, the nature of her breasts begins also to change.

10) A Yiddish term meaning "the eight-branched candelabrum lit on *Chanukah*, the Feast of Lights."
11) Philip Roth, *Portnoy's Complaint* (New York: Random House, 1969) 33-34. All the subsequent quotations from *Portnoy's Complaint* are from this edition, followed by page numbers in parentheses.
12) Melvin J. Friedman, "Jewish Mother and Sons: The Expense of *Chutzpah*," in *Contemporary American-Jewish Literature*, ed. Irving Malin (Bloomington: Indiana University Press, 1973) 167.
13) Friedman 172.

14) A Yiddish term meaning "plump, buxom, well-rounded (of a female)."
15) Irving and Harriet Deer, "Philip Roth and the Crisis in American Fiction," *The Minnesota Review* VI (No. 4, 1966): 358.
16) Philip Roth, *Goodbye, Columbus and Five Short Stories* (Boston: Houghton Mifflin, 1959) 145.
17) Sanford Pinsker, *The Comedy That "Hoits"; An Essay on the Fiction of Philip Roth* (Columbia: University of Missouri Press, 1975) 6.
18) Philip Roth, *Reading Myself and Others* (New York: Farrar, Straus and Giroux, 1975) 127.
19) Victoria Sullivan, "The Battle of the Sexes in Three Bellow Novels," in *Saul Bellow: A Collection of Critical Essays*, ed. Earl Rovit (Englewood Cliffs, N. J. : Prentice-Hall, 1975) 101.
20) Saul Bellow, *The Victim* (New York: Vanguard Press, 1947) 54.
21) Irving Malin, *Saul Bellow's Fiction* (Carbondale: Southern Illinois University Press, 1969) 75.
22) Gilead Morahg, *Ideas as a Thematic Element in Saul Bellow's 'Victim' Novels* (Ann Arbor, Mich.: Xerox University Microfilms, 1973) 97.
23) Gilbert M. Porter, *Whence the Power?: The Artistry and Humanity of Saul Bellow* (Columbia: University of Missouri Press, 1974) 34.
24) Saul Bellow, *Seize the Day* (New York: Viking Press, 1956) 47. A subsequent quotation from *Seize the Day* is from this edition, followed by page number in parenthesis.
25) Sullivan 101.
26) Saul Bellow, *Herzog* (New York: Viking Press, 1964) 6. All the subsequent quotations from *Herzog* are from this edition, followed by page numbers in parentheses.

第VII章
崇高なる世界と俗悪の世界
―― Saul Bellow, *Humboldt's Gift*

I

　Humboldt's Gift（1975）は Saul Bellow の小説の第8作であり，彼が60歳のときに上梓された作品である。作中人物の Humboldt は John Berryman と Delmore Schwartz をモデルとしており，この作品の前半の部分はSchwaltzの死（1966）の直後に書き始められ，後半の部分は *Mr. Sammler's Planet*（1970）以後に書かれたということである。[1] またSaul Bellowが1976年にノーベル文学賞を受賞する直接のきっかけとなったのは，この作品であった。

　Eusebio L. Rodrigues の表現を借りるなら *Humboldt's Gift* はエヴェレスト山に比せられるべきものであり，*Herzog* と *Henderson the Rain King* という対をなす峰の上に高くそびえ，エヴェレストの壮大な山頂から見ると *The Adventures of Augie March* はその傍らにながながと横たわる尾根であり，*Seize the Day* はそれに接したほとんど完全な大地....ということになる。[2] この比喩の当否を論ずるのはここでは差し控えるとしても，この小説の語り手である Charles Citrine がヒマラヤ的なパースペクティヴを与えられ，前作までの主人公たちが苦しみながら考えてきた「人間とは何なのか」「人間に救いがあるか」「死とは何なのか」という基本的な問題を考察し，解決を与えようとした，壮大でしかもコミックな特色ある一級の作品であることに異論はない。

Saul Bellow の小説に，目まぐるしいプロットの展開を期待するのは無理というものだ。あまりに多くの人物が登場し，あまりに多くの哲学的思弁や微に入り細をうがった記憶とエピソードが合い間に記述され，観照的瞑想が繰り返し反芻されて挿入される。*Humboldt's Gift* も例外ではない。

　物語は，成功した60歳近くのユダヤ系劇作家・伝記作家 Charles Citrine によって語られる仕組みとなっている。彼は1918年生まれ，若いときウィスコンシン州 Appleton からニューヨークに出てきて詩人の Von Humboldt Fleisher に師事し，10年前の1960年代前半ブロードウェイで映画 *Von Trenck* によって大成功を収め，名声とささやかな富を得た。Woodrow Wilson や Harry Hopkins の伝記も出版しており，ピュリッツァー賞を受け，レジォン・ドヌール勲章受賞者でもある。

　この小説の最初の34頁は，共に故人となった Humboldt や愛人だった Demmie Vonghel に対する回想で占められ，プロットの展開はようやくその後「そして，いまは現在。人生のちがった側面——現にいま起こりつつある人生なのだ。」(And now the present. A different side of life—entirely contemporary.)[3] という文章で始まる。所はシカゴ，時は1970年代前半のある年の12月の朝。Citrine が起きてみると，彼のメルセデス280-SLが夜の間に襲われ，野球のバットでめった打ちにされている。暴力団くずれの男 Donald Cantabile の仕業である。この男は，小説の最後までダニのようにしつこく出没して Citrine に取り付き，悩ませる。Schlemiel としての Citrine に対する加害者は Cantabile 一人にとどまらない。離婚訴訟によって彼の財産をまき上げようとする彼の妻だった Denise，裁判にかかわる弁護士たちと判事，友人のような顔をして彼から金を絞り取る Alec Szathmar や Pierre Thaxter。義兄弟の誓いのあかしとして白地で交換した小切手によって，彼の知らぬ間に預金口座から6千数百ドルを引き出した Humboldt，金が目当ての白痴美人 Renata Koffritz。それぞれの人物に対するCitrineの愛憎や思い入れは異なるが，彼を取り巻くschlimazel にも全くこと欠かない。

　こうした輩からむしり取られ破産寸前の状態にあるCitrine は，Renata とヨーロッパに旅すべく，シカゴを出てまずニューヨークに赴く。コニー・アイラ

ンドの老人ホームに住む Humboldt の叔父 Waldemar Wald 老人から，今は亡き Humboldt からの贈り物，Citrine と上書きされた分厚い大きな封筒を受け取る。またニューヨークのホテルで，兄の Ulick 手術の知らせを受けた彼は，Renata をミラノに先行させ一人でヒューストンの兄を見舞う。マドリードのホテルで待っている筈だった Renata は，葬儀屋 Flonzaley のもとに走る。見捨てられて失意の Citrine はまた皮肉にも，Renata と Koffritz の間の子供 Roger を預かる破目となる。裁判所の命令で20万ドルの保証金を積まなければならなくなった彼は，金もなくなりホテルを出て，しばらくの間 Roger と 2 人でペンション住いをする。

　Waldemar 老人から受け取った封筒のなかには Humboldt が死の直前に書いた手紙と封緘された小さな封筒が 2 通入っていた。長い手紙の最後に，映画のシナリオの梗概が書かれていた。封緘封筒の中身は，共に版権を証明するためのもので，もう 1 通の方には以前 2 人で考えたシナリオ「映画のための原案—Chales Citrine と Von Humboldt Fleisher による合作」が入っていた。後者によって得られた示談金8万ドル（興行大成功中の映画 Caldofreddo が，2 人の書いたこのシナリオの盗作であることが証明され，交渉の結果示談金を得た），前者によって得られそうな売買特権5万ドルの半分を Citrine は Waldemar 老人に与え，友人を助け，ばらばらになっていた Humboldt 一家の墓を一カ所に集めることにする。4 月の暖かいある日，Waldemar Wald と彼の友人 Menasha Klinger，それに Citrine が加わり，Valhalla 共同墓地に並んだ 2 つの新しい墓に Humboldt と彼の母を改葬する場面で，この小説は終わっている。

　小説のプロットは大体以上のごとくであるが，前述したように，現実の物語の進展の合い間に回想や瞑想が延々と繰り返し記述される。それは友人 Humboldt に対する思い入れであったり，死や霊魂不滅の問題であったり，俗物的アメリカや現代資本主義批判，詩人と金，芸術とアメリカ，詩的力と科学的力との対立，詩的幻想を奪われた現代人の窮境であったりする。また，このような高尚な瞑想に耽る Citrine が，現実には Renata のような若い肉感的美人を盲目的に追っかけ，捨てられるフウテン老人であること——崇高なるものと俗悪なるものとの mixture が，Bellow 独特の巧みな語り口でしかもコミックに

描かれているのが，この小説の特質の一つであろう。以下，この小説の本質に迫るべく，具体的に考察を進めてみたい。

II

　Citrine の相手として登場する女性群は，年代順に Naomi Lutz, Demmie Vonghel, Denise, Renata である。Naomi Lutz は Citrine が15歳だったころの恋人であった。彼がこれまでに出会ったなかで一番美しく一番完全な女性だと，今でも彼は信じている。「ネイオミ・ルーツを愛しているとき，わたしは安全に人生の内側にいた。」(When I love Naomi Lutz I was safely *within life*.)（大井86;76）と述べ，Naomiを抱きしめて1万5000回の夜を過ごせたら，墓場の孤独と倦怠にもほほ笑みかけることができただろう，業績も財産も勲章なんか必要でなかっただろうに，と回想している。また小説の半ばで，40年ぶりにNaomiに偶然再開したCitrineは，直接同じ内容の言葉を投げかけ，君と一緒に人生を送れなっかたばっかりに，僕の性格はすっかり変わってしまった。完全にねじくれてしまった，と言っている。Naomi が "common" と言い，Doc Lutz (Naomi の父で足の治療師）が "Republican" と言うとき，2人は偉大なアメリカ大衆の一部であってそのことに満足していることを意味するに反し，自分は完全なアメリカ人ではないのだと，Citrine は述懐している。

　Citrine の文学修行時代の恋人 Demmie（正式名は Anna Dempster Vonghel）は，ワシントン・アーヴィング・スクールのラテン語教師で，名門 Bryn Mawr College の出身だが，15歳ごろ非行グループに入っていた経緯もある。父親は田舎の百万長者で，昔風の正統派キリスト教主義者の最後の生き残りのような人物である。その影響もあるのか，彼女のキリスト教は，激しい興奮状態に陥るタイプで，不眠に悩み，夜の世界に入り込もうとする際，病気・殺人・自殺・永却の罰・地獄の火などの話題を好んでする。ようやく眠りについたと思ったら，数分もしないうちに目を覚まして，うめき声を上げる。地獄がこわい。邪悪な精神が宿っているので追放しなければならぬ，と言うのである。「その声には，この不可思議な地球という場所と，この不可思議な生きるという状態

に対する恐怖があらわされている。もがき，うめきながら，そこを脱出しようとしているのだ。」(The voice expressed her terror of this strange place, the earth, and of this strange state, being. Laboring and groaning she tried to get out of it.)（大井163；147）それが，百姓女・学校教師・エレガントな女性の背後に潜んでいる原始的な Demmie なのだ。Citrine がこよなく愛していた Demmie はしかしながら，父親と共にDC-3でCaracasの空港を発ち，ジャングルに墜落，死亡してしまう。

　別れた妻の Denise とは離婚訴訟中であり，Denise は復讐心に燃えた冷たくあくどい徹底した悪女として描かれる。2人の間の娘 Lish と Mary にとっても悪い母親で，裁判所に Citrine を縛りつけ，弁護士に彼の金をしこたま絞り取らせているという訳だ。この作品を書いている頃 Bellow は，3番目の妻と離婚したばかりで，彼の怨念のようなものを窺い知ることができると言うのは，言い過ぎであろうか。Denise は Vassar College の卒業，父親は連邦判事でCitrine と同じくウェスト・サイド・シカゴの出身。Bellasco 劇場で Von Trenckの舞台稽古のとき最初に出会って10年後離婚し，Kennedy 大統領夫妻に招かれ正装して2人で出席したこともあった。Denise が自宅に招くシカゴの一流人に対し，Citrine はそりが合わなかった。彼にとって，シカゴの知的上流社会の連中は，「真」「善」「美」(the True, the Good, the Beautiful)（大井68；60）に背を向け，「知性の光」(the light)（大井68；60）理性では説明できない類の喜びを味わせてくれる生命の息吹きそのもの，存在の光を否定しているからだ。Denise は，Citrine の幼友達 George Swiebel が大嫌いである。George が家のソファーに触れたり，じゅうたんの上を歩くのにも Denise は我慢がならない。それに反し，「ジョージは自然の代弁者をもって自認している。彼を導いているのは，自然，本能，心情なのだ。生命を中核的な事実とみなしているジョージ。」(George feels that he can speak for Nature. Nature, instinct, heart guide him. He is biocentric.)（大井49；42）つまり George は外的世界に属しながらも肉的世界・原始主義の世界により近く位置し，Denise は俗悪な外的世界・アメリカ性を代弁していることが暗示されているのである。

　Renata Koffritz は，今の Citrine が最も愛している肉感的な若い美人である。

いかれた母親の一人娘で，父親は不明。高校時代，美術の教師とメキシコに駆け落ちして連れ戻され，墓石や納骨堂のセールスマン Koffritz と結婚，Roger という男児をもうけたが，現在離婚訴訟中。その担当弁護士の Alec Szathmar から紹介されて2人の関係が始まる。Renata の美，彼女の肉体の完璧さは，古代ギリシャか盛期ルネッサンスに属するタイプのもので，今日の時代にそぐわないものだ，と Citrine は考える。すなわち，人間が自らの存在を自然的な存在と区別することをしなかった時代の美だという訳だ。Renata が Citrine を捨てて葬儀屋の Flonzaley と結婚する際，彼によこした手紙のなかで，Citrine を批判して次のような趣旨のことを言っている。私は淫売婦みたいな立場に置かれていた。私はあなたのすてきなセックスの道化となったのよ。あなたは退屈に関する大論文を書こうとしているけど，さぞかし全人類が感謝することでしょうね。でも，そんな精神的で，知的で，普遍的なことには一切かかわりたくないの。私には退屈なだけですから，と。

　Denise は Citrine をどのように見ているのであろうか。Denise にとって今の彼は信じられない。あんなに素晴らしい洞察力を持っている人，世界中の学者や知識人に尊敬されている人間が，今は一体何をしているというの？　この醜くて，いやらしく，危険がいっぱいのシカゴにどうして戻ってきたの？「あなたという人間が，心底はスラム生まれの若僧だからなのよ。あなたの心は，ウェスト・サイドの古ぼけた貧民街と縁が切れないのね．．．．」(Because at heart you're a kid from the slums, your heart belongs to the old West Side gutters. . . .)（大井48；41）と手厳しい。

　Demmie の Citrine 批判の言葉は見当たらないが，40年後に会ったときの Naomi も彼を難詰している。ベリー・ダンスの踊り子みたいな体格の大きな黒い目の東洋風の女（Renata）とまだ手が切れていないのでしょう。「あなたって，どうなっているんでしょうね——偉くて，頭の切れる有名人のあなたが女から女へせっせと渡り歩いているなんて。もっと大切なお仕事はないの？．．．」(I wonder what it is with you—a big important clever man going around so eager from women to women. Haven't you got anything more important to do?. . .)（大井，下78；302-03）と。

Ⅲ

　暴力団くずれのRonald Cantabileは，どうしようもない悪漢であるが，この小説においては一つの重要な役割を演ずる人物である。世間知らずのCitrineは，実人生のガイド役を自認するGeorge Swiebelの案内で，悪い連中のポーカー・ゲームに連れてゆかれ，Cantabileに450ドルの借金を負う。イカサマだから払うことはないと助言するGeorgeに従って，小切手の支払停止の処置をしたのがCantabileの癇に障り，停車中のベンツをめった打ちにされる。ある日，50ドル紙幣で450ドルを準備しロシア風呂に来るよう呼び出されたCitrineは，Cantabileにトイレの個室のなかまで付き合わされ，プレイボーイ・クラブやハンコック・ビルの宝石商に連れてゆかれる。ようやく受け取った50ドル紙幣のほとんどを，Cantabileは建築中のビルの上から紙飛行機の折り紙にして飛ばすなど，数々の彼の愚行にCitrineは1日中，暴力によって付き合わされる。また別の日に，Stronsonを一緒に脅迫したような格好となり，警察から捕らえられ留置場に入れられそうになる。Citrineは彼に辟易しながらも，最初からすごく変わった強い印象をCantabileから受ける。人間とは何かを考える対象として，いろいろなことをCantabileは教えてくれるように思えたからである。

　小説の後半でも，Cantabileは大きな役割を果たす。CitrineとHumboldtの共作シナリオが盗作され，今大評判のCaldofreddoとして上映されていることを知らせてくれたのは，他ならぬCantabileである。そのおかげでCitrineは，調停示談金8万ドルその他を得て破産寸前の経済的危機から救われ，これまでと違った新しい生活に入ることができたのであった。Cantabileは迷惑な男だけれども，Citrineにはなぜか彼が憎めない。Cantabileは何か精神的な役割を果たすことを目的として，ふっと湧いたように自分の行く手に姿を現し，"dead center"（288）の位置から自分を動かそうと努力しているように，Citrineには思われるのである。それにCitrineはまた，普通の分別のある連中だと本来の自分になることができないが，Cantabileのような連中を相手にすればそれができる，と告白している。

同じようなことが Citrine を取り巻く何人かの男たちに対しても言える。Denise が言うところの「世間なみの人間」("common clay")（大井47；40）でなく「悪い仲間」("vulgar company")（大井47；40）の連中である。原始主義者、自然の代弁者で幼友達の George Swiebel、同じく幼友達で夜学出の弁護士 Alec Szathmar、Citrine と共同して雑誌 Ark の発刊準備をしている友人 Pierre Thaxter、そして極め付きは Humboldt である。

George Swiebel は元は俳優であったが、何十年も前舞台を去って、今は建設業者となっている。Citrine のために、暗黒街の知識——犯罪者、売春婦、競馬、暴力団組織、麻薬など——に関する指南役を演ずる。破損したベンツの売却、じゅうたんを売ってお金を調達してくれるのも彼であり、Cantabile との縁ができたのも George が用意したポーカー・ゲームが契機であった。夢を見て Renata にすっかり熱をあげている Citrine に対し、自分で自分がやっていることが分からなくなっている、そこがまたイカしているし尊敬もすると言う George。文無しになって、裁判所でグルになっている連中に一泡ふかせてやればいいんだ、と言う George。アフリカの叢林地でベリリウムの鉱山探しを試み、無残にも失敗する George。それでも Citrine は、人を騙すことなどとてもできない男だと George を信頼しきっている。

Alec Szathmar の紹介で Renata との関係が始まったことは前にも述べたが、Denise に訴えられた Citrine のために、Alec は大物だが無能の弁護士 Forrest Tomcheck を紹介し担当としてくれる。Tomcheck にかかると、大型電気掃除機の前に紙幣の紙吹雪を置くようなものだ、とんだペテン師をお前は世話してくれたものだと託ちながらも、Citrine の Alec に対する友情は変わらず、結局家族ぐるみの感情だなと思ったりするのである。

興味が多様であり、文化なら何でも首を突っ込む野次馬根性豊かなジャーナリスト Pierre Thaxter も、Citrine に随分迷惑をかける。コンドミニアム (condominium) を買うというので貸してやった金を Thaxter が返さなかったために、担保に入れてあった IBM の株を50株もフイにしてしまう。なかなか発刊の運びとならない Ark のために新しい棟を建てたり、大量の紙を買い込んだりしているが、支払いは Citrine が負っている。遂にはアルゼンチンで誘拐さ

れ，世界中の新聞に，Citrine に助けを求め身元保証人になってくれと公表されるのだが，この誘拐事件そのものも実際にあったのか Thaxter の作り話か真意のほどが分からない始末である。Renata は Thaxter をインチキな人間として信用していない。どうして文無しの Thaxter がヨーロッパに行くのに豪華船のファースト・クラスで行かなければならないのかと非難するが，Citrine は Thaxter 流のやり口のパトロンをもって自任している。他の人から Thaxter の悪口を言われると，彼はあれで結構いい男なんですよ，私自身も彼の悪口を言いますが，彼が何をやらかしたとしても，本当は大好きなんです，という意味の返事をする。

　昔の人間関係に依存し過ぎるというひどい弱点について何度も忠告され，自覚もしているのだが，Citrine にとって，親友は神聖なカテゴリーに属するものである。彼らのおかげで踏んだり蹴ったりの目にあい，自分はいつも文無しの状態でありながら，彼にとって友情は金よりも大切な掛け替えのないものなのである。

IV

　Humboldt は成功というテーマを情熱的に生き，失敗者として死んだ。1930年代の終わりごろ *Harlequin Ballads* で一躍有名となり，その成功は10年ばかり続いたが，40年代の終わりごろからパッとしなくなり，酒と薬に溺れ，そううつ病患者となり，狂気と対決しながら失意のうちに急死した。彼は *King Lear* の「あらゆる無残な混乱が声をあげてわれらを墓場まで追ってくる」("Ruinous disorders follow us disquietly to our graves.")（大井9；5）[4]という言葉を好んで引用したが，その無残な混乱が7年前墓場まで彼の後を追いかけてきたのだった。Citrine が50年代初めに成功を収めたころから，Humboldt は金銭のことで Citrine を恨み続けた。Humboldt のパーソナリティーを盗んで映画の主人公を作り上げているなどと言いふらし，Citrine と彼の富に関するあらゆる中傷を，ニューヨーク中に触れ回っていた。Demmie の飛行機事故死直後の悲しみのさなかに，Citrine の口座から6,763ドルを黙って引き出しもした。

Magnascoを脅迫して警察に拘束されBellevue病院センターに監禁され，それをCitrineのせいだと非難した。それでもCitrineはHumboldtが好きだった。いや愛していたと言ってもよかった。Humboldtの死は，自分の死を考えるとき以上のショックだったし，晩年の彼を見殺しにしたことを何度も後悔した。彼はしょっちゅうHumboldtの夢を見た。Citrineは，死者のことをぼんやりと考えたり，交感し合ったりする時間が多かったが，Humboldtは彼にとって重要な意味を持つ死者の一人となった。

詩人で，思想家で，天才で，驚くべき雄弁家，即興の語り手で比類なき毒舌家でもあったHumboldt，そのHumboldtとCitrineは，機械を，奢侈を，支配を，資本主義を，テクノロジーを，黄金の神を，アメリカや世界文明などを論じ合った。Humboldtは，精神の解釈者，神秘的指導者にも心を惹かれていた。彼の関心事は，生と死のはざまで何をなすべきかということであり，お得意のテーマの一つは，かつて存在した根源的世界，古典的世界が失われてしまったという人間的感情であった。また，詩人はプラグマティックなアメリカを打ち負かす道を見付けてしかるべきという主張を持っていた。晩年の彼は詩が書けなかった。書かれざる詩作品が彼を殺していた。古代においては詩は力だった。詩人は現実世界に実際的な力を持っていた。今のアメリカという大規模な企業では，詩人の影は薄くなる。美の神秘，芸術なんて話をすると，アメリカ合衆国の人間は全く関係ないとよそよそしい顔をする。詩人は，アルコール中毒者や異常性格者や落後者たちと同じように悲惨さのなかに沈んでゆく。アメリカのように物質主義の社会では，詩人は弱き者のシンボルであり，Humboldtはその体現者であった，とCitrineは考える。

Humboldtの贈り物には，具体的なものと精神的なものとの両側面があった。前者は，後に十数万ドルの金を与えてくれることになった封緘された2通の映画シナリオであり，後者はHumboldtが最後に書いたCitrine宛の長い手紙の内容である。この手紙のなかで，彼はこれまでのCitrineに対する不実を詫び，体力が弱り，頭が正気になる日が去来するにつれてCitrineのことを度々考えるのだと述べる。そしてさらに，この数年間詩を書くことはおろか，読むことさえできない有り様であることを告白している。今世紀の偉大なアメリカ詩人

になるとCitrineに期待されていた重圧に反比例する現実と，それに伴うむなしい挫折感，狂気となり，零落の果てに侘びしく，タイムズ・スクエアはずれの安宿でこの世を去ってゆく経緯が暗示されている。この手紙の最後の個所でHumboldtは「ぼくらはぼくらの同類のために何かをしなくちゃならない。カネのことでかっかするなよ。欲張りはやめることだ。女運がよくなることを祈る。最後に一言——ぼくらは自然的存在ではなくて，超自然的存在であることを忘れるなよ。」(We are supposed to do something for our kind. Don't get frenzied about money. Overcome your greed. Better luck with women. Last of all— remember: we are not natural beings but supernatural beings.) (大井，下130；347)と書いている。Citrineは実際的なHumboldtの贈り物によって経済的破産状態から救われ，無形のgiftによってHumboldtノイローゼから解放され，人類のために何かをしなければならないという彼の精神を継承して，新しい生活に入ることができたのである。

V

　Citrineは死の問題に必死に取り組んでいる。オーストラリアの社会哲学者Dr. Rudulf Steinerの人知学（anthroposophy）に共鳴し，Steiner式瞑想に長時間をかけ，死者たちに近付こうと最善の努力を続けている。死者の魂との交流を待ちわびており，そのような接触にふさわしい状態に身を置くために，故人となったDemmie，とりわけHumboldtを絶えず回想し精神を集中させている。彼の考えは，プラトンやダンテやドストエフスキーが支持した霊魂不滅説であり，眠っているとき魂は肉体を離れ，死者は我々に近付いてくると信じている。ヒンズー教の因果応報（Karma）にまで関心を持っている。また最近のCitrineは，Steinerの人知学のおかげで，かつてのように死の恐怖を感じることはめったになく，永遠に続く倦怠を恐れることもない。

　Citrineは，どうしてこんなに死んだ人間に忠義立てをするのか，自分でも分からないと言う。死んだ人のやり残したことを片付けてやらねばならないと思う。「そのかわりに，気がついてみると，その人たちの特徴のいくつかがわた

しにこびりついて, 離れなくなりはじめている。たとえば, 時がたつにつれて, 自分がフォン・フンボルト・フライシャー風の変人になりはじめていることに気づくといったあんばいだ。生前の彼はわたしの代弁者を務めていたという事実が, 次第に明らかになってくる。」(Instead I found that certain of their characteristics were beginning to stick to me. As time went on, for instance, I found myself becoming absurd in the manner of Von Humboldt Fleisher. By and by it became apparent that he had acted as my agent.)（大井119；107）つまり, Citrineという非常に落ち着いた人間の代弁者として, Humboldt が自由に言いたい放題のことを言って, Citrine の願望のいくつかを満足させてくれていたという訳だ。

　ノーベル賞受賞記念講演のなかで Saul Bellow は, 物体と行為と外観からなる外的世界と, 善も幻想ではないと我々を信じさせる内的世界があり, この2つの世界の間を, 小説は往来しているという意味のことを言っている。この小説では, 前者はただ単に自然だけに留まらず, 俗悪なシカゴであり, 裸のエゴや合理性や計算ずくに満ちたアメリカであり, ウォール街に象徴される現代資本主義であり, セックスの世界であり, したたかな現実を教えてくれるビジネスや権力の世界である。後者は, 知覚の世界だけでなく, 人の心を落ち着かせる瞑想の世界であり, 死の問題をめぐる思考の世界であり, 決して破滅することのない気高き霊魂の世界であり, 原始的・根源的なものを重んずる世界であり, プラトン的な宇宙であり, 詩や芸術の世界である。前者は natural で mortal な領域であり, 後者は supernatural で immortal な世界である。

　人間は俗悪な側面と崇高な側面とを併せ持つ複雑で不可解で, ある意味ではコミックな存在であるが故に, 登場人物をどちらかに截然と区別することは難しい。俗悪の外的世界に深く足を踏み入れていて救いようのないのは, シカゴの上流社会の連中であり, Denise であり, 彼女の離婚訴訟を担当する弁護士 Tomchek, Pinsker, そして Urbanovich 判事などである。詩も真・善・美も解せず, 存在の光を否定しているグループである。これに対し, 俗悪の世界に属していて崇高の世界に縁なき衆生でありながら, まだ稚気があり, 原始的な側面を留めているのが, Naomi Lutz, Demmie Vonghel であり, なかんずく Renata Koffritz である。人知学の先生の娘 Doris Scheldt を加えてもよい。彼女たちは,

Citrine の死に取り憑かれた気分を，愛し合うことによって慰めてくれる。さらにこのグループに入れるべき人物として，Ronald Cantabile, Alec Szathmar, George Swiebel, そして兄の Ulick を挙げることができる。これらの人物は，自らの欲望を目覚めた状態で追求する Citrine にとって愛すべき存在であり，彼に対し人間とは何かを教えてくれるありがたい見本なのである。

　崇高なる内的世界に深く，またより多く沈潜している人物は Humboldt と Citrine である。Citrine の登場人物に対する尊敬と愛情と執着の度合いは，逆順にまず Denise の言う "common clay" がきて，次いで "vulgar company"，そして最後に Humboldt と Citrine 自身がくるという訳だ。アメリカ的非難攻撃にさらされてズタズタに引き裂かれ，現代社会の虚無にじっと耐え，黙々とそれが過ぎ去るのを待っている人間である。Humboldt は詩人だった，高貴な人間だったと Citrine は回想する。Citrine は最近，存在の光，生命の息吹きを経験する。不正な世界，グロテスクな世界，狂気の世界などとは対照的に異なる世界が発見され，自己保存や生存競争のために消えてなくなっていたものが，よみがえってくるのを感じている。このような高尚な瞑想に耽る Citrine も，一方現実には，取り巻き連中に金をまき上げられて破産状態になったり，死の想念が漁色へと走らせるのか Renata のような若い女性に年甲斐もなく執着し，捨てられた後もなお彼女を思ってメソメソしている間抜けな男なのである。崇高なるものと俗悪なものとの間の大きな落差と矛盾を併せ持つことから醸し出されるおかしみは，ユダヤ的ユーモアというよりも，人間の愚かしさ不可解さをコミックに諷刺したものであろう。

　ともあれ，Humboldt の贈り物は，Citrine の当面もろもろの問題をかき消してしまった。前述したように，有形な贈り物によって自らも経済的破綻から救われ，Humboldt 一族のただ 1 人の生き残った老人を援助することができた。無形の贈り物，墓を乗り越えてやって来た Humboldt の声によって Citrine は，Humboldt を裏切ったことへの自己批判と羞恥から解放され，埋葬という通過儀礼を経て，Humboldt に取り憑かれたオブセッションからも解き放たれる。そしてある意味では，Humboldt が生存中に俗悪なるものに押しつぶされてなし得なかった崇高なる意図の一部分を継承し，死の問題を巡る正しい思考法を

自らに課し，人類の想像力を回復し，魂に加えられるあらゆる侮辱を排除し，生ける思想と真実の存在とを回復すべく，新しい生活に"supernatural being"として入ってゆくのである。

≪Notes≫

1) Daniel Walden, ed., *Twentieth-Century American-Jewish Fiction Writers* (Detroit: Gale Research Co.,1984) 21.
2) Eusebio L. Rodrigues, *Quest for the Human: An Exploration of Saul Bellow's Fiction* (Lewisburg, Pa.: Bucknell University Press, 1981) 225.
3) ソール・ベロー，大井浩二訳『フンボルトの贈り物，上』(東京：講談社，1977) 41. Saul Bellow, *Humboldt's Gift* (New York: Viking Press,1975) 34. 以下この作品からの引用はすべてこの版により，引用英文末尾の括弧内に頁数を記す。和文と英文を併記する場合は（大井41;34）と記す。訳本が下巻の場合は（大井，下78;302-03）とする。
4) William Shakespeare, *King Lear*, V.ii.119-20からの引用。
5) Saul Bellow, "The Nobel Lecture," *The American Scholar* XLVI (Summer 1977): 325.

第VIII章
東西都市文明批判とCordeの内省
—— Saul Bellow, *The Dean's December*

　The Dean's December（1982）の舞台は，クリスマスが押し迫った酷寒のブカレストで始まる。元ジャーナリストで今はシカゴのある大学の学生部長を務めている Albert Corde は，重症の義母を見舞うため，はるばるシカゴから妻と共にルーマニアの首都ブカレストにやって来た。秘密警察が跳梁する社会主義体制のこの町の雰囲気は，暗く荒涼としていて泥の色のように黒い。妻が少女時代を過ごしたアパートの小部屋に閉じ込められた Corde は，秘密警察の検束を恐れて外出も思うに任せない。暖房も利かず，骨身にこたえる寒さの部屋のなかで，学生部長は強いプラムブランディーをすすりながら，シカゴでの数々の出来事を何度も反芻し内省に耽ける。

　パリで *Herald Tribune* の記者をしていた Corde は40代半ばで転身し，郷里のシカゴに帰ってジャーナリズム科の教授となった。シカゴの現実を見て止むに止まれず書いた *Harper's* の2つの記事は，アメリカ文明の崩壊と道徳的危機，シカゴの腐敗を糾弾したものであった。読者の反応は決して好意的ではなかった。特に反感を抱いたのはマス・メディアの世界であった。今裁判になっている大学生 Rickie Lester 死亡事件に Corde が学生部長として取った措置に対し，マス・メディアはここぞと反撃し，身内からの攻撃批判さえもあった。この死亡事件に関連した Lucas Ebry 裁判事件の経緯も気になっている。牢獄のように閉塞された小部屋のなかで，Corde はアメリカ合衆国の狂った状態，共産国

における官僚世界・監獄社会の独特な考え方と精神異常——西と東の腐敗に想いを馳せる。なぜ自分はあの *Harper's* の記事を書いたのか，未成熟の印ではないか，という自己反省も執拗と思えるほど繰り返される。

この小説は19章で構成されているが，その大半の15章が終わるまで主人公 Albert Corde とその妻 Minna Raresh が滞在する場所は，物理的には少なくともブカレストである。16～18章で2人はシカゴに帰り，最後の19章はカリフォルニア州南西部の山峰にある Paloma 天文台が舞台となっている。これまで筆者は Corde の回想に重点を置いて記述してきたが，学生部長夫妻ブカレスト滞在中の約2週間にも，いろいろな外的事件が起きる。

Minna の母で Corde の義母に当たる Dr. Valeria は高名な精神分析医で，30年前コスモポリタン心理主義あるいはフロイト主義のかどで共産党から追放され，ルーマニア厚生大臣の地位を失脚した。1950年代の末に赦免されて名誉回復，年金も復活したが党に再加入することを彼女は拒否した。そのため，現在入院中の，彼女自身が在任中に建てた共産党病院でも，死亡後の葬儀においても，その前歴にふさわしい扱いを受けることができない。Dr. Valeria が入院している病院の実権は，秘密警察の大佐である病院監督官に握られていて，Corde 夫妻が母の見舞いに出かけるのも思うに任せない。死亡証明書を得るのに必要な社会主義体制特有の面倒な手続きは，門番 Ioanna のいとこ Traian の助けがなければ不可能であった。Dr. Valeria の葬儀の準備，上流階級出身の彼女のいとこたちの対応，葬儀の実態，火葬から墓地への納骨のプロセスが，事細かに記述される。不幸なこの実態の進展する約2週間のブカレスト滞在中に，Corde はまた黒人のアメリカ大使や，いとこで国際的コラムニストの Dewey Spangler と2度も会見し，シカゴから送られた小包を受け取る。暗く陰気で気分の滅入るブカレストの現実のなかで，会見や小包の中身の吟味の度ごとに，Corde の想念は絶えず過去へとさかのぼり，7000マイルも離れたシカゴに飛び，自己の内面や死の問題にも及ぶのである。

むろん，Corde の意識というフィルターにかけられて抽出される数々の世界と問題の探求は，2人のブカレスト滞在中のみならず，シカゴに帰った後も，最後の舞台のパロマ天文台でも続けられる。本論では以下 Corde による東西都

市文明の糾弾，自己の人間としての内省と観照と苦悩について，具体的に研究を進めてゆきたい。

I

　ブカレストとシカゴの二都物語でもあるこの小説において，まず学生部長の目に映ったブカレストの町の印象は"terrible"[1]であり"heavy"(17)であり"dreary"(6)であった。共産圏のこの町の商店と農作物，陰気な行列を見てCordeは「灰色，褐色，黒色，泥の色，そして刑務所の庭での強制運動の雰囲気。」(brown, gray, black, mud colors, and an atmosphere of compulsory exercise in the prison yard.)（渋谷56；52）と形容している。強制労働，反体制者の精神病院送り，検閲，部屋には盗聴器が仕掛けられている。外国人との会話はすべて報告しなければならないし，アメリカ文化センターの読書室を訪れる勇気のある人は少なかった。テレビの画面に見えるのは独裁者だけで，彼が庶民を検閲し点検し統括していた。何千万人の人たちを封じ込めているのは共産主義の最大の業績の一つであり，検閲手段が伝達技術に匹敵対抗している状況は今日考えられないと Corde は考える。この国では何をするにしても鼻薬が必要だし，秘密警察の大佐は厚生大臣なんて屁とも思っていない。この町のホテルIntercontinental で，いとこの Dewey Spangler も Albert Corde に対し，ブカレストの印象を次のように述べている。

> "Yes, this must be a hell of a place seen from inside. You're *in* it. I'm just another VIP, passing through. But my impression riding around the city is that it's got to be a miserable damn comfortless life, and scary as well as boring...."(119)

　鉄のカーテンの背後では，歴史学・文学は"phony"(25)な学問だが，数学や自然科学は不滅であり賞揚されている。Dr. Valeriaの死，その葬儀に関連して，Corde は閉塞的な小部屋——Minna の娘時代の部屋で，今は Corde の隠れ家，彼の聖域，彼の独房——から外に出て，この専制主義体制支配下の生活の一端に触れる。そして，誰ひとり個人的権利を持っていないこの都市の現実を，

これでもかこれでもかと繰り返し見せ付けられる。

　Blanche Housman Gelfant はその著書 The American City Novel (1954) のなかで，都市小説を① "portrait" 型，② "synoptic" 型，③ "ecological" 型に分類している。[2] ① は一人の主人公の体験を通して都市を描いていくタイプで Theodore Dreiser の Sister Carrie (1900) をその代表として挙げている。②は主人公のいない小説で，都市そのものを一つの人間として描こうとし Dos Passos の Manhattan Transfer (1925) にその典型を見る。③は1つの狭い地域，例えば近隣とかあるいは街の一画などに焦点を置いて，その地域を詳細に描くもので，その実例として James T. Farrel の Studs Lonigan: A Trilogy (1935) が相当するとしている。[3] The Dean's December はこの3つのタイプのいずれにも属さない。西と東の退廃した都市を比較し，その現実を主人公 Corde の意識を通して回想し糾弾する新しい型の都市小説と言えよう。

　シカゴやアメリカ文明への批判は，Corde が Harper's に寄稿した記事に最も鮮明に表明されている。スラム，犯罪，刑務所，あの階級外の人間たち——ヤク中毒者，おいはぎ，売春婦たちが取り上げられる。彼らはコソ泥，強盗をやり，セックスをやらかせ，飲み，ヤクをやり，お互いに切り付け射ち合い，若くして死ぬ。彼は白昼の強姦，強盗，公の場所における性行為についても記述した。都市内部の黒人の子供たちを，鉛による中毒，あるいはヘロインなどの合成麻薬剤による中毒から救わなければならない。都市は，迷妄と捕らわれの一大センターなのであり，死でもある。半分破壊された都市の荒涼たる醜悪な背景のなかでの残された選択は「緩慢な死と突然の死，磨耗と急速な破壊，そのいずれかである」(. . . was between a slow death and a sudden one, between attrition and quick destruction, . . .) (渋谷198；193) と Corde はこの記事のなかで述べている。都市というものは抹消される可能性がある。死にかけている世代，黒人とプエルトリコ人，引っ越しの金もない老人たち。彼らは腐敗し，破壊し，死に，互いに排除し合っている。現代の達成，ジェット機，高層ビル，高度テクノロジーは，知性を枯渇させる大元凶であると学生部長は信じた。

　この国のムード，都市の内部，都市の腐敗，政治的問題。Corde が知っている町を描く目的は分析的であるよりは絵画的なものであった。Bellow がその

第Ⅷ章　東西都市文明批判とCordeの内省　*123*

作品のなかでしばしば指摘するように，アメリカの道徳的危機の最大の要件は，起こりつつあることを経験し，見なければならないものを見ることである。我々を驚かすのは，自分の内部に抱えているスラム，一人一人の内なる都市内部なのだ。シカゴというこの巨大な都市の恐るべきジャングルと戦慄について，ヤクについても銃についても，識者たちが言及もせず指摘もしないことにCordeは憤りを覚える。*Harper's* の記事を書いた真の目的は何だったのか，とCordeは自問する。

> Again, the *high* intention—to prevent the American idea from being pounded into dust altogether. And here is our American idea : liberty, equality, justice, democracy, abundance. And here is what things are like today in a city like Chicago. Have a look ! How does the public apprehend events? It doesn't apprehend them. It has been deprived of the capacity to experience them. (123)

現実を掘り起こすこと，ゴミ溜めからそれを掘り出し，これがあなた方のシカゴですよ，これがあなた方のアメリカの民主主義ですよ，と彼が見たままに描く権利をCordeは主張したのである。すなわち，西欧の崇高な考えを，そのアメリカ版の考えを擁護するために発言したのであり，シカゴやアメリカの現実を芸術が描出するであろうごとく描くことが *Harper's* の記事の意図であったと回顧するのである。

　それ故，道徳の第1の行為は「現実を掘り出すこと，現実を取り戻すこと，ゴミ溜めからそれを掘り起こし，それを芸術が描出するであろうように新しく描出すること」（to disinter the reality, retrieve reality, dig it out from the trash, represent it anew as art would represent it.）（渋谷129；123）なのである。Bellowは，そしてその分身でもあるCordeは，人文科学，芸術，なかんずく詩の重要性を強調する。*Harper's* の記事においても，おそらく詩だけが「"麻薬の魅力，テレビの磁力，性の興奮あるいは破壊のエクスタシーに拮抗できる"」（"to rival the attractions of narcotics, the magnetism of TV, the excitements of sex, or the ecstasies of destruction."）（渋谷192；187）力を持っていると書いたのであった。

　葬儀のためにシカゴからやって来た中年の女性科学者 Vlada Voynich との会

話のなかで，Corde は次のような意味のことを言う。ここブカレストでは，オリエント風，専制君主風の原始的基準がある。苦痛が生存の地盤，生存の現実の基礎として受け入れられている。政府が苦痛のレベルを設定し，また設定する力を持っている。民衆はこの独占を理解し，それを受け入れる用意ができていなければならない。西欧では違う。

> ". . . . America is never going to take an open position on the pain level, because it's a pleasure society, a pleasure society which likes to think of itself as a tenderness society. A tender liberal society has to find soft ways to institutionalize harshness and smooth it over compatibly with progress, buoyancy." (275)

Corde は続けて言う。それ故アメリカでは，非情な人，人殺しをする人が出てくれば，不遇な境遇のせいだ，鉛中毒にかかったからだ，後進部門の出身だからだとか，心理的治療を必要とする人だと説明する。ここブカレストでは，人民のうち，これこれの数の者は消される予定であるという立場は，ほとんど隠されることもないと。

Ⅱ

　この小説のなかで，主人公 Albert Corde を取り巻く多くの登場人物を，便宜上4つのグループに分類してみよう。Corde と敵対的というか相容れない関係にある人物として，病院監督官の Colonel，勤務する大学の教務部長兼事務局長 Alec Witt, Rickie Lester 殺人容疑者で黒人の Lucas Ebry, Lucas の友人で彼を弁護する側にいる Corde の甥 Mason Zaehner, Jr., Spofford Mitchell 殺人事件の公選弁護人 Sam Varennes などがいる。その対極にあって，Corde が共感を持てる人物群に，大学の同僚で地球物理学者・環境保護運動家の Sam Beech, Beech の研究グループの一員で有名な主任化学者 Vlada Voynich, 郡刑務所を改革しようとし囚人虐待のかどで起訴された元刑務所長の黒人 Rufus Ridpath, やはり黒人で元殺し屋・元ヘロイン中毒者で今は Operation Contact という救援センターを作っている Toby Winthrop, 殺された Rickie Lester の若い

第Ⅷ章　東西都市文明批判とCordeの内省　*125*

　白人の妻Lydia Lesterなどを挙げることができる。
　その中間に位置し *Humboldt's Gift* の「悪い仲間」[4]に近い存在として，共にCordeのいとこで幼友達でもあるDewey SpangerとMax Detilliionがいる。前者は有名なコラムニスト，後者は売名を好む悪徳弁護士。2人に対する愛憎併存感情の割合は異なるかもしれないが，Cordeはこの2人から裏切られ傷めつけ騙されても，心の底から彼らを憎むことができないのである。妻のMinna，義母のDr. Valeria，妹のElfrida，妹の夫のZaehner, Sr.やUncle Haroldなどに対する感情は，彼らが近い血縁関係にあるだけに別のカテゴリーに入れなければなるまい。ともあれ，この4つのグループの人物のCordeとのかかわりが，行動や会話が，この主人公の人物像と心のなかの動きや変化を，鮮明にクローズアップしてくれていることは申すまでもない。

Ⅲ

　東西の都市や文明に対するCordeの考えはこの小説の初めから終わりまで不変であるが，その墜落を糾弾する記事の性急な調子に対する自己反省は執拗に繰り返される。カッとなって冷静さと自制心を失い，怒りをナイーブにぶっつけた甘っちょろさを自嘲する。挑戦を神聖なcrusadeだとする生硬さを近視眼的であったと考えるようになる。明らかに，小説の初めと終わりのCordeには変化が見られる。
　Harper's の記事は，今回のトラブルの火種となったものだった。第1部では，郡立刑務所内の囚人たちの唖然たる状況が記されてあった。牢内ボスの支配，公然と行われる不正行為，殴打，鶏姦，刺殺。第2部では，主にRufus Ridpathスキャンダル，Spofford Mitchell裁判を扱っていて，市当局，ジャーナリズム，保安官，知事を立腹させる言辞が含まれていた。
　白人学生Rickie Lester死亡事件に対し，Cordeは学生部長として自分でも説明ができないほど積極的に対応した。殺人事件が横行し，それに対し何も対処されないことへの怒りがあった。Alec Wittを説いて，犯人に関する情報の報奨金を出させ，それで得た情報によりLucas Ebryを殺人容疑者として係争中

であった。Ebry の友人で Corde の甥にあたる Mason Zaehner, Jr. は，直ちに学生運動を組織し，学生新聞で大々的に学生部長に抗議した。急進派の学生たちの主張は「大学は黒人に対して密かな戦争を仕掛けており，学生部長は検察当局と共謀して大学の権力を使い黒人エブリを逮捕させた」(... the college waged a secret war against blacks and that the Dean was scheming with the prosecution, using the college's clout to nail the black man.)（渋谷35；30）というものだった。この事件の経緯は地元の新聞でも詳しく報道された。そんなある日，おせっかい屋で策謀家の Mason は何の前触れもなく学生部長室を訪れる。反体制派の代表として，バカでヘマで無知な Albert 伯父さんに，シカゴの社会的現実についてのレッスンを与えるつもりであった。高尚な感情や，人情味あふれた教訓や，信心や詩や「その他一切の愚にもつかぬ雑音は！」(and the rest of that jazz.)（渋谷46；41）を止めてくれと言いに来たのである。今は故人となったMasonの父親の見解によると，Cordeは「現実の世界を放棄して哲学と芸術に避難所を求めた」(... had given up the real world to take refuge with philosophy and art.)（渋谷47；42）人間なのであった。意志は強いが，周囲の人とは最小限の共通基盤しか持たず，紙面上以外ではめったに「"自分をさらけ出す"」("gave out")（渋谷47；42）ことをしないというのも，この義理の弟のCorde評である。その子のMasonは今Cordeの面前で反抗的態度をとっていた。それでもCordeは厳しく情熱的に公平になろう，考え直そうと必死の努力をした。「たぶん自分にも盲点があるだろう」(Maybe he [Corde] did have a blindspot.)（渋谷48；44）と思い直すのである。

　Dewey SpanglerもCordeの取った行動や記事に疑問を投げ掛け，批判の刃を向けた人物の一人であった。シカゴの歩道で共に遊び，Oscar WildやWalter Paterに共に夢中になった幼友達のSpanglerは，今や第2のWalter Lippmannとも言うべきシンジケート・コラムニストとなっている。超一流の国際世論形成者となり，彼の記事は現在30カ国で何百万もの人に敬意をもって読まれている。明敏なこの男にとって，Harper'sのあの2つの記事は不可解な自己破壊行為に思われた。ここかしこでCordeは名誉毀損すれすれのことを言い，怒りのため正気を失い，我と我が身を切りさいなんでいる，と思えるのであった。

ブカレストの Intercontinental のバーで久方ぶりに会った Spangler は，Corde に向かってなぜ君があの記事を書いたのか俺には分からない，君がシカゴに仕掛けた攻撃は一体何だったのかと尋ねる。君は一生涯のたまった怒りを一度に爆発させているのを意識していないのか？ Spangler はさらに畳み掛けて次のように言う。

> ". . . . In *Harper's* you crossed and offended just about everybody. You might have gotten away with it if you had adopted the good old Mencken *Boobus Americanus* approach. Humor would have made a difference. But you lambasted them all. . . . "(117)

自ら退行することを許している男。Albert は把握の力を失っていると，Spangler は考える。このような批判に対し，Corde も自分は自分の道徳的欲望に駆られ，人類の重荷を引き受けている，シカゴの連中が俺を憎むのは正しいかもしれない，俺はそれに値するすもしれない，と自省する。

Dr. Valeria の葬式の後，ブカレストのホテルであった 2 回目の会見でも Spangler は言う。君のあの記事を読んで，シカゴについて開眼することにはならなかったかもしれないが，君の正体は見た。君はものすごく変なことを書いた，と繰り返す。君の記事で我慢がならなかったのは，取り上げた材料ではなくて「いつわりの叙述あるいは非存在の瓦礫の下に埋められている世界を取り戻す」("To recover the world that is buried under the debris of false description or nonexperience.")（渋谷250 ; 243）ための事実の述べ方であり態度だと言うのである。Spangler は，Corde が絶望のドン底とか終末論をぶったと言って非難した。詩を持ち出したことにも罪があると言う。Spangler は「二都物語」("A Tale of Two Cities")（渋谷306 ; 298）と題するコラム記事のなかで，2 回目の会見を材料にして Corde を徹底的に攻撃する。学生部長は情緒的・神秘的な観察者で冥想的な人物である。学生部長の才能は最初から観察にあり，一般論や総合には向いていない。Corde は，仲間の市民にはほとんどアメリカ人と認められぬ奇異なアメリカ人である。そしてジャーナリズム・マスメディアや大学人に対する Corde の厳しい態度を論難する。この記事のため Corde は大学を辞

任することになるのだが，自分との友情を裏切った Spangler を本気で憎んではいない。Corde は言う。

"He [Dewey Spangler] was so delirious that he couldn't think what it might do to his pal. Maybe it was the cuts in his intestines that put him in such a state." (308)

Mason Zaehner の母であり Corde の妹でもある Elfrida もまた，Corde に対していささか批判的である。Albert は中庸であるとはどういうことであるかを知らないで，何でも誇張する。彼にはノーマルなところがなく，ヘマをやらかすにも，彼一流の最もオリジナルな不可解なやり方でやる。彼女は彼を非常に変わった人間だと思っているのである。インテリの読書家でハイブラウの教授・学生部長の兄貴よりも，低趣味のシカゴの男，彼女自身の父のような男が好きなのである。2人の父は大金持のホテル経営者であり，ユグノートとアイルランド人の血統である。5) 彼と娘婿の Mason Zaehner, Sr. は大体同じタイプの人間で，考え方も似ていた。

To Zaehner, Chicago had been the greatest city in the world, no place like it. And Corde's father had agreed with Zaehner, no place like Chicago—big, vital, new, the best! Old Corde . . . would have been bitterly annoyed with a son who knocked Chicago. Of course Elfrida *couldn't* approve. (98)

ラサール街で40年にわたって弁護士を務め，ループ・ジャングルでの生存競争を生き抜いてきた Zaehner には，シカゴで讃嘆されているあらゆる形の男性的強さが充電されていた。入院中の友人の見舞いに売春婦を派遣するタイプの男，タフで大柄で，押しが強く頭が切れ，シニカルで政治的で，金持ちで，そうでない人間を軽蔑した。彼にとって Corde は，「落後者，紳士気取りの俗物」(a cop-out, a snob)（渋谷89；84）であった。

共和党の政治屋だった Uncle Harold も同じタイプの人間だった。彼にとって Corde は「"耽美主義のチンピラ小僧"」("an aesthetic little sonofabitch")（渋谷248；241）だった。Corde の父も，Uncle Harold も，義弟の Zaehner も，そして妹の Elfrida も，彼女と結婚する判事の Stan Sorokin も，その弟の Ellis

第Ⅷ章　東西都市文明批判とCordeの内省　129

　Sorokin 夫妻[6]も，Johnson 大統領も皆，Corde から見みれば俗悪なアメリカ精神の代表者である。この都市，この国特有の生活をエンジョイしているこのような人たち，なかんずく Mason Zaehner, Sr. に代表される俗悪なアメリカ人のエトスに対する怒り，それも Corde をして一連の記事を書かせた大きな要因の一つである。彼はシカゴというこの都市の状況について，この都市を讃美し安住する俗悪なアメリカ人について，彼自身の経験を頼りにし，新鮮な観察を行い，自分自身の感情に照らし，自分自身の言語を用いて，思うことを言おうと考えたのだった。ただし Corde は，醜悪な現実を直視することの重要性，彼自身の感覚を信じ，現実をして自分自身の魂を通過させることを主張しているのであって，何ら社会的不正改革の具体的な方策や手段を提示している訳ではない。[7] それは小説家としての Bellow の意図するところではないのであろう。むしろ，この文明の腐敗は「"最後の日々"」(the 'last days') (渋谷286；278) の大破壊によってのみ解放されるのだという絶望的見解が仄見えるのである。
　Corde もまた，時に激しく怒り，また時には反省して傷つく弱き人間である。彼は記事を発表したことによって，この国の読者の感情のサンプルを知ったのであった。周辺の友人や親戚の者たちからの非難も受け，学生部長の服を着た馬鹿・変わり者であったと思い返し懊悩する。Corde は義弟 Mason Senior の意見にも半ばぐらいは同意する。既に述べてきたように，Spangler や Mason Junior の批判にさえ一度は振り返って自己反省をする善良さと柔軟性を持っている。妻の Minna からさえ「あなたはわたしが思っていたよりずっと情緒的な，おかしな人だったのね」("You turned out to be a much more emotional and strange person than I ever expected.") (渋谷266；259) と言われ，それを受け入れている。体制のなかに埋没した東の権力者や，退廃したアメリカ文明のなかに所属するアメリカ人たちには，苦悩もなく自己を振り返ってみる余裕もない。詩を愛し人文科学を尊重する，人間らしき人間 Corde にはそれがある。そしてそのことが大変重要なんだと，Bellow は言っているように思われる。

IV

　母の死に直面して衝撃を受け健康を害した妻の Minna を伴って，Corde は急遽シカゴに帰り，Minna の退院後2人はロスアンゼルス郊外の Paloma 天文台に赴く。広漠として凍てつく空間のなかで大宇宙の星を見つめながら，仕事に熱中する天文学者の Minna。これまでギクシャクとしていた夫婦間の感情も修復される。「独房・火葬場・天文台」[8] という移動のプロセスのなかで，Dr. Valeria の死が想起され，火葬場の下降運動と天文台の上昇運動が2重写しにされる。監獄都市ブカレストを脱出し，場所の概念を持たない住民が右往左往する犯罪都市シカゴを経て，広大な原風景のなかの宇宙空間に直面して，Corde はそこはかとなき自由と解放を感じる。病院・火葬場という死の暗うつさから離脱して，天文台の上の天空は生の喜びと躍動を与えた。

　　　Here the living heavens looked as if they would take you in. (311)

Corde の再生であり，安息への回帰である。天文台での経験の後この主人公は，俗悪なる人物群によって論難され脅威にさらされていた人生の意義と人間性を求め，将来にわたって道徳的探求を継続してゆくことであろう。

　なるほど Ellen Pifer も指摘しているように笑いもほとんど存在しない陰うつな小説であり，[9] Matthew C. Roudané も消極的に肯定しているように十分に描き切れていない登場人物と共にタドタドしく進展する小説という見方も，[10] いくぶん当たっているところがあるかもしれない。しかしながら Bellow は The Dean's December のなかで，現代アメリカ知識人の心に絶えず去来し揺曳している問題，すなわち眼前に展開する都市の恐るべきジャングルとそのなかに安住する俗悪なる人物を糾弾し，さらに東西両文明の憂うべき将来を一人一人が真っすぐに凝視することを訴え，また同時に，作者の分身とも言うべき Albert Corde の人間としての内省と観照と苦悩を生き生きと提示してくれたのであった。読者に訴えるその迫力は，指摘されている多少の欠陥をはるかに凌駕するものである。精神を集注して精読し何度も読み返さなければ，作品の方が読者をはねのけ寄せ付けない難解さも，またこの小説の魅力であろう。

第Ⅷ章　東西都市文明批判とCordeの内省　　*131*

≪Notes≫

1) Saul Bellow, *The Dean's December* (New York: Harper & Row, 1982) 19. 以下この作品からの引用はすべてこの版により，引用英文末尾の括弧内に頁数を記す。和文と英文を併記する場合は（渋谷56；52）と記す。和文はソール・ベロー，渋谷雄三郎訳『学生部長の十二月』（東京：早川書房，1983）による。
2) Blanche Housman Gelfant, *The American City Novel* (Norman, Okla. : University of Oklahoma Press, 1954) 11.
3) Gelfant 11-15.
4) 112頁を参照。
5) 自己嫌悪に陥りながら，生きるために戦い続け，人生の意味を見いだそうとするBellowの典型的主人公でありながら，Cordeがユダヤ人でないことは特筆されなければならない。
6) Ellis Sorokin夫妻主催のパーティは，兄の新婚夫婦のためのものではなく，飼い犬の誕生日だった。祝電もきており，陸軍元帥の本物の記章が付いた首輪もあった。デカダンス，ほとんど崩壊した文明とCordeは思う。
7) Matthew C. Roudané, "*Cri de Coeur*: The Inner Reality of Saul Bellow's *The Dean's December*," in *Saul Bellow in the 1980s: A Collection of Critical Essays*, eds. Gloria L. Cronin and L.H. Goldman (East Lansing, Mich.: Michigan State University Press, 1989) 257.
8) 渡辺克昭「独房・火葬場・天文台」藤井治彦編『空間と英文学』（東京：英宝社，1987）246-270.
9) Ellen Pifer, *Against the Grain* (Philadelphia: University of Pennsylvania Press, 1990) 164.
10) Roudané 245.

第IX章
結 論

I. Cahan, Singer のユダヤ人とユダヤ性

前述したように，Abraham Cahan（1860-1951）が最高傑作 *The Rise of David Levinsky* を出版する契機となったのは，雑誌 *McClure's* からの原稿依頼であった。その*McClure's* の副編集者Burton J. Hendrickは，Cahan の物語が連載される前に，Hendrick 自身の記事 "The Jewish Invasion of America" を掲載している。Cahan の物語は，ユダヤ人がなぜ他の移民集団に先駆けて成功したのか，ユダヤ人の頭の良さ（ずる賢さ）の例証であると Hendrick は結んでいる。にんまりとほくそ笑んだ，鉤鼻の好色そうなユダヤ人の挿絵が，Cahan のストーリーの一部に付けられたことからも，当時のジャーナリズムや編集者のユダヤ人に対する考え方を窺い知ることができよう。[1]

Dreyfus[2] がようやく釈放された20世紀の初頭に，換言すれば反ユダヤ主義がアメリカにおいても現在と比べてより強く残っていた時代に，Cahan は直接 *McClure's* に抗議もせず，素知らぬ顔で，ユダヤ系移民の内的生活を生き生きと描き続けた。社会主義の洗礼も受けていた Cahan は，自分の一生を回顧する一人称形式で，52歳で200万ドルを所有する衣料産業界の雄となった Levinsky を主人公とし，移民の生活に本質的に内在する心理的・文化的衝突を an immigrant novel として描いたのである。自己満足と後悔を併持しながら

Cahanは，Levinsky に物質的な成功よりも精神的な満足を重んじさせたのであった。

トルストイ，チェーホフ，ヘンリー・ジェームズ，ウィリアム・ディーン・ハゥエルズを尊敬し，その作品を愛読した Cahan が，ヨーロッパ的情感，ユダヤ人の生活，アメリカという土壌の3者を豊かに均衡させた，[3] ユダヤ系アメリカ文学の祖であるのは，なるほどと首肯できるのである。

The Rise of David Levinsky など文学作品の著者であるばかりでなく，彼のもう一つの存在価値は，ユダヤ系移民の教育者，労働運動の指導者，当代アメリカ文明の紹介者，啓蒙家であったことにある。Cahan が評価されるようになったのは1960年代後半で，Donald Sanders, The Downtown Jews: Portraits of an Immigrant Generation (1969) が上梓されたころと大体一致する。Cahanはまた，Sholem AschやIsrael Joshua SingerやIsaac Bashevis Singerを世に出した人物であることと共に付記しておきたい。

ユダヤ系アメリカ文学が黄金時代に入る Malamud や Bellow や P. Roth が活躍する時期の以前に，Abraham Cahan の後を受けて史上に残るユダヤ系作家について，ここで若干触れておきたい。Mary Antin (1881-1949) には，約束された国アメリカ，女性を尊重する国アメリカへの賛歌がある。Allen Guttman は The Jweish Writer in America のなかで「幸運なるわずかな人たちの台頭」(The Rise of a Lucky Few: Mary Antin and Abraham Cahan) という項目の下で，Antin と Cahan の2人を併せ論じている。[4] Anzia Yezierska (1885-1970) はユダヤ系移民の『飢えた心』(Hungry Hearts)[5] について書いたが，Samuel Ornitz (1890-1957)やMichael Gold (1893-1967) には，ユダヤ人内部批判，第2世代の軽薄なアメリカでの生き方が示唆され，ユダヤ性に対する反抗的態度が表れる。Philip Roth 出現の前兆とでも言うべきであろうが，アメリカ社会のユダヤ人差別に対する抗議小説 (protest novel) の要素は，黒人作家 Richard Wright (1908-1960) の Native Son (1940) などの厳しさとは比べくもなく薄い。

Isaac Bashevis Singer (1904-91) の作品は，父 Pinchos-Mendel の敬虔な宗教性と兄 Israel Joshua の世俗的合理主義の弁証法的止揚のなかで創造された。彼は神を信じると同時に神に対して疑念を抱いていた。1935年31歳のとき渡米し

た Singer は,結局アメリカに完全に同化することはできなかった。同化できないで迷い途方に暮れた彼の作品の登場人物は,神の善良さに疑念を抱きながら,ものに取り憑かれたように魔女のような女性の愛を求めて止まない。信仰への探求と喪失感や人間嫌い,そして禁じられた愛への激しい情熱,破滅・冷酷さ・激しい憎悪のテーマへの関心,この3者の融合が Singer 作品の主要なテーマである。彼がアメリカでいつまでも「グリーンホーン」("greenhorn")だと感じている敗北感が,作品の題材をユダヤの民間伝承,ユダヤ人の宗教的過去,ユダヤ人の歴史,彼の心の故郷に求めさせた。登場人物はユダヤ人,場所の多くはポーランド特にワルシャワの shtetl,時代は過去,なかには17世紀までさかのぼる作品さえあった。1970年代になって,アメリカを舞台にする物語もだんだんと増えてきた。それは,ニューヨークのマンハッタンやマイアミ・ビーチを歩きながら,寂しく東欧のshtetlの想い出に耽り,同化に苦悩する彼の半自叙伝的な男性主人公の登場であった。Singer にとって,文学とはリアリズムであり,リアリズムは叙述してそれだけで分かる語り口を必要とする。現代世界のリアリスティックな舞台装置ではそれが自由になし得なかったことも,彼が歴史的年代記や民間伝承の物語や超自然的なものに題材を求めた大きな理由であった。[6]

　Leslie Fiedler は "Isaac Bashevis Singer; or, The Americanness of the American Jewish Writer" という論文のなかで,彼は an American Jewish writer であっても,Bellow や Malamud や Roth のような a Jewish American writer ではないと述べている。彼の描くアメリカは現実のアメリカではなく,半ば神話的なニューヨークであり,登場人物も Yiddish の世界の彼の夢が白昼夢化したものに過ぎない存在だとする。これは Singer が,Cahan や Yezierska のようにユダヤ系移民の最盛期に渡米した一世とも遅れてアメリカを訪れ,移民でも避難民でもなく,同化の意志も実現も前2者よりも劣り,逆説的だがむしろ外観は Cahan などよりも二世か三世のユダヤ系アメリカ人作家に近いとさえ言っている。[7] しかしながら彼は,engagé(政治や社会の動きに参加している文学者)という視点からは,本書で論究した他の4人の作家の誰よりも超然とした存在であった。Talmud の教えだけが人間を教化し,道徳的規範を従順に守らせると信じてい

る点と併せ, 5人の作家群のなかで最もユダヤ的痕跡を留めている作家と言えるであろう。矛盾した言い方にみえるかもしれないが, Cahan は移民として同化に努力した時代に生き, Malamud, Bellow, Roth は（それぞれユダヤ性に対し異なった対応を示すのだが）同化の進んだ世代として執筆活動に従事した。しかし Singer は, アメリカの政治や社会に超然としていたが故に, 両極端に位置して外観的には二・三世作家に似ていても, 最も強くユダヤ的伝統を保持していたのではないか, という意味である。

II. Malamud, Bellow, Roth のユダヤ人とユダヤ性

　第I章でも述べたように, いわゆるアメリカのユダヤ系作家と呼ばれる人たちが, 常にその作品のなかでユダヤ人を主人公とし, ユダヤ人の問題を取り上げている訳では決してない。ユダヤ人の生活を investigate することに全く関心を示さない作家もあれば, 作品によって関心が異なる作家もある。
　アメリカ生まれの二世・三世の作家群のなかでは Bernard Malamud (1914-1986), Saul Bellow (1915-　), Philip Roth (1933-　) の3人が, 登場人物や題材や背景において最もユダヤ的な作家と言えよう。彼らは overtly であれ covertly であれ, いくつかの本質的にユダヤ的な性格が付随している作家であり, ユダヤ人を取り扱うとき, 作家としての最善の素質と深みが発揮される人たちである。Irving Malin も指摘しているように, Roth は Letting Go においてよりも "Eli, the Fanatic" において, より優れた芸術を生み出し, Bellowは The Adventures of Augie March よりも Seize the Day や The Victim において, Malamud は The Nature よりも The Assistant において, それぞれ, より強く読者に訴える作品を創り上げているのである。[1]
　本節では, このような作品に描かれているユダヤ人像とユダヤ性を浮き彫りにして, 3人の作家の同質性と異質性を明らかにしてみたい。

　Malamud, Roth, Bellow は, それぞれ異なるユダヤ人のタイプを創造した。しかし, 彼らの間には, いくつかの共通した絆も存在している。彼らは一様に,

どうしようもない schlemiels か schlimazels かであり，あるいはこの両者の性格を併せ持っている場合もある。Self-made men というよりは foolish inncoents であり，強く逞しく行動的であるというよりは，弱く受動的な人間である。彼らが等しく賞揚するのは「弱さ」と「敗北」と「徳性」である。初期のユダヤ系アメリカ人によって書かれた小説のなかの一部にあった，ヒステリックな反ユダヤ主義に対する抗議は影を潜めているが，彼らは依然として，罪悪感と恐怖に取り憑かれている。疑い深く，神経質で，感受性が強く，傷つきやすくて自己防御的であり，疎外感に悩んでいる。Ambivalent で優柔不断で，決然とした態度を取ることができない。犠牲者となる可能性をはらんだ性格を備え，現代アメリカ人の生活は，本質的に犠牲者のそれであるという共通の認識を持っている。各々の量と質に程度の差はあるが，感傷主義，苦悩の経験，歴史と神話の諸要素の融合がある。

　これら3人の作家の小説の世界は，金儲けに専念する人物の世界ではなく，人生に付き物の努力と犠牲と苦悩を通して真のアイデンティティを探求する人物の世界である。そして彼らは皆，ユダヤ系アメリカ人の生活のなかで，だんだんと消滅していこうとしているユダヤ性の意味にスポットライトを当てようと努力している。そしてまた，このユダヤ系アメリカ人の生活におけるユダヤ性の意義を認識しようとする努力の過程のなかで，人間の生きるべき最善の方法を探求しようとしているのである。

　Malamud の描くユダヤ人には，まがうことなきユダヤ臭が芬々としている。しがない倒産寸前の食料品店主である *The Assistant* の Morris Bober, その妻の Ida と娘の Helen, "The Magic Barrel" の Yeshivah 大学律法博士養成コースの学生 Leo Finkle と結婚ブローカーの Pinye Salzman, "The First Seven Years" の靴屋の Feld とその娘 Miriam それに靴屋の助手の Sobel, "The Loan" の貧しいパン屋 Lieb その妻 Bessie と亡妻の墓を建てるための借金を依頼に来た Kobotsky など，皆あたかも東欧の shtetl からタイムトンネルを通って，アメリカという舞台に突然姿を現したかのごとき感を与える。大抵ニューヨーク市に住み，貧しく，しみったれていて，重々しく，陰うつな，同化していない一世か二世の

ユダヤ人である。[2] 馬鹿に近いお人好しで,しばしば人に騙され,教育と結婚に夢を懸けるが,往々にして成功の夢は無残にも打ち砕かれる。彼らの一生は不運な事件の連続であるが,それでも正直一途の生涯を送り,苦悩はユダヤ人の宿命と諦めている。

　Malamud の小説が,人間として成長と昇華を描く苦難に満ちた過程であるなら,Philip Roth は現代アメリカの半ば同化したユダヤ人のアイデンティティ・クライシスについて書いている。Malamud の小説の世界が,苦悩するユダヤ人の息の詰まるような貧窮に色付けられているならば,Roth の世界には Yiddish 文学の臭いから解放されて,ほとんど同化したユダヤ人の物質的な豊かさから醸し出される明るい雰囲気がある。

　Roth の作品には,伝統的なユダヤ的価値,ユダヤ的遺産,アメリカの Jewish community に挑戦する若者が登場する。"The Conversion of the Jews" の13歳の Ozzie Freedman は Rabbi Binder に Judaism について質問をし,自己中心的で非論理的な Jewish community の堕落を攻撃する。Yeshivah school of Orthodox Jews を追放するよう町の人から依頼された "Eli, the Fanatic" の弁護士 Eli Peck,軍隊生活のなかで,部下のユダヤ人兵士から,同じユダヤ人であるという理由でさまざまな利己的要求を受ける "Defender of the Faith" の Marx 軍曹,金持ちの娘 Brenda Patimkin とひと夏のロマンスを楽しむ "Goodbye, Colombus" の図書館員 Neil Klugman, *Portnoy's Complaint* の中でニューヨーク市人権擁護副委員長に指名された切れ者の未婚弁護士 Alexander Portnoy,これらの主人公は皆,アメリカ人であることとユダヤ人であることとの中間にあってアイデンティティの危機に苦しんでいる。Philip Roth は,普通の状況下の極端な行動を通して,ユダヤ人のアイデンティティの問題と真剣に取り組んでいる。Roth の主人公は,アメリカの現代社会がいかに狂っており,その狂える社会がその構成要員にどんな影響を与えているかを描こうとしている。

　典型的な Bellow の主人公は,*Dangling Man* の入隊前の Joseph, *The Victim* の業界誌編集者で不当な言い掛かりに悩む Asa Leventhal, *Seize the Day* の妻にも父にも職にも金にも運にも見捨てられた男 Tommy Wilhelm, *Romanticism and Christianity* の著者で誰彼となく果てしなく投函しない手紙を書きまくる *Herzog*

の同名の大学教授, *Humboldt Gift* の60歳近くのユダヤ系劇作家・伝記作家 Charles Citrine, *More Die of Heartbreak* の（世界的な植物学者でありながら）女性にはめっぽう不器用な50代半ばの Benn Crader などで, のらくら男で怠け者の要素と, ノイローゼ的要素と, 哲学者的要素とを併持している。衝動的で子供っぽいところがあり, 陰うつで高踏的で, いつも物思いや哲学的な思弁に耽っている。Innocent で非現実的であることを自覚し, マゾヒスティックな自己嫌悪に陥りながら, 生きるために死に物狂いで戦い続け, 人生の意味を見いだそうと努力しているのが, Bellow のユダヤ人である。

　Malamud の典型的ヒーローは, 苦悩するユダヤ人の苦しい諦観や息の詰まりそうな窮乏の世界に住んでいる。Roth の登場人物は, 熱病的な自己批判に取り憑かれている。Bellow の主人公はノイローゼになったように, 人生の意味の心理学的探索に専念する。もしも Roth の登場人物が enfant terrible のユダヤ版で, 自信に満ちた都会的複雑さを持ち併せているなら, Malamud のそれは孤立した寄る辺のない敗北者であり, Bellow のそれは感傷的な宙ぶらりんの男である。Roth と Bellow のユダヤ人は, 取り憑かれたような自己告白者であることに喜びを感じ, 程度の差はあれいくぶん狂気の気味を帯びている。Malamud のそれは, 決して不平を言わない secular tzaddik[3] であることに満足している。Bellow は, 謎の笑いを浮かべた感受性の強いハイブラウのユダヤ人について書いているように思われる。Malamud が, 時代も場所も定かでない Lower East Side 的ユダヤ人のユダヤ性を取り扱う点にその特色を発揮すれば, Roth は主として, 中産階級に属する現代アメリカ人についての satirical comedy を描く。文体について言えば, Malamud のは簡潔で抑制されたところがあり, Roth のは, ウィットに富み諷刺的で, 明敏なピリッとした鋭さがあり現代的である。それに反して Bellow の文体は, 冗長で華麗であり, 哲学的でさえある。

　Malamudのmoral code は善良なユダヤ人でなければ善良な人間ではないということであり, 良いユダヤ人であることと良い人間であることは同じことを意味する。Malamud にとっては「人間はすべてユダヤ人である」("All men are Jews.")。[4] 彼の描くほとんどすべての小説の環境はユダヤ人社会であり, また

苦悩はユダヤ人であることの宿命であり，あかしでもあると言っているのだが，それはユダヤ人ばかりでなく普遍的に人間全体に通用するものだと比喩的に言っているのである。無条件にアメリカのユダヤ人の社会に埋没し，ユダヤ系アメリカ人の本質と現状に疑問を投げ掛けることが少ない Malamud のユダヤ性探求は，その意味では marginal なのかもしれない。Malamud が創り上げる典型的ユダヤ人は，人生において苦しみ耐えるが，しかし希望は失わないでいる。Malamud の小説の特色は，古風で流行遅れの，ばかばかしい程度を越した善良さにある。

　苦悩に対して Roth の抱いている考えは，それを受け入れることがユダヤ人の伝統だということである。Roth の小説のなかに出てくるほとんど同化したユダヤ人の苦悩は，現代の豊かな社会やその愚かな皮相性，安易な無味乾燥さに対する拒絶にその根源がある。彼らは，物質的な豊かさのなかに表面的な満足を見いだすことはできるが，精神的な安息を得ることはできない。Rothの主人公が，ユダヤ人の生活を拒絶するのは，それがあまりにユダヤ的であるからではなく，堕落し腐敗して本当の意味でユダヤ的でないからである。Rothの主要な関心は，世俗化の度合いの異なった段階にあるユダヤ人の間の対立関係を通して見た，アイデンティティの探求と同化の問題の複雑さである。Rothの特質は，normalcy や absurdity や苦悩の探求に安易に背を向けることに対する過酷なばかりの皮肉にある。

　Malamud のヒーローは，ユダヤ人であることを誇りとしている。Malamud は，現代アメリカでの伝統的ユダヤ人の価値を重んじ，またそれに対して忠実な登場人物——例えば，*The Assistant* の Morris Bober やその娘のHelenとそれにイタリア系で最後にユダヤ教に改宗する Frank Alpine，財はなくとも魂を持つユダヤ人Sobelと結婚する "The First Seven Years" の Miriam，ユダヤ人としての過去の苦難を重んじユダヤ人としか結婚しないとする "The Lady of the Lake" の Isabella del Dongo など——に共感し，惜しみない愛情を注ぎ，拍手と賛辞を呈しているようだ。

　Philip Roth の登場人物は，一見したところ，ユダヤ人であることをひどく嫌っているように思われる。事実 Roth は，小説のなかであまりにユダヤ人社会

を非難攻撃するとして，伝統的価値を保持しようとするユダヤ人グループから，厳しく批判されてきた。しかし彼は，本質的には決して徹底した同化論者ではない。ユダヤ的なものに対する嫌悪の叫びのようにみえるものの背後に隠されて，伝統的ユダヤ的諸価値に対するノスタルジックな愛情が潜在している。彼が拒絶しているのは Judaism ではなく，アメリカのユダヤ人，それも現代アメリカ人の諸特性を体現している者としてのユダヤ人の不安やディレンマや堕落腐敗である。Malamud も Roth も，厳しいモラリストであるが，そのタイプは異なっている。Roth の批判は，物質的豊かさにもかかわらず精神的には不安定な状態にあり，祈りは覚えているが，神についてすべて忘れてしまったユダヤ人に向けられている。特に初期の短編小説において，人間と神との問題に固執しているようだ。Ozzie Freedman, Eli Peck あるいは Nathan Marx のような信仰の殉教者的擁護者は，最後には，各々異なった種類の改宗を経て，伝統的 Judaism の精神に返ってゆく。

　作家が年令を重ねるにつれて，全部がそうとは限らないが，後期作品の作中人物は年寄りとなる傾向が強く，自分の人間としての人生・過去を振り返り，病気や死の問題を考究し，人間的には頑固・迷妄となる例が多い。Malamud 作 *Dubin's Lives* (1979) の主人公で伝記作家の William Dubin も 60 代に近付き，自分の娘ぐらい若い Fanny Bick と逢瀬を重ね，妻の Kitty を裏切る。D. H. Lawrence の伝記を書くためには passion の実践が必要だという理由付けであるが，失われた青春への悔恨と願望が仄見える。Bellow の *Mr. Sammler's Planet* の主人公 Mr. Sammler もナチによる大虐殺を奇跡的に逃れてニューヨークに住み現在 70 歳を超え，Bellow の後期の作品にしばしば描かれるように，アメリカの大都市の退廃・狂気性・phoney liberalism にひんしゅくするばかりでなく，近親者の狂気の沙汰に近い行動も理解できない。ただし，体力の不足をかこち，過去の人間になったと痛感する Mr. Sammler が延々と説教を続けるだけで，プラスのイメージが乏し過ぎること，換言すれば，Mr. Sammler の schlemiel 性の欠如がこの作品の欠点であるという田畑千秋氏の意見には同感できる。[5] 次に，Bellow のもう一つの後期の作品 *The Bellarosa Connection* (1989) について若干

触れておきたい。この中編小説では，多少悪辣な手段も使って今やアメリカ・ショービジネス界の大立物として成功した Billy Rose が，マフィアの手を借りて Harry Fonstein をナチの手から救出する。Newwark 出身のユダヤ人女性 Sorella と結婚した Harry は，暖房機具改良特許を取り富を得，一度 Billy に直接会って感謝の気持ちを伝えたいと思うのだが，Billy は頑として応じない。Billy の目的は，寛大な心根からのユダヤ人救済というよりはむしろ，個人としての弱み（体も小さく，ハンサムでもなく，性的にも弱く女性に屈辱を味わってきた）を隠すために，名声を求めて，エルサレムに巨額を投じて彫刻庭園を築き，結婚相手も WASP の女性を選ぶ。この物語の無名の語り手（記憶力の天才）によって記述されるテーマは，Bellow の一貫した主題，アメリカに渡ってきたユダヤ人のアイデンティティの問題，アメリカ化したユダヤ人の堕落，アメリカの夢，記憶の問題などである。批評家のなかには *The Dean's December* や *More Die of Heartbreak* は，Bellow の老化による質の低下を感じさせる作品だと言う人もいる。しかしながら，*The Bellarosa Connection* は "a classic Bellow story"[6] と David Denby も賞揚しているように，決して駄作ではない。Bellow の後期の作品のなかには第Ⅶ章や第Ⅷ章で詳述したように，アメリカ文明の崩壊と道徳的危機，都市の腐敗が執拗に追究される。[7] 死や霊魂不滅の問題，現代社会の虚無に耐えるための瞑想の世界・超自然的存在との交流も描かれる。*Mr. Sammler's Planet* は Bellow が55歳，*Humboldt's Gift* は60歳，*The Dean's December* は66歳，*More Die of Heartbreak* は72歳，The Bellarosa Connection は実に74歳ごろに書かれた作品である。

　Philip Roth は多才であり多作である。1959年の処女作以来1998年の *I Married a Communist* までの約40年間，2年か1年あるいは少なくとも3年の間隔を置いて24冊の作品を上梓している。それだけに，後期には1作ごとに新しい作風を心掛け，時には読者の意表をついた小説を公表する。その一例として *Zuckerman Bound*(1985) を紹介しよう。この作品は，既に出版された3つの小説 *The Ghost Writer*(1979)，*Zuckerman Unbound*(1981)，*The Anatomy Lesson* (1983) から構成され，それに *Epilogue: The Prague Orgy*(1985) を付け加え，784頁の大冊として刊行された。自伝的色彩の濃いビルドゥングスロマンであ

って，主人公 Nathan Zuckerman はおそらく Philip Roth 自分自身をモデルとしたものであろう。第1作は，無名時代の Nathan がユダヤ系作家 E. I. Lenoff (Malamud かあるいは I. B. Singer かと思われる) を訪れ，師としてまた精神的な父としての助力を求めるシーンで始まる。ユダヤ人社会を批判した Nathan の小説 "Higher Educaion" は，彼の父の激怒を誘う。父は言う，「ネイサン，非ユダヤ人からみれば，おまえの小説はたったひとつのことしか言っていないんだ。たったひとつだ。聞くんだ，そしたら行ってもいい。あれはユダ公の話だ。我利我利亡者のユダ公の話だ。われらがキリスト教徒の友人たちはまちがいなくそういう風に読む。」(Nathan, your story, as far as Gentiles are concerned, is about one thing and one thing only. Listen to me, before you go. It is about kikes. Kikes and their love of money.)[8] と。第2作では，Carnovsky で有名になった Nathan に見知らぬ男 Alvine Pepler がストーカーのように付きまとい，母の安全も脅迫されるが，亡くなったのは父であった。葬儀の後，弟の Henry は，父を殺したのは「兄さん『解放をもたらす』小説のせいなんだぞ！」(You and your 'liberating' book!)[9] と論難する。第3作では，Nathan は病気になった。首と両腕と両肩が痛み，鎖骨は湾曲していた。肉体の不自由，知性の停滞，精神の憂うつ，本が書けないことからくる職業の不振，Carnovsky への酷評などが，作家の仕事を止める決心をさせ，医者になるため医学校への入学を試みる。孤独をいやすために付き合っている女たちからも相手にされなくなる。シカゴの病院で友人の医者に，医者となる希望を拒否され，患者として昼間は廊下を散歩し，夜はインターンと病棟を同行して，ユダヤ人としての宿命から自分自身を解放し，死の恐怖からも脱れようとするのである。ユダヤの伝統や規範から自由になりたいと思いながら，結局その束縛から逃れられないで，ユダヤ人の世界を素材としなければ小説も書けない Roth の苦悩。Philip Roth のよく取り扱うテーマを新しい形式で提示したものと言えよう。

　その後も Roth は精力的に書き続け，自伝的事実をストレートに語る *The Facts: A Novelist's Autobiography* (1988) や，虚構と現実の交錯を描いた *Patrimony: A True Story* (1991)，現実と虚構のぬきさしならぬ関係を描いた *Operation Shylock: A Confession* (1993) などばかりでなく，その他にも最近の3

作を出版しているが，これらの作品についての論評は他日を期したい。とにかく，（文学批評理論の動向はあまり気に留めなかったが）新しい小説形態の模索，性の問題のあくなき探究と固執，それが Roth の大きな特質と言えよう。

　後期の作品についてごく簡略に述べたが，3人の作家の社会的関心について話を戻すことにしよう。Roth も Bellow も，社会における自己との戦いを描くことに熱意を燃やしている。Roth と Bellow が異なるのは，Roth の方により社会的な関心があり，ユダヤ人社会の諸問題に confornt する意志を持っている点である。Bellow は，その小説のなかで，ユダヤ人ばかりでなくすべての人間が現代社会では不安定な状態にあり，社会の重圧のもとに苦しんで生き，制度や組織によって走らされねばならぬことを明らかにしようとする。現代社会の狂気性を批判するが，人間は未知の力に完全に屈従することなく威厳を持って生きていかねばならぬと主張する。苦悩を変えて人生の肯定に誘導し，絶望や挫折感に屈せず期待と野望を持って生きるよう説く。Bellow の顕著な特質は，自己発見への知的でしかも道徳的な探求にある。人間に対する悲哀を含んだ愛情と，一歩離れて客観的に人間を見る哲学的思弁もまたその特色と言えよう。

　Bellow の典型的ヒーローは，苦しみ悩む人間であり，感情をあらわに表現する古いユダヤ人のタイプである。登場人物のユダヤ性は，彼の小説の要素のなかで非常に重要なものであるが，しかし，彼の登場人物がユダヤ人としての役割と歴史を絶えず意識している訳ではない。Malamud と Roth にとってユダヤ性は中心的なテーマである（前者は温かい共感をもって，後者は辛辣さと怒りと悲しみを秘めた同情でもって）のに反し，Bellow はユダヤ性の問題に真正面から取り組んでいない。Malamud や Roth と違って Bellow の主要な関心は，ユダヤ的徳性やアメリカの社会におけるユダヤ人の役割にあるのではなく，たまたまユダヤ人としての遺産を祖先から受け継いだアメリカ人の道徳や役割にある。Bellow のユダヤ人は，代表的な人間であり，代表的なアメリカ人である要素が，またユダヤ人としての個人でなく，個人としてのユダヤ人である要素が，Roth や Malamud より，はるかに強いのである（そして，この点でのBellow と Malamud の隔りは，Bellow と Roth の距離よりも大きい）。換言すれば，

Bellowの作品のユダヤ性は残滓的なものなのである。

Malamud は，どっぷりとユダヤ的伝統の世界に重々しく安住沈潜し，Roth は，ユダヤ人社会の腐敗や不安を皮肉に攻撃しながらも，良き伝統にノスタルジアを感じ，Bellow は，ユダヤ人を素材としながら，より知的に，より general な人間生活の意味を探求しようとする姿勢が3人のなかで最も顕著である。同じくユダヤ人を主人公として選び，ユダヤ人の生活を描き，ユダヤ性の意味に光を当て，その意味を認識しようとする努力の過程のなかで，人間の生きるべき最善の方法を模索しながら，3人の作家のアプローチの上述のような相違が，作家の年齢と関係なく Bernard Malamud, Philip Roth, Saul Bellow の順に，現代ユダヤ系アメリカ人の同化の過程──その文化特性，意識態，価値体系の変化──を象徴的に示していると言えよう。

≪Notes≫
I.
1) この辺の事情の詳細は，Nancy Walker, *Abraham Cahan* (New York : Twayne Publishers, 1996)136-37. を参照。
2) 1894年フランスの砲兵大尉ドレフェスは，軍機密漏洩のかどにより Devil's Island に投獄された。フランスの反ユダヤ主義者の陰謀事件であった。Emile Zora をはじめ多くの国民の運動により1906年復職し叙勲された。
3) Jules Chametzky, "Abraham Caham" in *Twentieth-Century American-Jewish Fiction Writers*, ed. Daniel Walden, Vol. 28 of *Dictionary of Literary Biography* (Detroit : Gale Research, 1984) 34. を参照。
4) アレン・グットマン，佐々木肇訳『アメリカのユダヤ系作家たち』（東京：研究社, 1979）37-48. Allen Guttmann, *The Jewish Writer in America : Assimilation and the Crisis of Identity* (New York: Oxford University Press, 1971) 25-33.
5) Anzia Yezierska, *Hungry Hearts* (Boston : Houghton Mifflin, 1920).
6) Ruth R. Wisse, "Singer's Paradoxical Progress," in *Critical Essays on Isaac Bashevis Singer*, ed. Grace Farrell (New York : G. K. Hall & Co. ,1996) 105-06.
7) Leslie Fiedler, "Isaac Bashevis Singer; or The Americanness of the American Jewish Writer," in *Studies in American Jewish Literature* 1 (1981): 124-31.

Ⅱ.
1) Irving Malin, *Jews and Americans* (Carbondale and Edwardsville: Southern Illinois University Press,1965) 9-10.
2) Malamud の作品の舞台はニューヨークを setting にしたものが多いが, *Pictures of Fidelman* (1969) のようなイタリア物, *A New Life* (1961) のような西部物, *The Fixer* (1966) のように革命前のロシアを舞台にしたものなどに分かれる。彼は1945年イタリア系アメリカ人 Ann De Chiara と結婚し, 1956年には *Partisan Review fellowship* を得てイタリアに家族で長期滞在した。*A New Life* (1961) は, 彼が Oregon State University at Corvallis の講師として1949年から1961年まで勤めた経験をもとにしている。
3) "tzaddik" は Yiddish で *The Joys of Yiddish*, 414 では, その意味の一つとして "A holy man; a man of surpassing virtue and (possibly) supernatural powers." を挙げている。
4) フィリップ・ロス, 青山南訳『素晴らしいアメリカ作家』(東京：集英社, 1980) 145.
5) 田畑千秋,『ソール・ベローを読む』(京都：松籟社, 1994) 159-72.
6) David Denby, "Memory in America," in *The Critical Response to Saul Bellow*, ed. Gerhard Bach (Westport, Conn.: Greenwood Press, 1995) 333.
7) Bellow は戦争にも反対であったが, そのような戦争反対の新しい団体に加入することはしなかった。Philip Roth が *Our Gang* (1971) で, ニクソン大統領のヴェトナム政策を戯画化したのに反し, Bellow は具体的な事件や人物を取り上げて諷刺するようなことは望まなかった。
8) フィリップ・ロス, 青山南訳『ゴースト・ライター』(東京：集英社, 1984) 106. Philip Roth, *Zuckerman Bound: A Trilogy and Epilogue* (New York: Farrar Straus Giroux) 94.
9) フィリップ・ロス, 佐伯泰樹訳『解き放たれたザッカーマン』(東京：集英社, 1984) 236. Philip Roth, *Zuckerman Bound: A Trilogy and Epilogue* (New York: Farrar Straus Giroux) 398.

初出一覧

"Abraham Cahan"『別冊英語青年,特集：ユダヤ系アメリカ文学』(1983年11月).
「悪魔的激情の語り手：I. B. Singer」『広島女学院大学論集』第47集 (1997年12月).
「バーナード・マラマッドのニューヨーク」松山信直編『アメリカ文学とニューヨーク』(東京：南雲堂,1985年2月).
「"ユダヤ教への改宗"と"ユダヤ人の改宗"——バーナード・マラマッドとフィリップ・ロス」小川晃一・片山厚編『宗教とアメリカ』(東京：木鐸社,1992年2月).
"The Ordeal of Jewishness in the Works of Bernard Malamud, Philip Roth and Saul Bellow"(PartⅠ)『広島大学総合科学部地域文化研究』第4巻 (広島大学総合科学部,1978年3月)；(PartⅡ)『広島大学総合科学部地域文化研究』第5巻 (広島大学総合科学部,1979年3月).
「*Humboldt's Gift*：崇高なる世界と俗悪の世界」『広島文教女子大学紀要』第28巻 (広島文教女子大学,1993年12月).
「*The Dean's December*——東西都市文明批判とCordeの内省」『中・四国アメリカ文学研究』第32号 (中・四国アメリカ文学会,1996年6月).
「Malamud, Roth, Bellowのユダヤ人」『吉田弘重先生退官記念英米文学語学研究』(東京：篠崎書林,1980年3月).

Selected Bibliograpby

(1) Ⅱ.～Ⅵ.のPrimary Sources は出版年順に，Ⅰ.及びⅡ.～Ⅵ.の Secondary Sources はアルファベット順に配列した。

(2) Ⅰ.の2) 以降，Ⅱ.～Ⅵ.の Secondary Sources で挙げた文献のなかで翻訳のあるものは，その場で訳本を併記した。

(3) Ⅱ.～Ⅵ. Primary Sources 2) の邦訳書は，原則として出版年順に配列したが，同一訳者による同一書の場合は，出版年順にかかわらず併記した。

(4) Interviews は Primary Sources に入れる場合と Secondary Sources に分類するケースがあるようだが，本書では Secondary Sources のなかに入れた。

(5) 邦語雑誌論文及び単行本のなかの論文は，その数が膨大なのでここに列挙することは差し控えた。以下の文献を参照されたい。

『20世紀文献要覧大系.3. 外国文学研究要覧（1965-74）』1977年.
『20世紀文献要覧大系.18. 英米文学研究要覧（1975-84）』1987年.
『20世紀文献要覧大系.19. 英米文学研究要覧（1985-89）』1991年.
『20世紀文献要覧大系.23. 英米文学研究要覧（1954-64）』1994年.
『20世紀文献要覧大系.29. 英米文学研究要覧（1990-94）』1996年.

　　（以上，編者：安藤勝，発行所：日外アソシエーツ，発売元：紀伊國屋書店）

『雑誌記事索引—人文・社会編—累積索引編, 1948-54』1979年.
『雑誌記事索引—人文・社会編—累積索引編, 1955-64, 文学・語学』1977年.
『雑誌記事索引—人文・社会編—累積索引編, 1965-69, 文学・語学』1976年.
『雑誌記事索引—人文・社会編—累積索引編, 1970-74, 文学・語学』1975年.
『雑誌記事索引—人文・社会編—累積索引編, 1975-79, 文学・語学（下）』1981年.
『雑誌記事索引—人文・社会編—累積索引編, 1980-84, 文学・語学（下）』1986年.
『雑誌記事索引—人文・社会編—累積索引編, 1985-89, 文学・語学（下）』1994年.

　　（以上，監修国立国会図書館参考書誌部，編集：国立国会図書館逐次刊行物部，発行：紀伊國屋書店，協力：日外アソシエーツ）

Ⅰ. Jewish American Literature in General

1) General References:

American Jewish Year Book (A Record of Events and Trends in American and World Jewish Life) New York: The American Jewish Committee and Jewish Publication Society of America. Its recent publication is Vol.99 (1999).

Birnbaum, Philip. *Encyclopedia of Jewish Concepts.* New York: Hebrew Publishing Co., 1979.

Commentary (U.S. Jewish monthly). New York: The American Jewish Committee, 1945- .

Encyclopaedia Judaica 17 vols, Jerusalem, Israel: Keterpress Enterprises. (出版年は明記してないが Vol.17 の *Supplement* のなかの一節は Diary of Events 1972-1981 となっている。)

Gilbert, Martin. *The Atlas of Jewish History.* New York: William Morrow and Co., 1992.

Hart, James D. *The Oxford Companion to American Literature.* 6th ed. New York: Oxford University Press, 1995.

Midstream (U.S. Jewish monthly) New York: The Theodor Herzl Foundation, 1995-1964 (quarterly); 1965- (monthly).

Rosenbaum, Samuel. *A Yiddish Word Book for English-Speaking People.* New York: Van Nostrand Reinhold Co., 1978.

Rosten, Leo. *The Joys of Yiddish.* New York: McGraw Hill Book Co., 1968.

Saul Bellow Journal. (Spring/Summer. Semiannual) West Beloomfield, Mich.: Saul Bellow Society, 1982- .

Studies in American Jewish Literature (Annual journal). University Park, Pa.: Studies in American Jewish Literature, Inc., 1980- .

Thernstrom, Stephan, et al. eds. *Harvard Encyclopedia of American Ethnic Groups.* Cambridge: Harvard University Press, 1980.

常松正雄,田中久男,ハロルド・H・コルブ Jr.『アメリカ文学研究資料事典』東京：南雲堂, 1994.

2) Books Specifically about Jewish American Literature:

Aarons, Victoria. *A Measure of Memory: Storytelling and Identity in American Jewish Fiction.* Athens: The University of Georgia Press, 1996.

Alter, Robert. *After the Tradition: Essays on Modern Jewish Writing.* New York: E.P. Dutton, 1969.

Fried, Lewis. *Handbook of American-Jewish Literature: An Analytical Guide to Topics, Themes, and Sources.* New York: Greenwood Press, 1988.

Girgus, Sam. *The New Covenant: Jewish Writers and the American Idea.* Chapel Hill: University of North Carolina Press, 1984.

Guttmann, Allen. *The Jewish Writer in America—Assimilation and the Crisis of Identity.* New York: Oxford University Press, 1971. 佐々木肇訳『アメリカのユダヤ系作家たち』東京：研究社, 1979.

Harap, Louis. *In the Mainstream: The Jewish Presence in Twentieth-Century American Literature, 1950s-1980s.* New York: Greenwood Press, 1987.

Malin, Irving. *Jews and Americans.* Carbondale: Southern Illinois University Press, 1965.

―――, ed. *Contemporary American-Jewish Literature: Critical Essays.* Bloomington:

Indiana University Press, 1973.
Pinsker, Sanford. *Jewish American Fiction, 1917-1987*. New York: Twayne, 1992.
Sherman, Bernard. *The Invention of the Jew—Jewish-American Education Novels (1916-1964)*. New York: Thomas Yoseloff, 1969.
『別冊英語青年　特集：ユダヤ系アメリカ文学』東京：研究社，1983年11月
浜野成生『ユダヤ系アメリカ文学の出発』東京：研究社，1984．
広瀬佳司『ユダヤ文学の巨匠たち—シュレミールの批評精神』大阪：関西書院，1993．
中西勝之『現代ユダヤ系アメリカ文学』東京：原書房，1981．
20世紀文学研究会編『20世紀文学 9. 特集—ユダヤ系作家』東京：南雲堂，1969．
日本マラマッド協会編『ユダヤ系アメリカ短編の時空』東京：北星堂，1997．
小山田義文『アメリカユダヤ系作家』（英米文学シリーズ 5）東京：評論社，1976．

3) Parts of Books:
Bakker, J. *Fiction as Survival Strategy: A Comparative Study of the Major Works of Ernest Hemingway and Saul Bellow*. Amsterdam: Rodopi B. V., 1983.
Balakian, Nona, and Charles Simmons, eds. *The Creative Present: Notes on Contemporary American Fiction*. Garden City, N. Y.: Doubleday, 1963.
Baumbach, Jonathan. *The Landscape of Nightmare: Studies in the Contemporary American Novel*. New York: New York University Press, 1965.
Bryant, Jerry H. *The Open Decision—The Contemporary American Novel and Its Intellectual Background*. New York: Free Press, 1970.
Cheyette, Bryan, ed. *Between 'Race' and Culture: Representations of 'the Jew' in English and American Literature*. Stanford, Cal.: Stanford University Press, 1996.
Eisinger, Chester E. *Fiction of the Forties*. Chicago: University of Chicago Press, 1963.
Fiedler, Leslie A. *An End to Innocence: Essays on Culture and Politics*. New York: Stein and Day, 1971.
―――. *No! In Thunder—Essays on Myth and Literature*. Boston: Beacon Press, 1960.
―――. *The Jew in the American Novel*. New York: Herzl Press, 1959.
―――. *The Return of the Vanishing American*. New York: Stein dnd Day, 1969. 渥美昭夫，酒本雅之訳『消えゆくアメリカ人の帰還—アメリカ文学の原型Ⅲ』東京：新潮社，1972．
―――. *Waiting for the End*. New York: Stein and Day, 1964. 井上謙治，徳永暢三訳『終りを待ちながら—アメリカ文学の原型Ⅱ』東京：新潮社，1972．
Finkelstein, Sidney. *Existentialism and Alienation in American Literature*. New York: International Publishers, 1965.
French, Warren, ed. *The Fifties: Fiction, Poetry, Drama*. Deland, Fla.: Everett/Edwards, 1971.
Geismar, Maxwell. *American Moderns—From Rebellion to Conformity*. New York: Hill and

Wang, 1958.

Harap, Louis. *The Image of the Jew in American Literature*. Philadelphia: The Jewish Publication Society of America, 1974.

Harper, Howard M., Jr. *Desperate Faith: A Study of Bellow, Salinger, Mailer, Baldwin and Updike*. Chapel Hill: University of North Carolina Press, 1967. 渥美昭夫, 井上謙治訳『絶望からの文学』東京：荒地出版社, 1969.

Hassan, Ihab. *Contemporary American Literature 1945-1972: An Introduction*. New York: Frederick Ungar, 1973.

―――. *Radical Innocence: Studies in the Contemporary American Novel*. Princeton, N. J.: Princeton University Press, 1961. 岩本巌訳『根源的な無垢―現代アメリカ小説論―』東京：新潮社, 1972.

Hicks, Granville. *Literary Horizons—A Quarter Century of American Fiction*. New York: New York University Press, 1970.

Howe, Irving. *World of Our Fathers*. New York: Harcourt Brace Jovanovich, 1976.

Kazin, Alfred. *Contemporaries*. Boston: Little, Brown ,1962.

Klein, Marcus. *After Alienation: American Novels in Mid-Century*. Cleveland: Meridian, 1965.

―――, and Irwin Stark, eds. "Introduction." *Breakthrough—A Treasury of Contemporary American-Jewish Literature*. New York: McGraw-Hill, 1964.

Meeter, Glenn. *Bernard Malamud and Philip Roth—A Critical Essay*. Grand Rapids, Mich.: W. B. Eerdmans, 1968.

Pinsker, Sanford. *The Schlemiel as Metaphor—Studies in the Yiddish and American Jewish Novel*. Carbondale: Southern Illinois University Press, 1971.

Pughe, Thomas. *Comic Sense: Reading Robert Coover, Stanley Elkin, Philip Roth*. Basel: Birkhäuser Verlag, 1994.

Rupp, Richard H. *Celebration in Postwar American Fiction—1945-1967*. Coral Gables, Fla.: University of Miami Press, 1970.

Scott, Nathan A., Jr. *Three American Moralists: Mailer, Bellow, Trilling*. Notre Dame: University of Notre Dame Press, 1973.

Schulz, Max F. *Radical Sophistication: Studies in Contemporary Jewish-American Novelists*. Athens: Ohio Univrsity Press, 1969.

Tanner, Tony. *City of Words—American Fiction 1950-1970*. New York: Harper & Row. 1971.

Weinberg, Helen. *The New Novel in America: The Kafkan Mode in Contemporary Fiction*. Ithaca, N. Y.: Cornell University Press, 1970.

Wisse, Ruth R. *The Schlemiel as Modern Hero*. Chicago: The University of Chicago Press, 1971.

Yudkin, Leon Israel. *Jewish Writing and Identity in the Twentieth Century*. New York: St.

Martin's Press, 1982.
藤井治彦編『空間と英米文学』東京：英宝社, 1987.
浜野成生『今日のアメリカ作家群像』東京：研究社, 1978.
岩元巌『現代のアメリカ小説―対立と模索』東京：英潮社, 1974.
岩元巌『現代アメリカ作家の世界』東京：リーベル出版, 1988.
越川芳明編『アメリカ文学のヒーロー』東京：成美堂, 1991.
元山千歳, 金谷良夫, 清水一雄, 佐川和茂『アメリカ文学と暴力―ポオ／トウェイン／ヘミングウェイ／ベロウ／マラマッド』東京：研究社, 1995.
徳永暢三編『英米文学の新視点』東京：英潮社, 1976.

II. Abraham Cahan

PRIMARY SOURCES

1) Books (in English):

Yekl, A Tale of the New York Ghetto. New York: D. Appleton and Co., 1896. Also published in *Yekl and The Imported Bridegroom and Other Stories of the New York Ghetto.* Introduced by Bernard C. Richards. New York: Dover Publications, 1970.

The Imported Bridegroom and Other Stories of the New York Ghetto. Boston: Houghton Mifflin, 1898; later published as Vol.7 of the American Short Story Series, New York: Garrett, 1968. Also published in *Yekl and The Imported Bridegroom and Other Stories of the New York Ghetto.* Introduced by Bernard C. Richards. New York: Dover Publications, 1970.

The White Terror and the Red: A Novel of Revolutionary Russia. New York: A. S. Barnes & Co., 1905.

The Rise of David Levinsky: A Novel. New York: Harper & Bros., 1917. Reprint. New York: Grosset & Dunlap, 1928. With introduction by John Higham: New York: Harper & Bros., 1960. With introduction and notes by Jules Chametzky: New York: Penguin Books, 1994.

The Education of Abraham Cahan. Vols. 1 and 2 of *Bleter fun Mayn Lebn.* Trans. Leon Stein, Abraham P. Conan, and Lynn Davidson. Introduced by Leon Stein. Philadelphia: Jewish Publication Society of America, 1969.

A Bintel Brief: Sixty Years of Letters from the Lower East Side to the Jewish Daily Forward. Ed. Isaac Metzker. Garden City, N.Y.: Doubleday & Co. 1971.

Grandma Never Lived in America: The New Journalism of Abraham Cahan. Ed. and introduced by Moses Rischin. Rischin's comprehensive introduction is valuable for information on both Cahan and the *Commercial Advertiser.* Bloomington: Indiana University Press, 1984.

2) 邦訳書：なし

SECONDARY SOURCES
1) Bibliographic Aids:
Cronin, Gloria L., Blaine H. Hall, and Connie Lamb. "Abraham Cahan: 1860-1951." *Jewish American Fiction Writers: An Annotated Bibliography.* New York: Garland, 1991. 89-111.
Jeshurin, Ephim H. *Abraham Cahan Bibliography.* New York: United Vilner Relief Committee, 1941.
Marovitz, Sanford E. "Abraham Cahan." *American Literary Realism, 1870-1910* 8. 3 (Summer 1975): 206-8.
―――, and Lewis Fried. "Abraham Cahan (1860-1951): An Annotated Bibliography." *American Literary Realism, 1870-1910* 3. 3 (Summer 1970): 196-243.
Polster, Karen L. "Abraham Cahan: An Annotated Bibliography of Criticism, 1970-1988." *Studies in American Jewish Literature* 12 (1993): 25-35.

2) Books Specifically about Cahan:
Chametzky, Jules. *From the Ghetto: The Fiction of Abraham Cahan.* Amherst: University of Massachusetts Press, 1977.
Maroritz, Sanford E. *Abraham Cahan.* New York: Twayne Publishers, 1997.

3) Other Bocks and Articles:
Chametzky, Jules. "Abraham Cahan." *Twentieth-Century American-Jewish Fiction Writers.* Ed. Daniel Walden. Vol.28 of *Dictionary of Literary Biography.* Detroit: Gale Research, 1984. 29-35.
Engel, David. "The Discrepancies of the Modern: Reevaluating Abraham Cahan's *The Rise of David Levinsky.*" *Studies in American Jewish Literature* 5. 2 (1979): 68-91.
Fiedler, Leslie A. "Genesis: The American-Jewish Novel through the Twenties." *Midstream* 4. 3 (Summer 1958): 21-33.
Fine, David M. "Success as Failure: Abraham Cahan's Fiction." *The City, the Immigrant and American Fiction, 1880-1920.* Metuchen, N. J.: Scarecrow Press, 1977. 121-38, 160-62.
Girgus, Sam B. "A Convert to America: Sex, Self, and Ideology in Abraham Cahan." *The New Covenant: Jewish Writers and the American Idea.* Chapel Hill: University of North Carolina Press, 1984. 64-91.
Greenspan, Ezra. *The "Schlemiel" Comes to America.* Metuchen, N. J.: Scarecrow Press, 1983. 30-43.
Guttmann, Allen. *The Jewish Writer in America: Assimilation and the Crisis of Identity.* New York: Oxford University Press, 1971. 28-33.

Harap, Louis. *Creative Awakening: The Jewish Presence in Twentieth-Century American Literature: 1900-1940s.* Westport, Conn.: Greenwood, 1987.

―――. "Fiction in English by Abraham Cahan." *The Image of the Jew in American Literature from Early Republic to Mass Immigration.* Philadelphia: Jewish Publication Society of America, 1974. 485-524, 567-71.

Higham, John. Introduction to *The Rise of David Levinsky.* New York: Harper & Bros, Harper Torchbook, 1960. v-xii.

Kress, Susan. "Women and Marriage in Abraham Cahan's Fiction." *Studies in American Jewish Literature* 3 (1983): 26-39.

Levenberg, Diane. "David Levinsky and His Women." *Midstream* 26 (August-September 1980): 51-53.

Marovitz, Sanford E. "The Lonely New Americans of Abraham Cahan." *American Quarterly* 20. 2 (Summer 1968): 196-210.

―――. "The Secular Trinity of a Lonely Millionaire: Language, Sex, and Power in *The Rise of David Levinsky.*" *Studies in American Jewish Literature* 2 (1982): 20-35.

Pressman, Richard S. "Abraham Cahan, Capitalist; David Levinsky, Socialist." *Studies in American Jewish Fiction* 12 (1993): 2-18.

Rosenfeld, Isaac. "America, Land of the Sad Millionaire." *Commentary* 14 (August 1952): 131-35.

4) Cahanについての邦語単行本：なし

Ⅲ. Isaac Bashevis Singer

PRIMARY SOURCES

1) Books:

The Family Moskat. Trans. A. H. Gross. New York: Knopf, 1950.

Satan in Goray. Trans. Jacob Sloan. New York: Noonday, 1955.

Gimpel the Fool and Other Stories. Trans. Saul Bellow and others. New York: Noonday, 1957.

The Magician of Lublin. Trans. Elaine Gottlieb and Joseph Singer. New York: Noonday, 1960.

The Spinoza of Market Street. Trans. Martha Glicklich, Cecil Hemley, and others. New York: Farrar, Straus & Cudahy, 1961.

The Slave. Trans. Isaac Bashevis Singer and Hemley. New York: Farrar, Straus & Cudahy, 1962.

Short Friday and Other Stories. Trans. Joseph Singer and others. New York: Farrar, Straus & Giroux, 1964.

In My Father's Court. Trans. Channah Kleinerman-Goldstein, Gottlieb, and Joseph Singer. New York: Farrar, Straus & Giroux, 1966.

Zlateh the Goat and Other Stories. Trans. Elizabeth Shub and Isaac Bashevis Singer, illustrated by Maurice Sendak. New York: Harper & Row, 1966.

Selected Short Stories of Isaac Bashevis Singer. Ed. Irving Howe. New York: Modern Library, 1966.

Mazel and Shlimazel; or, The Milk of A Lioness. Trans. Shub and Isaac Bashevis Singer, illustrated by Margot Zemach. New York: Farrar, Straus & Giroux, 1967.

The Manor. Trans. Joseph Singer and Gottlieb. New York: Farrar, Straus & Giroux, 1967.

The Fearsome Inn. Trans. Shub and Isaac Bashevis Singer, illustrated by Nonny Hogrogian. New York: Scribners,1967.

When Shlemiel Went to Warsaw and Other Stories. Trans. Isaac Bashevis Singer and Shub, Illustrated by Zemach. New York: Farrar, Straus & Giroux, 1968.

The Séance and Other Stories. Trans. Roger H. Klein, Hemley, and others. New York: Farrar, Straus & Giroux, 1968.

A Day of Pleasure: Stories of a Boy Growing Up in Warsaw. Trans. Kleinerman-Goldsetin and others, illustrated with contemporary photographs by Roman Vishniac. New York: Farrar, Straus & Giroux, 1969.

The Estate. Trans. Joseph Singer, Gottlieb, and Shub. New York: Farrar, Straus & Giroux, 1969.

Joseph and Koza; or, The Sacrifice to the Vistula. Trans. Isaac Bashevis Singer and Shub, illustrated by Symeon Shimin. New York: Farrar, Straus & Giroux, 1970.

Elijah the Slave. Trans. Isaac Bashevis Singer and Elizabeth Shub, illustrated by Antonio Frasconi. New York: Farrar, Straus & Giroux, 1970.

A Friend of Kafka and Ohter Stories. Trans. Isaac Bashevis Singer Elizabeth Shub, and others. New York: Farrar, Straus & Giroux, 1970.

An Isaac Bashevis Singer Reader. New York: Farrar, Straus & Giroux, 1971.

Alone in the Wild Forest. Trans. Isaac Bashevis Singer and Shub, illustated by Zemach. New York: Farrar, Straus & Giroux, 1971.

The Topsy-Turvy Emperor of China. Trans. Isaac Bashevis Singer and Shub, illustrated by William Pène du Bois. New York: Harper & Row, 1971.

Enemies, A love Story. Trans. Aliza Shervin and Shub. New York: Farrar, Straus & Giroux, 1972.

The Wicked City. Trans. Isaac Bashevis Singer and Shub, illustrated by Leonard Everett Fisher. New York: Farrar, Straus & Giroux, 1972.

A Crown of Feathers and Other Stories. Trans. Isaac Bashevis Singer, Lauru Colwin and others. New York: Farrar, Straus & Giroux, 1973.

The Hasidim, with Ira Moskowitz. New York: Crown, 1973.
The Fools of Chelm and Their History. Trans. Isaac Bashevis Singer and Shub, illustrated by Uri Shulevitz. New York: Farrar, Starus & Giroux, 1973.
Why Noah Chose the Dove. Trans. Shub, illustrated by Eric Carle. New York: Farrar, Straus & Giroux, 1974.
Passions and Other Stories. Trans. Isaac Bashevis Singer and others. New York: Farrar, Straus & Giroux, 1975.
A Tale of Three Wishes. Illustrated by Irene Lieblich. New York: Farrar, Straus & Giroux, 1975.
A Little Boy in Search of God; or Mysticism in a Personal Light, with Moskowitz. Trans. Joseph Singer. Garden City, N.Y.: Doubleday, 1976.
Naftali the Storyteller and His Horse, Sus, and Other Stories. Trans. Joseph Singer, Isaac Bashevis Singer and others, illustrated by Zemach. New York. Farrar, Straus & Giroux, 1976.
A Young Man in Search of Love. Trans. Joseph Singer. Garden City, N.Y.: Doubleday, 1978.
Shosha. Trans. Joseph Singer and Isaac Bashevis Singer. New York: Farrar, Straus & Giroux, 1978.
Old Love. Trans. Joseph Singer, Isaac Bashevis Singer, and others. New York: Farrar, Straus & Giroux, 1979.
Nobel Lecture. New York: Farrar, Straus & Giroux, 1979.
Reaches of Heaven: A Story of Baal Shem Tov. New York: Farrar, Straus & Giroux, 1980.
The Power of Light: Eight Stories for Hanukkah. Illustrated by Lieblich. New York: Farrar, Straus & Giroux, 1980.
Lost in America. Garden City, N.Y.: Doubleday, 1981.
The Collected Stories. New York: Farrar, Straus & Giroux, 1982.
The Golem, illustrated by Uri Shulevitz. New York: Farrar, Straus & Giroux, 1982.
Yentl the Yeshiva Boy. Trans. Marion Magid and Elizabeth Pollet. New York: Farrar, Straus & Giroux, 1983.
The Penitent. New York: Farrar, Straus & Giroux, 1983.
Love & Exile: A Memoir. Garden City, N.Y.: Doubleday, 1984.
Stories for Children. New York: Farrar, Straus & Giroux, 1984.
The Image and Other Stories. New York: Farrar, Straus & Giroux, 1985.
Gifts. Philadelphia: Jewish Publication Society, 1985.
The Death of Methuselah and Other Stories. New York: Farrar, Straus & Giroux, 1987.
The King of the Fields. New York: Frarrar, Straus & Giroux, 1988.
Scum. New York: Farrar, Straus & Giroux, 1991.

2）邦訳書：
邦高忠二訳『短い金曜日』(*Short Friday and Other Stories*) 東京：晶文社, 1971.
田内初義訳『愛の迷路』(*Enemies, A Love Story*) 東京：角川書店, 1974；『敵, ある愛の物語』東京：角川文庫, 1990.
金敷力訳『ワルシャワで大人になっていく少年の物語』(*A Day of Pleasure*) 東京：新潮社, 1974.
井上謙治訳『奴隷』(*The Slave*) 東京：河出書房新社, 1975.
田内初義訳『羽の冠』(*A Crown of Feathers*) 東京：新書館, 1976.
木庭茂夫訳『メイゼルとシュリメイゼル』(*The Mazel and Shlimazel*) 東京：富山房, 1976.
関憲治訳『ヘルムのあんぽん譚』(*The Fools of Chelm and Their History*) 東京：篠崎書林, 1978；『ヘルム村の人々』(*The Fools of Chelm and Their History*) 1988.
工藤幸雄訳『やぎと少年』(*Zlateh the Goat and Other Stories*) 東京：岩波書店, 1979, 1993；東京：日本ライトハウス, 1980.
工藤幸雄訳『お話を運んだ馬』(*Naftali the Stroyteller and His Horse, Sus and Other Stories*) 東京：岩波書店, 1981, 1990, 1995.
飛田茂雄訳『カフカの友達』他4編 ("A Friend of Kafka," etc.) 『海』13（6），1981.
工藤幸雄訳『まぬけなワルシャワ旅行』(*Shlemiel Went to Warsaw and Other Stories*) 東京：岩波書店, 1983.
邦高忠二訳『愛のイエントル』(*Yentl the Yeshiva Boy*) 東京：晶文社, 1984.
工藤幸雄訳『喜びの日　ワルシャワの少年時代』(*A Day of Pleasure: Stories of a Boy Growing Up in Warsaw*) 東京：岩波書店, 1990.
広瀬佳司訳「メトセラの死」("The Death of Methuselah") ノートルダム清心女子大学『紀要』(外国語・外国文学編　第15巻), 1991.
広瀬佳司訳「ヘルシュレとハヌカ」(イディシュ語原文からの翻訳) ノートルダム清心女子大学『紀要』(外国語・外国文学編　第17巻), 1993.
島田太郎訳『罠におちた男』(*Scum*) 東京：晶文社, 1995.

SECONDARY SOURCES

1）Bibliographic Aids:
Bryer, Jackson R., and Paul E. Rockwell. "Isaac Bashevis Singer in English: A Bibliography." *Critical Views of Isaac Bashevis Singer*. Ed. Irving Malin. New York: New York University Press, 1968. 220-65.
Miller, David Neal. *Bibliogeraphy of Isaac Bashevis Singer: 1924-1949*. New York, Berne, Frankfort on the Main: Peter Lang, 1983.
―――. *A Bibliography of Isaac Bashevis Singer, January 1950-June 1952*. Working Papers in Yiddish and East European Jewish Culture, Vol.34. New York: YIVO Institute for

Jewish Research, 1979.

2) Interviews:
Andersen, David M. "Isaac Bashevis Singer: Conversations in California." *Modern Fiction Studies* 16 (Winter 1970-71): 424-39.
Blocker, Joel, and Richard Elman. "An Interview with Isaac Bashevis Singer." *Commentary* 36 (Noember 1963): 364-72.
Burgin, Richard, and Isaac Bashevis Singer. *Conversations with Isaac Bashevis Singer.* New York: Doubleday, 1985.
Farrell, Grace, ed. *Conversations with Isaac Bashevis Singer.* Jackson, Miss.: University Press of Mississippi, 1992.
Gilman, Sander L. "Interview/Isaac Bashevis Singer." *Diacritics* 4 (Spring 1974): 30-33.
Lee, Grace Farrell. "Stewed Prunes and Rice Pudding, College Students Eat and Talk with Isaac Bashevis Singer." *Contemporary Literature* 19 (Autumn 1978): 446-58.
Pinsker, Sanford. "Isaac Bashevis Singer: An Interview." *Critique* 11 (1969): 26-39.
Ribalow, Reena Sara. "A Visit to Isaac Bashevis Singer." *The Reconstructionist* 30 (29 May 1964): 19-26.
Rosenblatt, Paul, and Gene Koppel. *Isaac Bashevis Singer on Literature and Life.* Tucson: University of Arizona Press, 1971.

3) Books Specifically about Singer:
Alexander, Edward. *Isaac Bashevis Singer.* Boston: Twayne Publishers, 1980.
Allentuck, Marcia, ed. *The Achievement of Isaac Bashevis Singer.* Carbondale: Southern Illinois University Press, 1969.
Buchen, Irving. *Isaac Bashevis Singer and the Eternal Past.* New York: New York University Press, 1968.
Farrell, Grace, ed. *Critical Essays on Isaac Bashevis Singer.* New York: G. K. Hall & Co., 1996.
Friedman, Lawrence S. *Understanding Isaac Bashevis Singer.* Columbia: University of South Carolina Press, 1988.
Hadda, Janet. *Isaac Bashevis Singer, A Life.* New York: Oxford University Press, 1977.
Kresh, Paul. *Isaac Bashevies Singer.* New York: Dial Press, 1979.
Lee, Grace Farrell. *From Exile to Redemption: The Fiction of Isaac Bashevis Singer.* Carbondale and Edwardsvill: Southern Illinois University Press, 1987.
Malin, Irving, ed. *Critical Views of Isaac Bashevis Singer.* New York: New York University Press, 1969.
―――. *Isaac Bashevis Singer.* New York: Frederick Ungar, 1972.

Miller, David N. *Fear of Fiction: Narrative Strategies in the Works of Isaac Bashevis Singer.* Albany: State University of New York Press, 1985.

4) Other Books and Articles:

Alexander, Edward. "Isaac Bashevis Singer and Jewish Utopianism." *The Jewish Idea and Its Enemies.* New Brunswick and Oxford: Transaction Books, 1988.

——. "The Destruction and Resurrection of the Jews in the Fiction of Isaac Bashevis Singer." *The Resonance of Dust: Essays on Holocaust Literature and Jewish Fate.* Columbus: Ohio State University Press, 1979. 149-69.

Baumgarten, Murray. "Clothing and Character." *City Scriptures: Modern Jewish Writing.* Cambridge, Mass.: Harvard University Press, 1982.

Berger, Alan L. "Isaac Bashevis Singer." *Crisis and Covenant: The Holocaust in American Jewish Fiction.* Albany: State University of New York Press, 1985. 79-88.

Feldman, Irving. "The Shtetl World." *Kenyon Review* 24 (Winter 1962): 173-77.

Fixler, Michael. "The Redeemers: Themes in the Fiction of Isaac Bashevis Singer." *Kenyon Reiew* 26 (Spring 1964): 371-86.

Glatstein, Jacob. "The Fame of Bashevis Singer." *Congress Bi-Weekly* 32 (27 December 1965):17-19.

Howe, Irving. Introduction to *Selected Short Stories of Isaac Bashevis Singer.* New York: Modern Library, 1966.

——, and I. B. Singer. "Yiddish Tradition vs. Jewish Tradition: A Dialogue." *Midstream* 19 (June/July 1973): 33-38.

Milbauer, Asher Zelig. *Transcending Exile: Conrad, Nabokov, I. B. Singer.* Miami: Florida International University Press, 1985.

Miller, David N., ed. *Recovering The Canon.* Leiden: E. J. Brill, 1986.

Siegel, Ben. *Isaac Bashevis Singer.* Minneapolis: University of Minnesota Press, 1969.

Pinsker, Sanford. "The Fictive Worlds of Isaac Bashevis Singer." *Critique* 11 (1969): 26-39.

Prager, Leonard. "Isaac Bashevis Singer." *Encyclopedia Judaica,* Vol.4. B. Jerusalem: Keter, 1971.

Reichek, Morton A. "Storyteller." *New York Times Magazine* 23 March 1975: 16-18, 20, 22, 24, 26, 28, 30, 33.

Shmeruk, Chone. "Bashevis Singer—In Search of His Autobiography." *Jewish Quarterly* 29 (Winter 1981-82): 28-36.

Sontag, Susan. "Demons and Dreams" *Partisan Review* (Summer 1962): 406-63.

Trachtenberg, Joshua. *Jewish Magic and Superstition: A Study in Folk Religion.* Cleveland and New York: The World Publishing Company, 1961.

Wisse, Roth R. *The Schlemiel as Modern Hero.* Chicago: The University of Chicago Press,

1971.

Zamir, Israel. *Journey to My Father—Isaac Bashevis Singer.* Tel-Aviv: S. Poalin, 1994. 広瀬佳司訳『わが父　アイザック・B・シンガー』東京：旺史社，1999.

Zatlin, Linda G. "The Themes of Isaac Bashevis Singer's Short Fiction." *Critique* 11 (1969): 40-46.

5）Singer についての邦語単行本：
広瀬佳司『アウトサイダーを求めて―I. B. シンガーの世界』東京：旺史社，1991.

Ⅳ．Bernard Malamud

PRIMARY SOURCES

1）Books:
The Natural. New York: Harcourt, Brace, 1952.
The Assistant. New York: Farrar, Straus & Cudahy, 1957.
The Magic Barrel. New York: Farrar, Straus & Cudahy, 1958.
A New Life. New York: Farrar, Straus & Cudahy, 1961.
Idiots First. New York: Farrar, Straus, 1963.
The Fixer. New York: Farrar, Straus & Giroux, 1966.
A Malamud Reader. Ed. and with an introduction. Philip Rahv. New York: Farrar, Straus & Giroux, 1967.
Pictures of Fidelman: An Exhibition. New York: Farrar, Straus & Giroux, 1969.
The Tenants. New York: Farrar, Straus, & Giroux, 1971.
Rembrandt's Hat. New York: Farrar, Straus & Giroux, 1973.
Dubin's Lives. New York: Farrar, Straus & Giroux, 1979.
God's Grace. New York: Farrar, Straus & Giroux, 1982.
The Stories of Bernard Malamud. New York: Farrar, Straus & Giroux, 1983.
The People and Uncollected Stories. Ed. and with an introduction. Robert Giroux. New York: Farrar, Straus & Giroux, 1989.

2）邦訳書：
宮本陽吉訳『もうひとつの生活』（*A New Life*）東京：新潮社，1963，1970.
邦高忠二訳『魔法の樽』（*The Magic Barrel*）東京：荒地出版社，1968.
大竹勝訳「みずうみの女」（"The Lady of the Lake"）東京：荒地出版社，1968.（『現代アメリカ作家十二人集』）.
酒本雅之訳『アシスタント』（*The Assistant*）東京：荒地出版社，1969.
橋本福夫訳『修理屋』（*The Fixer*）東京：早川書房，1969.

繁尾久訳『魔法のたる』(The Magic Barrel) 東京：角川文庫, 1970.
鈴木武樹訳『汚れた白球』(The Natural) 東京：角川文庫, 1970.
西田実訳『フィデルマンの絵』(Pictures of Fidelman: An Exhibition) 東京：河出書房新社, 1970.
繁尾久訳『アシスタント』(The Assistant) 東京：角川文庫, 1971.
加島祥造訳『マラマッド短編集』(The Magic Barrel) 東京：新朝文庫, 1971.
繁尾久訳『アシスタント』(The Assistant) 東京：新潮文庫, 1972.
小島信夫・浜本武雄・井上謙治訳『レンブラントの帽子』(Rembrandt's Hat) 東京：集英社, 1975.
小野寺健訳『ドゥービン氏の冬』(Dubin's Lives) 東京：白水社, 1980.
小野寺健訳『コーンの孤島』(God's Grace) 東京：白水社, 1984.
真野明裕訳『奇跡のルーキー』(The Natural) 東京：早川書房, 1984.

SECONDARY SOURCES
1) Bibliographic Aids:
Habich, Robert D. "Bernard Malamud: A Bibliographical Survey." *Studies in American Jewish Literature* 4 (Spring 1978): 78-84.

―――――. "Bernard Malamud." *Contemporary Authors Bibliographic Series: American Novelists*. Ed. James J. Martine. Detroit: Bruccoli Clark/Gale, 1986. 261-91.

Kosofsky, Rita Nathalie. *Bernard Malamud: An Annotated Checklist*. Kent, Ohio: Kent State University Press, 1969.

―――――. *Bernard Malamud: A Descriptive Bibriography*. New York: Greenwood Press, 1991.

Grau, Joseph A. "Bernard Malamud: A Bibliographical Addendum." *Bulletin of Bibliography* 37 (October-December 1980): 157-66, 184.

―――――. "A Further Bibliographical Addendum." *Bulletin of Bibliography* 38 (April-June 1981): 101-04.

O'Keefe, Richard P. "Bibliograohical Essay: Bernard Malamud." *Studies in American Jewish Literature* 7 (Fall 1988): 240-50.

Salzberg, Joel. *Bernard Malamud: A Reference Guide*. Boston: G. K. Hall, 1985.

2) Interviews:
Field, Lislie A., and Joyce W. "An Interview with Bernard Malamud." *Bernard Malamud: A Collection of Critical Essays*. Ed. L. A. Field and J. W Field. Englewood Cliffs, N. J.: Prentice Hall, 1975.

Frankel, Haskel. "Interview with Bernard Malamud." *Saturday Review* 10 September, 1966.

Lasher, Lawrence, ed. *Conversations with Bernard Malamud*. Jackson, Miss.: University Press

of Mississippi, 1991.
Sheppard, Ronald Z. "About Bernard Malamud." *The Washington Post* 13 October 1963.
Wershba, Joseph. "Not Horror But 'Sadness'." *New York Post* 14 September 1958.

3) Books Specifically about Malamud:
Abramson, Edward A., ed. *Bernard Malamud Revisited*. New York: Twayne Publishers, 1993.
Alter, Iska. *The Good Man's Dilemma: Social Criticism in the Fiction of Bernard Malamud*. New York: AMS Press, Inc, 1981.
Astro, Richard, and Jackson J. Benson, eds. *The Fiction of Bernard Malamud*. Corvallis: Oregon State University Press, 1977.
Bloom, Harold, ed. *Bernard Malamud*. New York: Chelsea House Publishers, 1986.
————. *Saul Bellow's Herzog*. New York: Chelsea House Publishers, 1988.
Cheuse, Alan, and Nicholas Delbanco., eds. *Talking Horse: Bernard Malamud on Life and Work*. New York: Columbia University Press, 1996.
Cohen, Sandy. *Bernard Malamud and the Trial by Love*. Amsterdam: Rodopi N. V., 1974.
Ducharme, Robert. *Art and Idea in the Novels of Barnard Malamud: Toward the Fixer*. The Hague: Mouton, 1974.
Field, Leslie A., and Joyce W., eds. *Bernard Malamud: A Collection of Critical Essays*. Englewood Cliffs, N. J.: Prentice Hall, 1975.
————, eds. *Bernard Malamud and the Critics*. New York: New York University Press, 1970.
Helterman, Jeffrey. *Understanding Bernard Malamud*. Columbia: Unirersity of South Carolina Press, 1985.
Hershinow, Sheldon J. *Bernard Malamud*. New York: Frederick Ungar Publishing Company, 1980.
Richman, Sidney. *Bernard Malamud*. New York: Twayne Publishers, 1966.
Salzberg, Joel. *Critical Essays on Bernard Malamud*. Boston: G. K. Hall and Co., 1987.
Solotaroff, Robert. *Bernard Maramud: A Study of the Short Fiction*. Boston: Twayne Publishers, 1989.

4) Collection of Essays:
Studies in American Jewish Literature 4 (Spring 1978). Entitled "Bernard Malamud: Reinterpretations," this issue is devoted entirely to essays analyzing Malamud's work.
Studies in American Jewish Literature 7 (Fall 1988). Entitled "Bernard Malamud: In Memoriam," this issue is devoted entirely to Malamud's work, and contains what is probably his last interview and a useful bibliographic essay.
Studies in American Jewish Literature 14 (1995). Entitled five studies of "Bernard Malamud's

Literary Imagination: A New Look" are contained in this issue.

5) Other Books and Articles:
Alter, Robert. "Ordinary Anguish." *New York Times Book Review* 14 October 1983, 1, 35, 36.
Byer, James. "God's Grace and Bernard Malamud's Allusions: A Study in Art and Racial Insult." *The Changing Mosaic: From Cahan to Malamund, Roth and Ozick. Studies in American Jewish Literature* 12 (1993): 87-93.
Fiedler, Leslie. *To the Gentiles*. New York: Stein and Day, 1972.
Girgus, Sam. *The New Covenant: Jewish Writers and the American Idea*. Chapel Hill: University of North Carolina Press, 1984.
Guttman, Allen. *The Jewish Writer in America: Assimilation and the Crisis of Identity*. New York: Oxford University Press, 1971. 佐々木肇訳『アメリカユダヤ系作家たち』東京：研究社, 1979.
Knopp, Josephine Z. *The Trial of Judaism in Contemporary Jewish Writing*. Urbana: University of Illinois Press, 1975.
Lasher, Lawrence M. "An Early Version of Malamud's 'The German Refugee' and Other Early Newspaper Sketches." *The Changing Mosaic: From Cahan to Malamud, Roth and Ozick. Studies in American Jewish Literature* 12 (1993): 94-108.
Lyons, Bonnie. "The Contrasting Visions of Malamud and O'Connor" in *The Changing Mosaic: From Cahan to Malamud, Roth and Ozick. Studies in American Jewish Literature* 12 (1993): 79-86.
Malin, Irving. *Jews and Americans*. Carbondale: Southern Illirois University Press, 1965.
―――, ed. *Contemporary American-Jewish Literature*: Critical Essays. Bloomington: Indiana University Press, 1973.
Rahv, Philip. Introduction. *A Malamud Reader*. New York: Farrar, Straus & Giroux, 1967, vii-xiv.
Roth, Philip. "*Imagining Jews*." *Reading Myself and Others*. New York: Farrar, Straus & Giroux, 1976. 215-46.
Schulz, Max F. *Radical Sophistication: Studies in Contemporary Jewish-American Novelists*. Athens: Ohio University Press, 1969.
Shechner, Mark. "Sad Music." *Partisan Review* 5 (1984): 451-58.
Stern, Paniel. "The Art of Fiction: Bernard Malamud." *Paris Review* 16 (Spring 1975): 40-64.
Wegelin, Christof. "The American Schlemiel Abroad: Malamud's Italian Stories and the End of American Innocence." *Twentieth Century Literature* 19 (April 1973): 77-88.
Wisse, Ruth. *The Schlemiel as Modern Hero*. Chicago: Unirersity of Chicago Press, 1971.

6) Malamudについての邦語単行本（雑誌特集号を含む）：
『英語青年　特集：バーナード・マラマッド』東京：研究社，1986年9月号.
岩元巌『マラマッド―芸術と生活を求めて』東京：冬樹社，1979.
佐渡谷重信編『アメリカ小説研究第7号―バーナード・マラマッド特集』東京：泰文堂，1976.

V. Saul Bellow

PRIMARY SOURCES

1) Books:

Dangling Man. New York: Vanguard, 1944.
The Victim. New York: Vanguard, 1947.
The Adventures of Augie March. New York: Viking, 1953.
Seize the Day. New York: Viking, 1956.
Henderson the Rain King. New York: Viking, 1959.
Recent American Fiction. Washington, D.C.: Library of Congress, 1963.
Herzog. New York: Viking, 1964.
The Last Analysis. New York: Viking, 1965.
Mosby's Memoirs and Other Stories. New York: Viking, 1968.
Mr. Sammler's Planet. New York: Viking, 1970.
The Portable Saul Bellow. New York: Viking, 1974.
Humboldt's Gift. New York: Viking, 1975.
To Jerusalem and Back; A Personal Account. New York: Viking,1976.
Nobel Lecture. New York: Targ Editions, 1976.
The Dean's December. New York: Harper & Row, 1982.
Him with His Foot in His Mouth and Other Stories. New York: Haper & Row, 1984.
More Die of Heartbreak. New York: William Morrow and Company, Inc., 1987.
A Theft. New York: Viking Penguin Inc., 1989.
The Bellarosa Connection. New York: Penguin, 1989.
Something to Remember Me By. New York: Viking, 1991.
It All Adds Up; From the Dim Past to the Uncertain Future (A Nonfiction Collection). New York :Viking, 1994.
The Actual. New York: Viking, 1997.

2) 邦訳書：

刈田元司抄訳「オーギー・マーチの冒険」(The Adventures of Augie March) 東京：荒地出版社，1959 (『現代アメリカ文学全集』19) ; 1967 (『現代アメリカ文学選集』2).

大橋吉之輔・後藤昭次訳『犠牲者』(*The Victim*) 東京：白水社, 1966.
渋谷雄三郎『オーギー・マーチの冒険』(*The Adventures of Augie March*) 東京：早川書房, 1981.
佐伯彰一訳「雨の王ヘンダソン」(*Henderson the Rain King*) 東京：中央公論社, 1967 (『世界の文学』51巻)；東京：中公文庫, 1988.
井内雄四郎『宙ぶらりんの男』(*Dangling Man*) 東京：太陽社, 1968.
宇野利泰『ハーツォグ』(*Herzog*) 東京：早川書房, 1970, 1981.
徳永暢三訳『モズビーの思い出』(*Mosby's Memoirs and Other Stories*) 東京：新潮社, 1970.
栗原行雄訳『現在をつかめ』(*Seize the Day*) 東京：現代出版社, 1970；東京：河出書房新社, 1972.
大浦暁生訳『この日をつかめ』(*Seize the Day*) 東京：新潮文庫, 1971.
太田稔訳『宙ぶらりんの男』(*Dangling Man*) 東京：新潮文庫, 1971.
繁尾久訳『宙ぶらりんの男』(*Dangling Man*) 東京：角川文庫, 1972.
繁尾久訳『この日をつかめ』(*Seize the Day*) 東京：角川文庫, 1972.
太田稔訳『犠牲者』(*The Victim*) 東京：新潮文庫, 1973.
繁尾久訳『ソール・ベロー短篇集』東京：角川文庫, 1974.
橋本福夫訳『サムラー氏の惑星』(*Mr. Sammler's Planet*) 東京：新潮社, 1974.
大井浩二訳『フンボルトの贈り物 上・下巻』(*Humbolt's Gift*) 東京：講談社, 1977.
野崎孝訳『宙ぶらりんの男』(*Dangling Man*) 東京：講談社, 1977.
宮本陽吉訳『その日をつかめ』(*Seize the Day*) 東京：集英社文庫, 1978.
渋谷雄三郎訳『学生部長の十二月』(*The Dean's December*) 東京：早川書房, 1983.
宇野利泰訳『盗み』(*A Theft*) 東京：早川書房, 1990.
宇野利泰訳『ベラローザ・コネクション』(*The Bellarosa Connection*) 東京：早川書房, 1992.

SECONDARY SOURCES

1) Bibliographic Aids:

Cronin, Gloria L. "Saul Bellow Selected and Annotated Bibliography." *Saul Bellow Journal* 4. 1 (1985): 80-89.

―――, and Liela H. Goldman. "Saul Bellow." *American Novelists*. Detroit: Gale, 1986. 83-155. Vol.1 of *Contemporary Authors Bibliographical Series*. 3 vols. to date. 1986- .

―――, and Blaine H. Hall. *Saul Bellow: An Annotated Bibliography*. 2nd ed. New York: Garland, 1987.

―――. "Selected Annotated Critical Bibligraphy for 1984." *Saul Bellow Journal* 6. 1 (1987): 55-68.

―――. "Selected Annotated Critical Bibligraphy for 1985." *Saul Bellow Journal* 6. 2

(1987): 76-80.

Cronin, Gloria L. and Blaine H. Hall. "Selected Annotated Critical Bibliography for 1986." *Saul Bellow Journal* 7. 1 (1988): 79-95.

——. "Selected Annotated Critical Biblioraphy for 1987." *Saul Bellow Journal* 8. 1 (1989): 74-96.

——. "Selected Annotated Critical Bibliography for 1988." *Saul Bellow Journal* 9. 2 (1990): 82-94.

——. "Selected Annotated Critical Bibliography for 1989." *Saul Bellow Journal* 10. 2 (1992).

Field, Leslie, and John Z. Guzlowski. "Saul Bellow: A Selected Checklist." *Modern Fiction Studies* 25. 1 (1979): 149-71.

Galloway, David D. "A Saul Bellow Checklist." *The Absurd Hero in American Fiction: Updike, Styron, Bellow, Salinger.* Austin: University of Texas Press, 1966. 210-26; Rev. ed. 1970. 220-39.

Lercangee, Francine. *Saul Bellow: A Bibliography of Secondary Sources.* Brussels: Center for American Studies, 1977.

Nault, Marianne. *Saul Bellow: His Works and His Critics: An Annotated International Bibliography.* Garland Reference Library of the Humanities 59. New York: Garland, 1977.

Noreen, Robert G. *Saul Bellow: A Reference Guide.* A Reference Publication in Literature. Boston: Hall, 1978.

Sokoloff, B. A., and Mark Posner. *Saul Bellow: A Comprehensive Bibliography.* Folcroft, Penn.: Folcroft Library Editions, 1972.

2) Interviews

Bellow, Saul. "On John Cheever: Speech to the American Academy of Arts and Letters." *New York Review of Books* 17 Feb. 1983: 38.

Breit, Harvey. "A Talk with Saul Bellow." *New York Times Book Review* 20 Sept. 1953:22.

Bruckner, D. J. R. "A Candid Talk with Saul Bellow." *New York Times Magazine* 15 Apr. 1984: 2.

Clemons, Walter, and Jack Kroll. "America's Master Novelist: Interview with Saul Bellow." *Newsweek* 1 Sept. 1975: 33-35.

Cronin, Gloria L., and Ben Siegel, eds. *Conversations with Saul Bellow.* Jackson, Miss.: University Press of Mississippi, 1994.

Epstein, Joseph. "A Talk with Saul Bellow." *New York Times Book Review* 5 Dec. 1976: 3+.

Gutwillig, Robert. "Talk with Saul Bellow." *New York Times Book Review* 20 Sept. 1964: 40-41.

Howard, Jane. "Mr. Bellow Considers His Planet." *Life* 3 Apr. 1970: 57-60.

Kakutani, Michiko. "A Talk with Saul Bellow: On His Work and Himself." *New York Times Review of Books* 13 Dec. 1981: 28-30.

Kulshreshtha, Chirantan. "A Conversation with Saul Bellow." *Chicago Review* 23.4-24.1 (1972): 7-15.

Roudané, Matthew. "An Interview with Saul Bellow." *Contemporary Literature* 25.3 (1984): 265-80.

3) Books Specifically about Bellow:

Bach, Gerhard, ed. *Saul Bellow at Seventy-Five: A Collection of Critical Essays*. Tübingen: Gunter Narr Verlag, 1991.

———, ed. *The Critical Response to Saul Bellow*. Greenwood Press, 1995.

Bloom, Harold, ed. *Saul Bellow*. New York: Chelsea House Publishers, 1986.

———, ed. *Saul Bellow's Herzog*. New York: Chelsea House Publishers, 1988.

Bradburry, Malcolm. *Saul Bellow*. London: Methuen, 1982.

Clayton, John J. *Saul Bellow: In Defense of Man*. Bloomington: Indiana University. Press, 1968. 2nd ed. 1979.

Cohen, Sarah Blacher. *Saul Bellow's Enigmatic Laughter*. Urbana: University of Illinois Press, 1974.

Cronin, Gloria L., and L. H. Goldman, eds. *Saul Bellow in the 1980s*. East Lansing, Mich.: Michigan State University, 1989.

Detweiler, Robert. *Saul Bellow: A Critical Essay*. Grand Rapids, Mich.: Eerdmans, 1967.

Dutton, Robert R. *Saul Bellow*. Twayne's United States Author Series 181. New York: Twayne, 1971. Rev. ed. 1982.

Friedrich, Marianne M. *Character and Narration in the Short Fiction of Saul Bellow*. New York: Peter Lang Publishing, Inc., 1995.

Fuchs, Daniel. *Saul Bellow: Vision and Revision*. Durham, N. C.: Duke Universitiy Press, 1984.

Goldman, Liela H. *Saul Bellow's Moral Vision: A Critical Study of the Jewish Experience*. New York: Irvington, 1983.

Harris, Mark. *Saul Bellow: Drumlin Woodchuck*. Athens, Ga.: University of Georgia Press, 1980.

Hollahan, Eugene, ed. *Saul Bellow and the Struggle at the Center*. New York: AMS Press, Inc., 1996.

Kiernan, Robert F. *Saul Bellow*. Literature and Life. American Writers. New York: Continuum, 1989.

Kulshrestha, Chrirantan. *Saul Bellow: The Problem of Affirmation*. New Delhi: Arnold-

Heinemann, 1978.

Machida, Tetsuji. *Saul Bellow, A Transcendentalist.* Osaka: Kyoiku Tosho, Co. Ltd., 1993.

McCadden, Joseph F. *The Flight from Women in the Fiction of Saul Bellow.* Washington: University Press of America, 1981.

Malin, Irving. *Saul Bellow's Fiction.* Crosscurrents/Modern Critiques. Carbondale: Southern Illinois University Press, 1969.

————, ed. *Saul Bellow and the Critics.* New York: New York University Press, 1967.

Miller, Ruth. *Saul Bellow: A Biography of the Imagination.* New York: St. Martin's Press, 1991.

Newman, Judie. *Saul Bellow and History.* New York: St. Martin's; London: Macmillan, 1984.

Opdahl, Keith M. *The Novels of Saul Bellow.* University Park: Pennsylvania State University Press, 1967.

Pifer, Ellen. *Saul Bellow Against the Grain.* Philadelphia: University of Pennsylvania Press, 1990.

Porter, M. Gibert. *Whence the Power? The Artistry and Humanity of Saul Bellow.* Columbia: Univercity of Missouri Press, 1974.

Roderigues, Eusebio L. *Quest for the Human: An Exploration of Saul Bellow's Fiction.* Lewisburg, Pa.: Bucknell Univresity Press, 1981.

Rovit, Earl, ed. *Saul Bellow.* Minneapolis: Univresity of Minnesota Press, 1967.

————, ed. *Saul Bellow: A Collection of Critical Essays.* Englewood Clifffs, N. J.: Prentice-Hall, Inc., 1975.

Scheer-Schaetzler, Brigitte. *Saul Bellow.* New York: Ungar, 1972.

Tanner, Tony. *Saul Bellow.* New York: Barnes & Noble, 1965; New York: Chips, 1978.

Trachtenberg, Stanley, ed. *Critical Essays on Saul Bellow.* Boston: G. K. Hall, 1979.

Wilson, Jonathan. *Herzog: The Limits of Ideas.* Twayne's Masterwork Studies 46. Boston: Twayne, 1990.

4) Collections of Essays:

Critique: Studies in Modern Fiction 7 (Spring-Summer 1965). Five studies of Bellow's writings: "Bellow's View of the Heart" by James Dean Young; "Theme in *Augie March*" by Robert D. Crozer, S. J.; "Bellow's Henderson" by Allen Guttman; "The Theme of *Seize the Day*" by James C. Mathis; and "Clown and Saint: The Hero in Current American Fiction" by David D. Galloway.

Critique: Studies in Modern Fiction 9. 3(1967). Three studies of Bellow's writings: "Saul Bellow's *Luftmenschen*: The Compromise with Reality" by Stanley Trachtenberg; "Water Imagery in *Seize the Day*" by Clinton W. Trowbridge; and "Bellow and Milton: Professor Herzog in His Garden" by Franklin R. Baruch.

Modern Fiction Studies 25 (Spring 1979). This is a special Saul Bellow issue with eleven essays on his writing, most of them centering on a particular novel, with others more general. An excellent introductory essay on Bellow by Field, and a comprehensive bibliography of criticism on Bellow.

Salmagundi 30 (Summer 1975). Included are five essay on various aspects of Bellow and his fiction, along with Robert T. Boyers's "Literature and Culture: An Interview with Saul Bellow."

5) Other Books and Articles :

Baumbach, Jonothan. "The Double Vision: *The Victim* by Saul Bellow." *The Landscape of Nightmare: Studies in the Contemporary Novel.* New York: New York University Press, 1965. 35-54.

Davis, Robert G. "Individualist Tradition: Bellow and Styron." *The Creative Present: Notes on Contemporary Fiction.* Ed. Nona Balakian and Charles Simmons. New York: Doubleday, 1963. 111-41.

Eisinger, Chester E. "Saul Bellow: Man Alive, Sustained by Love." *Fiction of the Forties.* Chicago: University of Chicago Press, 1963. 341-62.

Fuchs, Daniel. "*More Die of Heartbreak* and the Question of Later Bellow." *Saul Bellow Journal* 11-1 (Fall 1992): 33.

Galloway, David G. "The Absurd Man as Picaro: The Novels of Saul Bellow." *The Absurd Hero in American Fiction: Updike, Styron, Bellow, Salinger.* Austin: University of Texas Press, 1966. 82-139.

Geismer, Maxwell. "Saul Bellow: Novelist of the Intellectuals." *American Moderns: From Rebellion to Conformity.* New York: Hill and Wang, 1958. 210-24.

Hassan, Ihab. *Radical Innocence: The Contemporary American Novel.* Princeton: Princeton University Press, 1961. 290-324.

Hoffman, Frederick. "The Fool of Experience: Saul Bellow's Fiction." *Contemporary American Novelists.* Ed. Harry T. Moore. Carbondale: Southern Illinois University Press, 1964. 80-94.

Klein, Marcus. "A Discipline of Nobility: Saul Bellow's Fiction." *After Alienation: American Novels in Mid-Century.* New York: World, 1964. 33-70.

Malin, Irving. *Jews and Americans.* Carbondale: Southern Illinois University Press, 1965. 73-75, 97-98.

McConnell, Frank D. "Saul Bellow and the Terms of our Contract." *Four Post-War American Novelists: Bellow, Mailer, Barth, and Pynchon.* Chicago: University of Chicago Press, 1977. 1-57.

Pinsker, Sanford. "Late Bellow and the Literary Scene." *Saul Bellow Journal* 11.1 (Fall 1992):

36.
Weinberg, Helen. *The New Novel in America: The Kafkan Mode in Contemporary Fiction.* Ithaca, N.Y.: Cornell University Press, 1970. 29-107.

6) Bellowについての邦語単行本（雑誌特集号を含む）:
安藤正瑛『ソール・ベローの世界―禅的視点による作品研究』東京：英宝社, 1984.
『英語青年　特集：ソール・ベロウ』東京：研究社, 1972年8月号.
佐渡谷重信編『アメリカ小説研究第5号―ソール・ベロー特集』東京：泰文堂, 1975.
坂野明子・町田哲司共編『ソール・ベロー論文集Ⅰ』大阪：大阪教育図書, 1995.
渋谷雄三郎『ベロー―回心の軌跡』東京：冬樹社, 1978.
田畑千秋『ソール・ベローを読む』京都：松籟社, 1994.

Ⅵ. Philip Roth

PRIMARY SOUCES
1) Books:
Goodbye, Columbus. Boston: Houghton Mifflin, 1959.
Letting Go. New York: Random House, 1962.
When She Was Good. New York: Random House, 1967.
Portnoy's Complaint. New York: Random House, 1969.
Our Gang (Starring Tricky and His Friends). New York: Random House, 1971.
The Breast. New York: Holt, Rinehart, 1972.
The Great American Novel. New York: Holt, Rinehart, 1973.
My Life as a Man. New York: Holt, Rinehart, 1974.
Reading Myself and Others. New York: Farrar, Straus and Giroux, 1975.
The Professor of Desire. New York: Farrar, Straus and Giroux, 1977.
The Ghost Writer. New York: Farrar, Straus and Giroux, 1979.
A Philip Roth Reader. New York: Farrar, Straus and Giroux, 1980.
Zuckerman Unbound. New York: Farrar, Straus and Giroux, 1981.
The Anatomy Lesson. New York: Farrar, Straus and Giroux, 1983.
The Prague Orgy. London: Jonathan Cape, 1985.
Zuckerman Bound (includes *The Prague Orgy*). New York: Farrar, Straus and Giroux, 1985.
The Counterlife. New York: Farrar, Straus and Giroux, 1987.
The Facts: A Novelist's Autobiography. New York: Farrar, Straus and Giroux, 1988.
A Theft. New York: Penguin, 1989.
Deception. New York: Simon & Schuster, 1990.
Patrimony: A True Story. New York: Simon & Schuster, 1991.

Operation Shylock: A Confession. New York: Simon & Schuster, 1993.
Sabbath's Theater. Boston: Houghton Mifflin, 1995.
American Pastoral. Boston: Houghton Mifflin, 1997.
I Married a Communist. Boston: Houghton Mifflin, 1998.

2) 邦訳書：
佐伯彰一訳『さようならコロンバス』(*Goodbye, Columbus*) 東京：集英社 (『世界文学全集』19巻), 1969；集英社 (『世界の文学』34巻), 1976；集英社文庫, 1977.
宮本陽吉『ポートノイの不満』(*Portnoy's Complaint*) 東京：集英社, 1971；集英社文庫, 1978.
斎藤忠利・平野信行訳『ルーシィの哀しみ』(*When She Was Good*) 東京：集英社, 1972；集英社文庫, 1977.
佐伯彰一・宮本陽吉訳『狂信者イーライ』("Eli, the Fanatic, and Other Four Short Stories.") 東京：集英社, 1973.
大津栄一郎訳『乳房になった男』(*The Breast*) 東京：集英社, 1974.
中野好夫・常盤新平訳『素晴らしいアメリカ野球』(*The Great American Novel*) 東京：集英社 (『世界の文学』34巻), 1976；集英社文庫, 1978.
青山南訳『われらのギャング』(*Our Gang*) 東京：集英社, 1977.
宮本陽吉訳『乳房になった男』(*The Breast*) 東京：集英社文庫, 1978.
大津栄一郎訳『男としての我が人生』(*My Life as a Man*) 東京：集英社, 1978.
青山南訳『素晴らしいアメリカ作家』(*Reading Myself and Others*) 東京：集英社, 1980.
佐伯泰樹訳『欲望学教授』(*The Professor of Desire*) 東京：集英社, 1983.
青山南訳『ゴースト・ライター』(*The Ghost Writer*) 東京：集英社, 1984.
佐伯泰樹訳『解き放たれたザッカーマン』(*Zuckerman Unbound*) 東京：集英社, 1984.
宮本陽吉訳『解剖学講義』(*The Anatomy Lesson*) 東京：集英社, 1986.
宇野利泰訳『盗み』(*A Theft*) 東京：早川書房, 1990.
宮本陽吉訳『背信の日々』(*The Counterlife*) 東京：集英社, 1993.
宮本陽一郎訳『いつわり』(*Deception*) 東京：集英社, 1993.
柴田元幸訳『父の遺産』(*Patrimony*) 東京：集英社, 1993.

SECONDARY SOURCES
1) Bibliographic Aids:
Leavey, Ann. "Philip Roth: A Bibliographic Essay (1984-1988)" *Studies in American Jewish Literature* 8 (Fall 1989): 212-18.
Rodgers, Bernard F., Jr. *Philip Roth: A Bibliography*, 2nd ed. Metuchen, N. J.: The Scarecrow Press, 1984.
Solinger, Jason D. "Philip Roth: An Annotated Bibliography of Uncollected Crticism, 1989-

1994." *A Tragedy Full of Joy: From Malamud, Ozick and Heller to I.B. Singer and Celia Dropkin.* Special issue of *Studies in Amerikan Jewish Literature* 15, (1996): 61-72.

2) Interviews:

Atlas, James. "A Visit with Philip Roth." *New York Times Book Review* 2 September 1979: 1.

Davidson, Sara. "A Talk with Philip Roth." *New York Times Book Review* 18 September 1977: 1.

Kakutani, Michiko. "Is Roth Really Writing About Roth?" *New York Times* 11 May 1981: 17.

Lelchuk, Alan. "On Satirizing Presidents." *Atlantic* December 1971: 81-88. Collected as "On *Our Gang*" in *Reading Myself and Others.*

————. "On The Breast." *New York Review of Books* 19 October 1972: 26. Collected in *Reading Myself and Others.*

May, Helen. "An Interview with Philip Roth." *New York Post* 29 September 1979: 11.

Oates, Joyce Carol. "A Conversation with Philip Roth." *Ontario Review* 1(1974): 9-22. Collected as "After Eight Books" in *Reading Myself and Others.*

Plimpton, George. "Philip Roth's Exact Intent." *New York Times Book Review* 23 February 1969: 2. Collected as "On *Portnoy's Complaint*" in *Reading Myself and Others.*

Raymont, Henry. "To Philip Roth Obscenity Isn't a Dirty Word." *New York Times* 11 January 1969: 20.

Saxon, Martha. "Philip Roth Talks About His Own Work." *Literary Guild* June 1974: 2. Collected as "On *My Life as a Man*" in *Reading Myself and Others.*

Searles, George J., ed. *Conversations with Philip Roth.* Jackson and London: University Press of Mississippi, 1992.

3) Books Specifically about Roth

Baumgarten, Murray, and Barbara Gottfried. *Understanding Philip Roth.* Columbia: University of South Carolina Press, 1990.

Bloom, Harold, ed. *Philip Roth* (Modern Critical Views). New York: Chelsea House, 1986.

Copper, Alan. *Philip Roth and the Jews.* Albany: State University of New York, 1996.

Halio, Jay. *Philip Roth Revisited.* New York: Twayne Publishers, 1992.

Jones, Judith Paterson, and Guinevera A. Nance. *Philip Roth.* New York: Frederick Ungar, 1981.

Leavey, Ann. "Philip Roth: A Bibliographic Essay (1984-1988)." *Studies in American Jewish Literature* 8 (Fall 1989) : 212-18.

Lee, Hermione. *Philip Roth.* New York: Methuen, 1982.

McDaniel, John N. *The Fiction of Philip Roth.* Haddonfield. N. J.: Haddonfield House, 1974.

Meeter, Glenn. *Bernard Malamud and Philip Roth: A Critical Essay.* Grand Rapids, Mich.: Eerdsmans, 1968.

Milbauer, Arthur Z., and Donald Watson, eds. *Reading Philip Roth*. New York: St. Martin's Press, 1988.

Pinsker, Sanford. *The Comedy That "Hoits": An Essay on the Fiction of Philip Roth*. Columbia: University of Missouri Press, 1975.

―――, ed. *Critical Essays on Philip Roth*. Boston: G. K. Hall, 1982.

Rodgers, Bernard F., Jr. *Philip Roth*. Boston: Twayne Publishers, 1978.

―――. *Philip Roth: A Bibliography*, 2nd ed. Metuchen, N. J.: Scarecrow Press, 1984.

Walden, Daniele, ed. *The Odyssey of a Writer: Rethinking Philip Roth*. Special issue of *Studies in American Jewish Literature* 8 (Fall 1989).

4) Other Books and Articles:

Alter, Robert. "Defenders of the Faith." *Commentary* July 1987: 55-56.

―――. "Deja Jew: *The Counterlife* by Philip Roth." *New Republic* 2 February 1987: 37.

―――. "The Spritzer." *New Republic* 15 April 1993: 32.

―――. "When He Is Bad." *Commentary* Novrmber 1967: 86-87.

Atlas, James. "A Postwar Classic." *New Republic* 2 June 1982: 26-32.

Barnes, Julian. "Philip Roth in Israel: *The Counterlife*." *London Review of Books* 5 Mar. 1987: 3-9.

Barret, William. "Let Go, Let Live." *Atlantic* July 1962: 111.

Baumbach, Jonathan. "What Hath Roth Got?" *Commonweal* 11 August 1967: 498.

Bellow, Saul. "The Swamp of Prosperity." *Commentary* July 1959: 77-79.

Berman, Jeffrey. *The Talking Cure: Literary Representations of Psychoanalysis*. New York: NYU Press, 1985.

Bettelheim, Bruno. "The Ignored Lesson of Anne Frank." *Surviving and Other Essays*. New York: Alfred A. Knopf, 1952.

―――. "Portnoy Psychoanalyzed." *Midstream* June-July 1969: 3-10.

Borowitz, Eugene. "Portnoy's Complaint." *Dimensions* Summer 1969: 48-50.

Brown, Georgia. "Shiksa Bashing." *7 DAYS* 30 November 1988: 66.

Charney, Maurice. *Sexual Fiction*. New York: Methuen, 1981.

Cohen, Roger. "Roth's Publishers: The Spurned and the Spender." *New York Times* 9 April 1990: C11.

Cohen, Sarah. "Philip Roth's Would-Be Patriarchs and their *Shikses* and Shrews." *Studies in American Jewish Literature* 1 (1975): 16-22.

―――, ed. *Jewish Wry*. Bloomington: Indiana Universicty Press, 1987.

Cooper, Alan. "Philip Roth Between The Peaks (Piques?)." *The Jewish Frontier* August/September 1984: 20-23, 25.

―――. "The Jewish Sit-Down Comedy of Philip Roth." *Jewish Wry*. Ed. Sarah Blacher

Cohen. Bloomington: Indiana University Press, 1987: 158-77.

Cooperman, Stanley. "Philip Roth: 'Old Jacob's Eye' With a Squint." *Twentieth Century Literature* July 1973: 203-16.

Deer, Irving, and Harriet. "Philip Roth and the Crisis in American Fiction." *The Minnesota Review* VI, 4 (1966): 353-60.

Feldman, Irving. "A Sentimental Education Circa 1956." *Commentary* September 1962: 273-76.

Fiedler, Leslie A. "The Image of Newark and the Indignaties of Love: Notes on Philip Roth." *Midstream* Summer 1959: 96-99.

———. "Philip Roth: Days of Whine and Moses." *Studies in American Jewish Literature* 5. 2 (1979): 11-14.

Furman, Andrew. "The Ineluctable Holocaust in the Fiction of Philip Roth." *The Changing Mosaic: From Cahan to Malamud, Roth and Ozick*. Special issue of *Studies in American Jewish Literature* 12 (1993): 109-21.

Gass, William H. "Deciding to Do the Impossible." *New York Times Book Review* 4 January 1987: 1, 24-25.

Goldman, Albert. "Wild Blue Shocker." *Life* 7 February 1969. 58-64.

Gray, Paul. "The Varnished Truths of Philip Roth." *Time* 19 January 1987: 78-79.

———. "Two Serious Comic Writers." *Time* 10 November 1980: 102-07.

Gross, Barry. "Sophie Portnoy and 'The Opossum's Death': American Sexism and Jewish Anti-Gentilism." *Studies in American Jewish Literature* 3 (1983): 166-78.

Gross, John. "Marjorie Morningstar PhD." *New Statesman* 30 November 1962:784.

———. *Shylock: A Legend and Its Legacy*. New York: Simon & Schuster, 1993.

Halkin, Hillel. "How to Read Philip Roth." *Commentary* February 1994: 43-48.

Hentoff, Nat. "The Appearance of Letting Go." *Midstream* December 1962: 103-06.

Hicks, Granville. "Hammer Locks in Wedlock." *Saturday Review of Literature* 16 June 1962: 16.

Hochman, Baruch. "Child and Man in Philip Roth," *Midstream* XIII (December 1967): 68-76.

Howe, Irving. "Philip Roth Reconsidered." *Commentary* December 1972: 69-77.

Howe, Irving. "The Suburbs of Babylon." *New Republic* 15 June 1959: 17-18.

Isaac, Dan. "In Defense of Philip Roth." *Chicago Review* XVII 2 & 3 (1964): 84-96.

Janowsky, Oscar. *The American Jew*. Philadelphia: Jewish Publication Society, 1964.

Kaminsky, Alice. "Philip Roth's Professor Kepesh and the 'Reality Principle.'" *Denver Quarterly* 13, 2 (1978): 41-54.

Katz, Jacob. "Accounting for Anti-Semitism." *Commentary* June 1991: 52-54.

Kazin, Alfred. "The Earthly City of the Jews." *Bright Book of Life*. New York: Little, Brown, 1973. 144-49.

Kliman, Bernice. "Women in Roth's Fiction." *Nassau Review* 3, 4 (1978): 75-88.

Kozodoy, Neal. "His Father's Son." *Commentary* May 1991: 52-54.

Landis, Joseph C. "The Sadness of Philip Roth: An Interim Report." *Massachusetts Review* 3 (Winter 1962): 259-68.

Larner, Jeremy. "The Conversion of the Jews." Review of *Goodbye, Columbus*. *Partisan Review* 27 (Fall 1960): 760-68.

Lee, Hermione. "Kiss and Tell." *New Repubic* 30 April 1990: 39-42.

———. "The Art of Fiction LXXXIV: Philip Roth." (originally in *Paris Review* 1984) Ed. George J. Searles. *Conversations with Philip Roth*. Jackson: University of Mississppi Press, 1992.

Lee, Judith. "Flights of Fancy." *Chicago Review* 31. 4 (1980): 46-52.

Lehmann-Haupt, Christopher. "The Counterlife." *New York Times* 29 December 1986: C19.

Lelyveld, Arthur J. "Old Disease in New Form: Diagnosing 'Portnoy's Complaint'." *Jewish Digest* Summer 1969: 1-4; a reprint with omissions of a longer sermon delivered at Fairmount Temple, Cleveland, Ohio, 7 March 1969.

Levine, Mordecai H. "Philip Roth and American Judaism." *CLA Journal* 14 (Dcember 1970): 163-70.

Liebman, Charles S. *The Ambivalent American Jew*. Philadelphia: Jewish Publication Society, 1973.

Maloff, Saul. "The Uses of Adversity." *Commonweal* 106 (19 November 1979): 628-31.

Margulies, Donald. "A Playwright's Search for a Spiritual Father." *New York Times* 21 June 1992: H5.

Mizener, Arthur. "Bumblers in a World of Their Own." *New York Times Book Review* 17 June 1962: VII: 1, 28-29.

Mudrick, Marvin. "Who Killed Herzog? Or, Three American Novelists." *Denver Quarterly* 1 (Spring 1966): 61-97.

Pinsker, Sanford. "Joseph in Chederland: A Note on 'The Conversion of the Jews.'" *Studies in American Jewish Literature* I (Winter 1975): 36-37.

———. "Surviving Jewish History: Updated Notes on the American-Jewish Dream." *Jewish Spectator* Summer 1988: 21.

Podhoretz, John. "Philip Roth, The Great American Novelist." *The American Spectator* September 1981: 12-14.

Podhoretz, Norman. "The Gloom of Philip Roth." *Doings and Undoings*. New York: Farrar, Straus, & Giroux, 1964. 236-43.

———. "Laureate of the New Class." *Commentary* December 1972: 4.

Prescott, Peter. "Sermons and Celery Tonic." *Newsweek* 12 January 1987.

Quart, Barbara Koenig. "The Rapacity of One Nearly Buried Alive." *Massachusetts Review* 24

Selected Bibliography   175

(1983): 590-608.
Retik, H. E. "Postscript to *Portnoy's Complaint.*" *Israel Magazine* Summer 1969: 40-42.
Rockland, Michael Aaron. "The Jewish Side of Philip Roth." *Studies in American Jewish Literature* I (Winter 1975): 29-36A.
Schechner, Mark. "Philip Roth." *Partisan Review* Fall 1974: 410-27.
Scholem, Gershom. *"Portnoy's Complaint."* Trans. E. E. Siskin. *CCARJ* (Central Conference of American Rabbis) June 1970: 56-58.
Searles, George J. *The Fiction of Philip Roth and John Updike.* Carbondale: Southern Illinois University Press, 1985.
Shaw, Peter. "Portnoy & His Creator." *Commentary* May 1969: 77.
Sheed, Wilfred. "The Good Word: Howe's Complaint." *New York Time Book Review* 6 May 1973: 2.
Solotaroff, Theodore. "Philip Roth and the Jewish Moralists." *Chicago Review* 13, 1 (1959): 87-99.
———. "The Journey of Philip Roth." *Atlantic Monthly* April 1969: 64-72.
———. "The Diasporist." *The Nation* 7 June 1993: 778-84.
Solotaroff, Theodore. and Nessa Rappoport. *Writing Our Way Home: Contemporary Stories by American Jewish Writers.* New York: Schocken Books, 1992.
Stampfer, Judah. "Adolescent Marx Brothers." *Jewish Heritage* Summer 1969: 13.
Syrkin, Marie. "The Fun of Self-Abuse." *Midstream* April 1969: 64-68.
Tanner, Tony. "Fictionalized Recall—or 'The Settling of Scores! The Pursuit of Dreams!' (Saul Bellow, Philip Roth, Frank Conroy)." *City of Words: American Fiction 1950-1970.* New York: Harper & Row, 1971: 295-321.
Toynton, Evelyn. "American Stories." *Commentary* March 1993.
Updike, John. "Recruiting Raw Nerves." *New Yorker* 15 March 1993: 32.
Walden, Daniel. "From Columbus to Portnoy: The Evolution of Philip Roth's Jewish American." *Studies in American Jewish Literature* I (Winter 1975): 38-39.
Weinberg, Helen. "Growing Up Jewish." *Judaism* Spring 1969: 241-45.
Weiss-Rosmarin, Trude. "On Jewish Self-Definition." *Reconstructionist* XXV, 2. 6 (March 1959): 22-25.
Weiss-Rosmarin, Trude. "Portnoy's Complaint" (editorial). *Jewish Spectator* April 1969: 6, 31; reprinted *Jewish Spectator* Winter 1985/Spring 1986: 46-47.
Wisse, Ruth. "Philip Roth Then And Now." *Commentary* Summer 1981: 56.
———. *The Schlemiel as Modern Hero.* Chicago: University of Chicago Press, 1971.
Wistrich, Robert S. "Once Again, Anti-Semitism Without Jews." *Commentary* August 1992: 45-49.
Wirth- Nesher, Hana. "The Artist Tales of Philip Roth." *Prooftexts* 3 (1983): 263-72.

Zimring, Franklin. "Portnoy's Real Complaint." *Moment* December 1980: 58-62.

5) Rothについての邦語単行本：
佐渡谷重信編『アメリカ小説研究第8号—フィリップ・ロス特集』東京：泰文堂，1977.

あとがき

　本書は，1999年度広島女学院大学学術図書出版助成による刊行である。関係の諸先生，事務担当の方々，特に1995～96学年度英米文学科長内藤裕子教授，Ronald D. Klein 教授・図書館の宍戸露子主任には，大変お世話になった。
　筆者がユダヤ系アメリカ文学研究を志したのは，もう四半世紀以上も前のことであったろうか。古い記録をひもといてみると，1973年のアメリカ学会年次大会部会「ユダヤ系アメリカ人の同化と疎外」(発表者：野村達朗・岩本巌・岡節三の3氏) で司会を務めている。翌1974年春，アメリカ国務省の招待により38日間全米各地の諸大学・機関を訪問したのも，1976～77年フルブライト上級研究員としてコロンビア大学及びニューヨーク市立大学で研究を続けたのも，「現代ユダヤ系アメリカ人作家の小説にみられるユダヤ系アメリカ人の同化と疎外とアイデンティティの危機」の研究がその目的であった。Leslie A. Fiedler, Norman Podhoretz, Ruth Wisse, Irving Howe 氏らに会えたのも，このどちらかの機会であった。ことにニューヨーク滞在中 Irving Malin 教授は，2週間に1回筆者の論文草稿に目を通し，コメントを付して郵送してくださった。Saul Bellow がノーベル賞を受賞した直後,「Norman Mailer でなく彼が受賞したのが嬉しい」との Malin 教授の言葉と共に，忘れられないありがたい想い出である。また1984年秋，財団法人浦上育英会 (福山通運) から研究助成金を頂き「イスラエル・イギリス・フランス・イタリアのユダヤ教とユダヤ人研究」のため渡欧，エルサレムに約10日間滞在することができた。アメリカ大使館の斡旋による E. L. Doctrow, Ihab Hassan, Robert Giroux, Allen Guttmann の諸氏の広島での講演の司会を務めたことも深く印象に残っている。
　日本アメリカ文学会，アメリカ学会，中・四国アメリカ文学会及び中・四国アメリカ学会においても，学会活動を通じて多くの刺激を得た。吉田弘重先生，故大橋吉之輔先生を始め，学会関係の諸先生から数々の貴重なご指導とご助言

を得た。深くお礼を申し上げたい。順序は逆になったが，筆者の受けた最も長く深い学問的恩恵はここにある。

　以上感謝と共に言及させて頂いた皆様のおかげで，筆者はこの約25年以上の間一貫して同じテーマで，同じ伝統的方法で，ユダヤ系アメリカ文学の研究を続けることができた。これまでに既に論文として発表したものに手を加え，第IX章のIIは大幅に改訂し，新たに第I章と第IX章のIを書き加え，このような形で一冊の単行本として世に残すことができたのは，望外の喜びである。紙面の関係もあり，取り扱えなかった作品も多い。とりわけRothの後期の作品について，また（文学の背景的知識として）アメリカのユダヤ人の歴史と現状の概略について，それぞれ一章をもうける当初の予定であったが，家庭の事情もあって残念ながら実現できなかった。「日暮れて道遠し」の感，しきりである。至らぬ点も多々あろうが，諸賢のご叱正をお願いする。

　最後になったが，（株）大学教育出版専務取締役佐藤守氏は，本書の出版を快諾され，編集上のご助言と誠心誠意のご協力を頂いた。本学大学院生，平田ユミさん，平井久美子さんには，校正その他の面で有益な援助を得た。

　学恩は深く重い。これまで列挙させて頂いた皆々様の寛容なサポートがなければ，本書は日の目を見なかったであろう。重ねて衷心より謝意を表明したい。

2000年1月

　　　　　　　　　　　　　　　　　　　　　　　　　　　　　　筆者

■著者略歴

陣﨑　克博（じんざき・かつひろ）

〈現在〉
広島女学院大学教授（大学院言語文化研究科博士課程「現代アメリカ・ユダヤ系作家研究」など担当），広島大学名誉教授，文学博士（慶應義塾大学）

〈学歴・職歴〉
広島文理科大学英文科卒（1951年）。長崎大学講師・助教授・教授（教授就任1965年）を経て広島大学に転任（1972年），総合科学部教授（1974年）となり，その後大学院修士課程・博士課程を担当。その間1961～62年にフルブライト留学生として米国ペンシルヴァニア大学院に留学，1976～77年にはフルブライト上級研究員としてコロンビア大学などにおいて研究に従事。1989～91年広島大学評議員・附属図書館長。1991年定年退職，広島文教女子大学教授を経て現職（1995年），現在に至る。

〈学会役職〉
1994～98年　日本アメリカ文学会代議員，中・四国アメリカ文学会会長
1986～91年　中・四国アメリカ学会会長
1974～97年　（日本）アメリカ学会理事
現　　　在　中・四国アメリカ文学会顧問，中・四国アメリカ学会理事

〈著書・論文〉
単　著：『アメリカ研究序説』（東京：英潮社，1967）
編　著：『アメリカ——その特質と諸相』（東京：英潮社新社，1982）
　　　　他2編
編注書：5編
論　文：57編

ユダヤ系アメリカ文学研究

2000年3月30日　初版第1刷発行

■著　者——陣﨑　克博
■発行者——佐藤　正男
■発行所——株式会社 大学教育出版
　　　　　〒700-0951　岡山市田中124-101
　　　　　電話 (086) 244-1268　FAX (086) 246-0294
■印刷所——原多印刷（株）
■製本所——平田製本（株）
■装　丁——ティー・ボーンデザイン事務所

© Katsuhiro Jinzaki 2000, Printed in Japan
検印省略　　落丁・乱丁本はお取り替えいたします。
無断で本書の一部または全部を複写・複製することは禁じられています。

ISBN4-88730-382-3